"I am Westray," he told her. **"More to the point, madam, who are *you*?"**

She bit her lip. He was dressed fashionably and a diamond twinkled from the folds of his neckcloth. Could he really be the missing earl?

"Well?" he said when she did not speak. "Pretending to be someone you are not is a crime, you know. I think I am entitled to an explanation."

She looked at him defiantly and wanted to retort that *he* was the criminal. He appeared relaxed, but there was a steely strength about him. She knew he would not be fobbed off with anything less than the truth.

"I am Arabella Roffey."

"Go on."

His eyes were glinting, but they were not unkind. She said impulsively, "I needed to be here. Pray do not expose me!"

"How intriguing," Randolph said. "You had best explain it to me."

She clasped her hands, squeezing them together to steady her nerves. "I am trying to find out who killed my husband."

Author Note

Readers of *Pursued for the Viscount's Vengeance* will remember Randolph as Deborah Meltham's ne'er-do-well brother, Lord Kirkster. I had never intended for him to be anything more than a weak, spoiled young man who caused a great deal of trouble for his long-suffering sister, but somehow the character I had created refused to remain a minor player. His actions, in owning up to his crimes, resulted in transportation to Australia.

There are many fascinating accounts of what happened to the men and women who were transported to the colonies. Randolph's survival is based on true-life accounts. Some went on to become successful businessmen and farmers. Randolph intended to become just such a man with the land he had been granted, but when he receives an unexpected inheritance, he realizes it is an opportunity to return to his homeland and shoulder responsibilities he had shirked as a younger man.

Compared to Randolph, Arabella has led a very sheltered life, but her calm existence is shattered by the sudden death of her husband. He was her hero, her childhood sweetheart, and Bella is determined to discover the truth about his death. With Ran's help she discovers just what happened, but along the way Bella also learns uncomfortable truths about her late husband. And her own heart.

I loved bringing Randolph back home and giving him his own happy ending. It was not an easy journey, for either of us, but I hope you will think it was worth it.

SARAH MALLORY

---

*His Countess
for a Week*

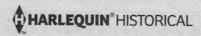
HARLEQUIN® HISTORICAL

Recycling programs
for this product may
not exist in your area.

ISBN-13: 978-1-335-50524-8

His Countess for a Week

Printed in U.S.A.

Sarah Mallory grew up in the West Country, England, telling stories. She moved to Yorkshire with her young family, but after nearly thirty years living in a farmhouse on the Pennines, she has now moved to live by the sea in Scotland. Sarah is an award-winning novelist with more than twenty books published by Harlequin Historical. She loves to hear from readers and you can reach her via her website at sarahmallory.com.

Books by Sarah Mallory

Harlequin Historical

The Scarlet Gown
Never Trust a Rebel
The Duke's Secret Heir
Pursued for the Viscount's Vengeance
His Countess for a Week

Saved from Disgrace

The Ton's Most Notorious Rake
Beauty and the Brooding Lord
The Highborn Housekeeper

The Infamous Arrandales

The Chaperon's Seduction
Temptation of a Governess
Return of the Runaway
The Outcast's Redemption

Brides of Waterloo

A Lady for Lord Randall

Visit the Author Profile page
at Harlequin.com for more titles.

To Sylvia T—who encouraged me not to wait for my dreams to come true but to go out and make them happen. And who would probably think RIP is a pretty boring thing to do.

Chapter One

The short November day was coming to an end when the *Apollonia* entered Portsmouth Harbour, its sails turned pink by the setting sun. On the bustling deck one figure stood motionless, a gentleman wrapped in a heavy cloak. He wore no hat and his thick blond hair was ruffled by the breeze as he stared out across the water, his eyes narrowed against the evening sunlight. He did not look at the sturdy walls and menacing fortifications rearing up around them, but back out through the narrow harbour entrance towards the open sea.

The Captain approached him. 'Beggin' your pardon, sir, we'll be docking shortly.'

'What?' He turned, his gaze and his mind taking a moment to focus on the Captain. 'Ah, yes. You'll be wanting me below decks, out of the way, I suppose.'

Reassured by the friendly tone, the Captain allowed himself a grin.

'Aye, sir, if you will. There's that many sacks and crates piled here...'

'And you don't want your men tripping over the

passengers. Very well, Captain. I'll go below, out of your way.'

'I thank 'ee for it, sir. We'll get you off as soon as we can, rest assured o' that.'

With a smile and a nod, Randolph made his way back to the dark, airless cabin. It had been his home for the past six months; another few minutes could be easily borne. He threw himself down on the bunk and put his hands behind his head, listening to the shouts and thuds from the deck above him and wondering, not for the first time, if he had been wise to return to England.

He had been in Australia for six years and had made a good life for himself. He had maintained his health and had enjoyed running his own farm in Airds, on the land granted him following his pardon. However, when Chislett's letter had arrived, it had not taken him long to convince himself it was his duty to return.

But now he wondered what awaited him. When he had left England, the country was recovering from the long and bruising campaign against Bonaparte. Randolph had taken little interest in English affairs since leaving the country, because he had never expected to return. He had not even expected to survive.

A gentle knock on the door roused him from his reverie.

'Excuse me, my lord, I see your valise is not yet packed. If you will allow me…'

'Oh, yes, Joseph. Come in.'

Randolph swung his feet to the ground and watched as his man collected up the few remaining items. He wrapped the folding bootjack in a cloth and pushed it into the already bulging bag, followed by the hairbrush and comb. When he picked up a pen-knife, Randolph held out his hand.

'I'll take that, Joseph. Thank you.' He pushed the small knife into the pocket of his coat. 'Are you sorry to have come back to England?'

'It makes no odds to me either way, my lord. If you'd wanted to remain at Airds, I'd have been content to see out the rest of my life there.'

'If this current venture turns out badly, we may yet return,' said Randolph.

'As you wish, my lord.'

'Confound it, Joseph, must you always be so damned cool?'

The grey-haired servant gave one of his rare smiles. 'Why, sir, I'd not have survived so long if I'd been anything else.'

'True!' Randolph laughed. He rose to his feet and put a hand on the older man's shoulder. 'What a sad trial I have been to you over the years, Joseph. I owe you a great deal. I should not have survived if it had not been for you. I wish you would let me——'

'If you are going to offer me a pension for life, my lord, let me tell you now I don't want it. Why, what should I do with myself, if I wasn't looking after you?'

'Aye, you've said that before, Joseph, but now we are back in the old country you might want to consider taking it a little easier. Settle down, perhaps. Find yourself a wife. I remember you and my sister's maid were on good terms at one time.'

Something flickered in Miller's eyes, but whether it was alarm, a fond memory or embarrassment, Randolph could not tell.

'Let us get you settled first, my lord, and then we'll see' was all his man would say.

A voice could be heard in the passage, inviting all passengers to disembark. Joseph fastened the valise and picked it up.

'Well, my lord, shall we go ashore?'

After so long at sea, it felt strange to Ran to have hard cobbles beneath his feet rather than wooden planking and constant movement, but he had little time to grow accustomed. The shadows were lengthening and he looked about him, his eyes coming to rest on a closed carriage with a soberly dressed figure standing by the door. Even after all these years Randolph recognised his family's lawyer. He strode towards him, his hand held out.

'Mr Chislett, good day to you.'

The man bowed low. 'My lord.'

'Come, man, take my hand,' barked Randolph. 'I've lived without ceremony for the past six years and I have no mind to begin yet, especially with such an old friend as yourself. And take note, I am travelling as plain Mr Randolph Kirkster for the moment.'

'As you wish, sir.' Chislett briefly shook hands, then waved towards the carriage. 'I have only the one vehicle. We may need to hire another, if you have a deal of baggage.'

'A couple of trunks and a few bags,' said Randolph. 'I think we shall manage.'

Within minutes the luggage was strapped to the coach and he and Joseph were settling themselves inside, together with Mr Chislett.

'I have booked rooms for you at the Admiral,' said

the lawyer. 'I am staying there myself and I hope it will suit. I thought that we might meet after breakfast tomorrow to discuss your situation.'

'Why wait until the morning?' said Randolph. 'The sooner this business is concluded the better.' He looked out of the window as the carriage began to slow. 'Are we here already? Capital. Let us go in. Arrange dinner for the three of us in a private parlour, if you please, Mr Chislett. In, say, an hour. Joseph, I will leave you to organise our bags while I go and order hot water sent up to our rooms.'

With that he jumped out of the carriage and strode into the inn, leaving the lawyer staring in surprise after him.

Joseph Miller chuckled. 'His Lordship's not one to stand back and let others do all the work. Nor will he walk if he can run. Come along, Mr Chislett, let us get on with it!'

Ran sat back in his chair and gave a loud sigh of satisfaction.

'After months of ship's rations, I enjoyed that meal!'

He was sitting at the table in the private parlour of the Admiral with Joseph and Mr Chislett. The dishes had been cleared away and a decanter of the landlord's finest brandy now stood on the table beside a jug of small beer.

Miller filled two glasses with brandy and pushed one towards the lawyer.

'You'll be wanting to get down to business,' he remarked, picking up the second glass and preparing to leave.

Ran waved him back to his seat. 'No need to go, Joseph. Heaven knows I have no secrets from you.' He poured himself a tankard of small beer and turned to the lawyer. 'Now, Mr Chislett, if you are ready, let us proceed with the business. Perhaps you might start by explaining to me again, and not in the legal jargon you used in your letter, just how it comes about that a disgraced baron, who was transported from this country in chains, is suddenly become the Earl of Westray? The connection was never even mentioned in my family.'

Mr Chislett picked up his glass and warmed it between his hands for a moment.

'It is a simple story, my lord, but a tragic one,' he began. 'The Seventh Earl had two healthy sons and three younger brothers. As a mere cousin, your grandfather never considered the title would come down through his line. The youngest brother died without issue, the second had a son who was killed at Waterloo, and still no one saw it as a cause for concern. Then the Earl's two sons were taken—one by fever, the other in a hunting accident—and the remaining brother discovered he had left it too late to marry and have a child. Thus, when the Earl died eighteen months ago, his brother succeeded to the title, but lived to enjoy it for only a few months. The Earldom therefore falls to the next male relative. That is you, my lord. You are now the Ninth Earl.'

'And if I do not want it?'

'As I advised you in my letter, the Earldom of Westray is an ancient title and includes several properties. There are any number of tenants, staff and their families all dependent upon the successful running of the estates. If you do not wish to claim the title, then we would do our best to administer the estates from London, as we have done since the Eighth Earl died nine months ago. The title would be dormant and pass on to your son in due course. If you die without issue, the title becomes extinct.' The lawyer's thin mouth turned down a little, expressing his disapproval of such a thought. He continued, his voice devoid of emotion, 'Of course, my lord, you might choose to leave the administration to your stewards and enjoy the…er…fruits of your new station. That, of course, is up to you.'

'You mean live like a lord while someone else does all the work? No. I thank you. If I decide to take this on, I would do my utmost to improve the estates, not milk 'em dry!'

Randolph sipped his beer. He had made a good life for himself in Australia. He had revelled in the outdoor life, running his farm, building it up into a thriving business. Also, the climate suited him and he was healthier than he had ever been, so much so that he had positively enjoyed the long sea voyage. It had been very different from the first one, when only Joseph Miller's devotion had kept him alive.

'Lord knows I don't want the title,' he said slowly, 'but it is mine now and I cannot ignore it. As a boy I evaded all my responsibilities, leaving my sister to bear the consequences. I am deeply ashamed of the hell she went through for me. I will not shirk my duty a second time.'

The merry crackling of the fire filled the awkward silence. At last Joseph Miller spoke.

'So, *Lord Westray*, we stay in England?'

Ran met his eyes, read the same affection and faith in them that had helped him through the darkest days. He smiled and raised his glass.

'We stay in England.'

With the decision made, the atmosphere in the little room lightened. The canny lawyer was not given to displays of emotion, but Ran could almost feel the older man's relief.

'Very well, my lord. Firstly, I must give you the Westray ring.' He pulled a small velvet pouch from his pocket and handed it over, watching as Randolph took out the ring and tried it first on one finger, then another. 'If it does not fit, my lord, we can have it made larger.'

'No, no, it fits snugly on my little finger,' said Ran, holding up his hand. The gold signet ring felt heavy, but he would get used to that, as he would accustom himself to being Earl and all that entailed.

The lawyer looked relieved and permitted himself a little smile.

'I am glad. Now.' He fetched a thick wallet from the sideboard and carried it to the table. 'I have one or two documents here that require your attention.'

When Randolph walked into the private parlour the following morning, he was surprised to see the lawyer already there and finishing his breakfast.

'Good God, man, do you never sleep? It was well after midnight when we went to bed!'

'I find a few hours is sufficient for me,' replied Chislett. He nodded to Joseph, who was following his master into the room, then turned back to Ran. 'If you have no further questions or instructions, I plan to set out for London as soon as I have broken my fast.'

'I am sure I shall have a hundred more questions,' retorted Ran cheerfully. 'However, for the moment I am content with all we have arranged.'

'Then I shall be on my way.' Chislett drained his coffee cup and got to his feet. 'Do not hesitate to write to me, my lord, if anything else comes to mind, and I shall look forward to seeing you in town in the spring. Good day to you, Lord Westray. Mr Miller.'

The lawyer went out and Ran walked to the window to watch his departure. Only when the carriage had drawn away did he turn back to survey the breakfast table.

'By heaven, I have an appetite this morning, Joseph. I want more than bread rolls and coffee! Will you go and see if the landlord can provide us with eggs and perhaps some ham?'

'Aye, willingly.' Miller grinned at him. 'Do you wish me to tell him who you are, puff off your consequence?'

'No, damn you! I am not dressed for the part yet and want to enjoy my anonymity for a little longer.' He hesitated. 'You realise, old friend, our lives are going to be very different from now on. There are estates to be managed, staff and tenants to be considered.'

'Aye, sir, but it's nothing we can't handle. Now, you sit down while I go and chase up this rascally landlord!'

Chapter Two

Randolph spent the day going over the paperwork Chislett had left him, putting it away only when it was time to change for dinner. He went off to dine with Lord and Lady Gilmorton at the King's Arms, the hostelry that was enjoying their patronage.

Apart from the lawyer, whom he had sworn to secrecy, Ran had told only his sister, Deborah, and her husband that he was bound for England, and he was not surprised to receive a message that they planned to meet him at Portsmouth. He was delighted they should come so far, but slightly apprehensive, too, and he could not help putting a hand up to his neck-cloth before he entered the inn.

As the tap boy showed him into the private parlour, Ran looked over the man's shoulder to catch his first glimpse of his sister in six years. His heart swelled. He would have known her anywhere, neat as a pin in her Pomona-green gown and her brown hair swept up.

'Deborah.'

She barely waited for the servant to close the door

before she flew across the room, her green eyes over-bright with tears.

'Oh, Ran, Ran. Is it really you?'

He caught her to him, laughing. 'Well, I hope you wouldn't throw yourself like this at a stranger!' Keeping his arms tightly about her, he nodded to his brother-in-law. 'How are you, Gilmorton?'

The Viscount came forward to meet him, a smile lightening his rather serious countenance, made all the more sombre by the scar running down his left cheek.

'Very well, Randolph, thank you. If you put my wife down, I will shake hands with you!'

The tension melted away. Between laughter and tears he was dragged to the settle close to the fire while Deborah bombarded him with questions.

'My love, give the poor fellow a chance to catch his breath,' murmured Gil. He added, with a glint of humour, 'She has been in alt ever since you wrote to say you were coming home.'

'Then I pity you,' replied Ran, dodging a playful blow from his sister.

'Your letters were always so cheerful,' she said now, clinging still to his hand and her eyes searching his face. 'And you are well, now. Really well?'

He squeezed her hand, knowing what was behind the question.

'Yes, truly. I avoid laudanum, never drink spirits and partake sparingly of wine. I have never felt better.'

Her eyes misted. 'Then you were telling the truth in your letters, when you said transportation saved your life.'

'Aye. I believe it did.'

He had told them nothing of the arduous months he'd spent aboard the transport ship to Sydney Cove. All the prisoners suffered from the harsh conditions, the sickness and deprivation, but he had also had to endure the unbearable craving for laudanum. There had been periods of delirium, even longer stretches of dark despair. He knew he was lucky to be alive and how much he owed to his valet. It had been Joseph's diligent care that had saved him. His valet had given up his freedom to accompany him and it was a debt Ran could never repay.

'Is Miller still with you?' asked Gil, as if reading his thoughts.

'Aye. I suggested he might remain and run the farm for me, but he preferred to come back. Mayhap he thought I would be as ill on this journey as the first time, but apart from a few days of seasickness at the start, the voyage was uneventful. Even enjoyable.'

'So Joseph Miller has returned with you,' murmured Deborah, her eyes twinkling with mischief. 'My maid, Elsie, will be pleased to hear that.'

'Do not tell me she has been pining for him all these years!' exclaimed Ran, alarmed.

Deborah laughed. 'No, no, of course not. But they were very friendly, at one time, and I *did* wonder—'

'My wife is an inveterate matchmaker,' the Viscount interrupted her, shaking his head. 'Let it be, Deb. Give your brother and his man time to settle into their new life!'

Dinner was brought in and they moved to the dining table, where the talk continued, Ran describing his life in Airds, where he had been granted land following his pardon. He made light of the hardships leading up to that time, knowing that as an educated man he had received far better treatment than many of his fellow prisoners.

'And what are your plans now?' asked Deb.

'He is going to transform himself into an earl,' put in Gil. 'Why else did he send us his measurements and ask that we have some fashionable clothes made up?'

Ran laughed. 'That was Joseph's idea. He knows I own nothing suitable.'

'No, I regret I must agree,' drawled his brother-in-law, casting an eye over him. 'In that coat you would at best pass for a gentleman farmer. Thankfully, we have fulfilled your commission and you may carry away the trunk with you when you leave us tonight. Next time we meet I hope I shall not be ashamed to own you as my brother.'

'Mighty good of you!' retorted Ran, grinning.

'But where will you go?' asked Deb. 'Why not come back with us to Gilmorton? Little James and Randolph would like to meet their uncle, I am sure, and you might remain with us for the winter.'

'Aye, but do not come merely for your nephews' sake,' added her husband. 'We'd be delighted to have you stay. For as long as you wish.'

'Thank you, but that must wait, I am afraid. I have estates of my own that I need to visit first.'

'Ah, yes. You are a wealthy man now, Ran.' Gil sat back, cradling his glass between his hands. 'A fortune and a title—you have become something of a catch!'

'Gil!' Deb gasped, half-laughing, half-outraged. 'And you said *I* was a matchmaker!'

The Viscount raised his brows at her.

'What have I said that is not true? The society pages may be agog with the fact that the new Lord Westray is a pardoned felon, but let me tell you, Ran, it does not diminish your attraction with scheming mothers one jot!'

'We do not know…' Deborah glanced shyly at her brother. 'Perhaps there is a lady, back in Australia.'

Ran shook his head. 'There was little opportunity to meet *ladies* in Sydney Cove, or Airds. Besides, I was too busy making a life for myself. Now, I suppose, I must consider the idea of marriage.'

'By heaven, Ran, you are taking your duties seriously indeed!' exclaimed the Viscount.

'There is the succession to be considered.' He shrugged. 'It should not be difficult. There must be any number of eligible ladies who would suit. I am not that particular. I only need someone who will make me a comfortable wife.'

Gil snorted. 'There is nothing *comfortable* about falling in love, my friend. It can be joyous, but it is also painful.' He grinned at his wife. 'Believe me, it is anything but comfortable.'

'Then I shall not fall in love,' said Ran simply. 'I am too old for that nonsense.'

'At eight-and-twenty?' Deborah gave a little trill of laughter. 'You are perfectly poised to make a great fool of yourself over a woman!'

Ran was unoffended. 'Perhaps, but I doubt I shall have much time for that sort of thing for a while, at least. I have told Chislett he may now write to the steward at the Earl's—that is, at *my* principal seat, Westray Priors in Oxfordshire, telling him I am in England and that I intend to travel there in a few weeks. However, from the papers Chislett left with me yesterday, I realise there is a small property in Devon, Beaumount Hall. It is near Tavistock, I understand. It seems a pity not to see it, since I am so close.'

'Close!' Gil frowned. 'Why, that must be all of a hundred and fifty miles from here and I wager the roads will be shocking.'

'But I am not going by road,' Ran replied. 'I have my sea legs now, you know.' He grinned. 'Joseph and I have booked a passage with a local vessel sailing to Plymouth on the morning tide!'

The weather proved fair for Randolph and Joseph's journey to Plymouth, where they hired a coach to take them to Beaumount Hall. Ran looked about him with interest.

'I had forgotten how it is here in autumn,' he murmured, 'the blaze of colour before the trees lose their leaves in winter. And it is greener, too.'

A contentment settled over him. A feeling that he had come home.

As the Viscount had predicted, away from the towns the roads were not good and they were relieved when, after an hour's bumpy travel, the carriage turned to pass between open gates and into a small park.

'The drive appears to be in good order for a property that has been vacant for at least a year,' remarked Ran. 'Let us hope the house is similarly up together.

Chislett said there were a handful of staff in residence. Now, what did he say was the name of the butler? Meavy. And his wife is housekeeper.'

'I still think we should have sent word we were coming,' muttered Joseph.

'Devil a bit,' replied the new Earl cheerfully.

'You will look no-how if they can't accommodate us and we have to find lodgings in Tavistock!'

'Oh, I doubt it will come to that. We have slept under the stars before now.'

'Aye, but that was on the other side of the world!'

Ran merely laughed at his companion's retort and leaned forward, eager for a glimpse of Beaumount Hall. He was not disappointed. It had been a fine day and the sun was setting in a blaze of golden light as the carriage swung around a bend and the house came into view.

It was an impressive building over three floors. There was more than a hint of the baroque in the redbrick exterior with its creamy pilasters reaching to the roof line on the corners of the house. More pilasters flanked the door, which was topped by a stone hood, richly carved like a shell. Randolph grinned at his companion.

'You may be easy, Joseph! The roof looks sound, so at the very worst we may sleep on the floor here tonight.' The carriage stopped at the shallow steps and Ran jammed his hat on his head. 'Come along, then. Let us see how Meavy reacts to our arrival.'

However, when they were admitted to the house the butler looked surprised to see the new Earl, but not as shocked as Randolph had expected. Joseph had the letter of introduction from Chislett ready to wave before any suspicious custodians, but the butler scarcely glanced at it.

'Welcome, my lord,' he said, bowing. 'It is unfortunate we had no notice of your coming today.'

'There was no time,' replied Ran, handing over his hat and coat. 'If there is anything to eat in the house, then bring it to the drawing room, if you please.'

'Very good, my lord. And what will you drink?'

'I doubt you have any coffee.'

'Lord love you, of course we have coffee, my lord. And tea.'

'A pot of coffee, then.' He glanced at Joseph. 'You will come with me.'

His valet maintained his silence only until Meavy had shown them into the drawing room and closed the door.

'They will think it a pretty rum do, my lord, you taking refreshment with a servant.'

'They will grow accustomed to it! And you are not a servant. You are my aide-de-camp. I have promoted you!' He threw himself down into a chair beside the marble fireplace, where cheerful flames blazed. 'Later I shall demand to know what the devil they are doing keeping fires burning here when there is no one in residence, but for now I am damned glad of it.'

'Aye,' said Joseph, sitting down. 'Seems a strange set-up to me, however. Servants in livery and fires burning when they did not know the master was coming.'

'Mayhap they light a fire occasionally to drive off the damp—' Ran broke off as the door opened and Meavy came in with a tray of glasses and a decanter. He was followed by a plump woman in a white apron and with a snowy lace cap over her grey curls. She introduced herself as Mrs Meavy, the housekeeper.

'The coffee will be ready in a trice, my lord, but I thought, in the meantime, you might like to take a glass of wine.' She put a tray of cakes and biscuits down on a side table and turned back to the Earl. 'Well, my lord, this is a to-do,' she said cheerfully. 'If I'd known you was coming, I'd have prepared a dinner for you, but with Her Ladyship being out for the day, all I have ready is an egg-and-bacon pie—'

'Wait a moment.' Ran raised one hand to stop the garrulous flow. 'Her Ladyship?'

The old lady blinked at him. 'Why, yes, my lord. The Countess.'

It was Ran's turn to blink. 'Countess? You mean the old Earl's widow is in residence here?'

He swore silently. He had not considered that possibility. Damn Chislett for not warning him!

The housekeeper gave a fat chuckle. 'Why, no, my lord. I means *your* Countess, o' course!'

Randolph ignored the choking sound coming from Joseph and concentrated on concealing his own astonishment.

'Ah, yes. Lady Westray,' he said, not betraying himself by the flicker of an eyelid. 'She is gone out, you say?'

'Aye, my lord. She went off to Meon House this morning to ride out with Lady Meon and then she is to dine there and stay the night.'

'Is she indeed?' He felt a laugh bubbling up and grinned at Joseph, who was still red in the face from coughing. 'Then we shall join her there, once we have eaten something. Please bring us some of that pie,

Mrs Meavy, and after we have dined, Joseph, you had best unpack and brush my evening coat!'

Ran gazed at himself in the long mirror, taking in the black coat with its gold buttons bearing the Westray crest. He had looked at it askance when he had pulled it out of the trunk of clothes the Gilmortons had procured for him, but now he gave a nod of approval.

'Deb and Gil have surpassed my expectations,' he declared. 'Coat, knee breeches, the finest linen shirt, even footwear! Everything that is needed to convince doubters that I am indeed the new Earl.'

He was in the master bedroom, where a fire had been hastily cobbled together. Joseph was tenderly brushing the new chapeau-bras that would complete his ensemble, but he threw his master a frowning look.

'Aye, my lord, but who is this mysterious lady masquerading as your wife?' He kept his voice low even though they were alone in the room. 'I've asked a few questions, discreetly, of course, but all the servants can tell me is that she arrived two weeks ago along with her maid and took up residence. Gave some taradiddle about your being on business at t'other end of the country.'

'And they believed it?' Randolph fixed a diamond pin into the folds of his snowy cravat.

'Why should they not?' Joseph spread his hands. 'They'd heard the new Earl had been found and summoned to come home and claim his inheritance. Nothing more.'

'I suppose I had ordered Chislett not to blab,' said

Ran, fairly. 'And the lady's maid, the one person who might be able to tell us what is going on, has accompanied her mistress to Meon House.' He took the hat from Joseph and adjusted it at a rakish angle on his fair head. 'This could prove an interesting evening.'

'Perhaps I should come with you, my lord. In case there is trouble.'

'I do not anticipate needing your help, my friend. You stay here and make sure the sheets on the bed are properly aired. It was made up in a hurry and I don't want to catch my death of cold.'

'After everything we've been through, it would take more than a damp sheet to carry you off, my lord,' muttered Joseph, as he opened the door for his master to go out.

Meon House was situated just a few miles from Beaumount Hall, but Randolph's coachman was unfamiliar with the territory and took a wrong turn. It was therefore nearly nine o'clock before the carriage arrived at its destination. Light poured from every window and the number of carriages he could make out on the drive suggested there was something more than a quiet dinner in progress.

It had started to rain and Ran hurried up the steps to the door, which a servant was holding open for him. In the hall a cheerful fire burned and Ran could hear the buzz of voices coming from the rooms beyond. The footman looked a little bemused when Ran gave him his name, but a lady, crossing the hall, stopped and came forward. By the way she dismissed the servant, Ran guessed this was Lady Meon. She was on the shady side of thirty, but taking in the voluptuous figure sheathed in gold satin and the glossy dark curls piled on her head, she dressed to advantage. She was an attractive woman, he thought, and she was well aware of it.

'Lord Westray, this is indeed a surprise.' The smile on her full red lips and the appraising look in her dark eyes suggested it was not an unpleasant one.

'Yes, I am Westray.' He smiled at her. 'I beg your pardon for coming unannounced, but I have just arrived at Beaumount and learned my wife is here. I hope I have not interrupted your dinner?'

Ran took her outstretched hand and bowed over it, then worried that perhaps it would be considered an old-fashioned gesture. To his relief, the lady was clearly charmed. Her smile grew.

'No, no, we are quite finished and everyone is in the drawing room. I shall take you in myself. That is—' She stopped suddenly. 'Have you dined, Lord Westray? If not, I am sure we can—'

'I dined at Beaumount, ma'am, thank you.'

'Ah, good.' She tucked her hand into his arm. 'Come along, then, my lord. Let us go in. But I must warn you, it is only a little party, just a few neighbouring families, which is all the society this isolated place can provide. Lady Westray was eager to meet her neighbours and I was delighted to oblige her. Heavens, how pleased she will be to see you!'

'Not nearly as pleased as I shall be to see *her*,' murmured Ran.

He accompanied his hostess into an elegant drawing room full of glittering light from the chandeliers and the jewels that adorned the necks of the ladies present. It might be a small party, but it was clear the guests considered it an important occasion.

There were only about a dozen persons gathered there, but from the level of noise in the room Ran thought the wine had been flowing freely. Two elderly matrons conversed on a sofa by the fire and an aged gentleman dozed in a chair. Everyone else was gathered by the large window bay. Lady Meon led Ran across the room towards them. The group consisted of three ladies and double the number of gentlemen, their attention fixed upon a lady who had her back to the room. She was talking in an animated fashion that set the skirts of her red silk gown shimmering.

As they approached, Ran took the opportunity to observe her. Even from the back the view was attractive. She had an elegant figure and her shoulders rose in smooth, creamy slopes from a low-cut bodice. Her graceful neck was adorned with a diamond collar and above that fair curls were piled artlessly upon her head. They glinted with her every movement, like newly minted sovereigns.

Ran glanced at the two other females, both matronly and grey-haired. Too old to be his Countess. His lips twitched and he felt a sudden kick of pleasurable excitement as they drew closer. By heaven, surely this vision in the red gown could not be…

Lady Meon reached out and lightly touched one scarlet sleeve.

'Well, well, Lady Westray, you do not know how delighted I am to be the bearer of good tidings, for here is your husband, arrived in Devon this very night and come to find you!'

The lady turned quickly and Ran was dazzled

by her smile of delight. It quickly faded as her lips formed a little 'oh' of surprise. She regarded him with a shadow of fear in the depths of her emerald-green eyes. His own smile grew.

'Well, my dear, I believe I have surprised you.'

He reached for her hand, but even as he clasped her fingers she collapsed into a dead faint.

Ran did not hesitate. He scooped her up, the red silk skirts sliding with a whisper over his arm.

One of the matrons laughed. 'There now, no one can doubt her astonishment! Poor little thing. Take her somewhere quiet, my lord, until she has recovered herself. We will happily wait for the pleasure of an introduction!'

'Yes, yes, this way,' cried Lady Meon, leading him away from the group. 'There is a little room across the passage. Here we are.' She opened a door and Ran stepped into a comfortable sitting room, where candles were already burning and there was a small fire in the hearth. 'Lay her on the sofa, my lord. I shall send for her maid.'

'No. No need for that.' Ran put his burden down gently and sat on the edge of the sofa, beside her. 'I shall take care of her now.'

'Ah, of course you will. Who better to do so than her own husband?'

His hostess looked on with approval as he began to chafe the little hands and Ran shot her a smile.

'No need for any fuss, Lady Meon. Her pulse has already grown steadier. Pray go back to your guests and assure them my lady has merely fainted. We shall join you again very soon.'

'Very well, my lord. I shall leave you to look after

your wife. I can see she is stirring. Good, good. But you must ring if there is anything you need, anything at all.'

Lady Meon departed, leaving Randolph alone with his lady.

Arabella surfaced from the dead faint, but kept very still, afraid the pain behind her eyes would be worse if she opened them. Someone was rubbing her hands, and a deep voice, rich with amusement, was speaking to her.

'Gently now, my lady. You are safe.'

Safe! Her heart began to pound as memory returned. She was at Meon House and had been regaling her new acquaintances with some tale. Then Lady Meon had said her husband was there. For one brief, blissful moment she had forgotten that George was no longer alive. She had turned eagerly, only to find herself looking into the face of a stranger. That had been a cruel blow. Shock, heartbreaking disappointment and alarm had combined to render her senseless, but now she was awake and all too aware that she was in trouble.

The pain in her head had faded and she risked opening her eyes. The stranger was still there, holding her hands in a firm, sustaining clasp. He was nothing like George. He was older and his hair was fair, not brown. It was lighter than her own and, unlike George in those last months, this man positively glowed with health and vigour.

He smiled and something twisted, deep inside. She wanted to smile back at this handsome stranger, to lie still and enjoy his ministrations for a little longer.

She quickly closed her eyes again. Heavens, what an alarming thought!

'We are quite alone,' he said. 'There is no need for pretence.'

'My fainting was no pretence,' she told him crossly as she struggled to sit up. 'Who are you?'

'I am Westray,' he told her. 'More to the point, madam, who are *you*?'

She bit her lip. He was dressed fashionably and a diamond twinkled from the folds of his neckcloth, but he wore no other jewellery save for a gold signet ring. Could he really be the missing Earl? A felon. True, the reports said he had received a full pardon and she knew that people were transported for crimes as trivial as stealing a length of cloth, but he was a convict nevertheless.

She looked at him now, the candlelight gleaming on his mane of fair hair, his skin glowing with the golden tan of a man who spent his time out of doors. Or on a long sea voyage.

'Well?' he said, when she did not speak. 'Personation, that is, pretending to be someone you are not, is a crime, you know. I think I am entitled to an explanation. Let us begin with your name.'

She looked at him defiantly and wanted to retort that *he* was the criminal, she had read about him in the newspapers. He was waiting patiently for her to respond and her defiance faltered. He did not *look* like a villain. Yet whatever he had done to earn his pardon, it did not mean she could trust him.

He appeared relaxed, even amused, but there was a steely strength about him. She knew he would not be fobbed off with anything less than the truth. She had no choice but to answer.

'I am Arabella Roffey.'

'Go on.'

His blue-green eyes were glinting with laughter but they were not unkind. She said impulsively, 'I needed to be here. It is very important. Pray do not expose me!'

She moved to the end of the sofa, not trusting her legs to support her if she tried to stand. He shifted his position to face her, sitting back, his arms folded and smiling as if he was completely at his ease, but a second glance confirmed her original thought: he was as relaxed as a cat watching its prey.

'How intriguing,' he said cheerfully. 'You had best explain it to me.'

'I…' She clasped her hands, squeezing them together to steady her nerves and gazing down at the white knuckles. 'I am trying to find out who killed my husband.'

Chapter Three

It was not the answer Ran had been expecting. She did not look old enough to be married, let alone a widow. A closer look at her face made him reconsider. She would be one- or two-and-twenty, he guessed. She was very pale; there were dark smudges beneath her eyes and faint lines of strain around them. Young she might be, but he could believe she had known grief.

'You think Lady Meon is responsible?'

'No. Possibly. George was staying here with friends, you see. Before he died. From what he told me, when he was sick, I suspect, I *believe* something happened here.'

'Why did you not write to the lady and ask her?'

She lifted her shoulders in a tiny shrug. 'If my suspicions are correct, I doubt Lady Meon would have told me anything if I had approached her as Mrs Roffey.'

'You decided you might have more success as a countess.' When she did not respond he continued. 'How long have you been masquerading as my wife?'

'Just over two weeks.' She added, as if in mitigation, 'But only here in Devonshire and until this evening I had met only Lady Meon. Then she invited me to her party and I thought I might learn something.'

Loud voices came from the passage beyond the door. A burst of laughter and heavy footsteps.

She looked at him, her green eyes wide with alarm. 'Will you tell them I am an impostor?'

'Not here,' he said, getting up. 'Not tonight.'

Ran noted the slight lessening of tension in her dainty form.

'I am most grateful, thank you.'

'I will send for your cloak and order the carriage.'

That startled her.

'But I cannot go now,' she protested. 'I have accepted Lady Meon's invitation to stay the night!'

A grin tugged at his mouth. 'Our hostess would hardly expect me to leave without you, but if you would rather I stayed, we could continue this charade until the morning.'

He let the words hang, watching with unholy amusement as the implication of his words sank in. She blushed furiously.

'No, of course I do not want that!' She rose and shook out her skirts. 'I came in my own carriage. I will go and find my maid and we shall follow you.'

'Oh, no, I do not intend to let you slip away from me. We shall return to the salon together and find our hostess. And then, my lady, I am taking you back to Beaumount. Your maid can pack your bags and follow later.'

Arabella wanted to protest, but she knew it would be useless. He was still smiling, but there was an implacable look in his eyes. She must capitulate. For now.

'Very well. I will go with you, Lord Westray.'

'How formal that sounds.' He grimaced. 'Very well, then. Let us take leave of our hostess.'

Arabella paused for a heartbeat. It was a risk to go off with this man, she knew that, but what choice did she have? She could confess everything and throw herself on the mercy of her hostess, but instinct told her not to trust Ursula Meon.

Did she trust the Earl of Westray? She looked at him again and realised that she did. She felt her world shift slightly, as if something momentous had occurred. It was irrational, illogical, but looking into his sea-blue eyes, she felt a connection, as if he would understand her. Nonsense, of course. Her thoughts were confused. She was still shaken, not yet recovered from her faint.

He held out his arm. 'Madam, shall we go?'

Taking a deep breath, she put her fingers on his sleeve and allowed him to lead her back to the salon.

The party had grown rowdier in their absence and they entered to a confusion of chatter and laughter. The noise died as they walked in and Arabella felt as if every eye was turned towards her. She could not help clutching more tightly at the Earl's arm. He put his hand over her fingers and squeezed them.

'Do not be afraid to lean on me, my dear. I have you safe now.'

Arabella knew the caressing tone was as much for the benefit of the gathered company as for her. Lady Meon had flown out of her chair and was beside them, begging the Earl to bring his lady closer to the fire, asking if she could fetch her anything.

'You might send for my carriage, madam,' replied the Earl. 'I would like to take my wife home.'

Home. Wife.

The words sent a chill through Arabella, dispelling the feeling of unreality that had possessed her since meeting the Earl. Common sense told her it was better to stay here, in company, rather than to leave with a stranger. To ride in a darkened coach with him and then to enter Beaumount. His house. As his wife. That would be foolhardy in the extreme. She needed time to think.

'Oh, but I am so much better now, my lord,' she said brightly. 'Indeed, I am mortified that I should be so silly as to faint off. I beg your pardon and hope you will forgive me. I should dearly like to remain here for a little longer yet, at least until after supper—'

'Alas, my love, I do not think that would be wise,' the Earl interrupted her smoothly. 'Lady Meon will understand, I am sure, that I want to have you to myself tonight.'

Arabella flushed at the inference, but she was also angered by the teasing note in his voice. It made her long to hit him.

'Of course I understand, my lord.' Lady Meon gave Arabella's arm a playful tap with her fan. 'You naughty puss, to tease him so, when I am sure you are just as eager to be away.'

The ladies were all smiling and nodding—one of the gentlemen even laughed. Arabella found herself blushing again, but she was not giving up just yet.

'Naturally, I should like to be at home,' she said

sweetly, 'and yet I think it would be better if I remained here, quietly, for a little while. Perhaps I might take a cup of tea before I leave.' She turned her head to look up at the Earl and gave him a false, glittering smile. 'That would also give my lord the opportunity to become acquainted with our new neighbours.'

His eyes gleamed appreciatively, acknowledging she had outmanoeuvred him.

'As you wish, my dear, we shall stay a little longer.'

The tea tray was summoned and the Earl guided Arabella to a chair. She sat down, fanning herself, and watched through half-closed eyes as Lady Meon and her guests vied for Lord Westray's attention.

There was no doubting their eagerness to become acquainted with the new Earl. Over the course of the evening she had learned that in recent times the Westray family had made little use of Beaumount. Everyone was aware of the present Earl's history, but it made no odds to them. It was more important to be on good terms with their exalted neighbour than to worry about his past.

'Do you intend to make this a long visit to Devonshire, my lord?' asked Lady Trewen, wife of the local squire.

'I hardly know, ma'am. A week, perhaps.'

'There is good sport, sir, if you are a hunting man,' declared her husband. 'Plenty of fish and fowl to be had. And of course, fox and stag hunting. If you haven't brought your own horses, I'd be happy to mount you on one of mine. I believe I have a couple that would be up to your weight.'

The Earl inclined his head. 'Thank you, but I doubt

we shall be in the area long enough for that. I have business in London that requires my attention.'

'And your good lady is pining for society, I don't doubt,' said a bewhiskered gentleman. 'You should come back in the spring or summer, my lord. Lady Meon's house parties would be very much in your line, I am sure. Any number of young bucks from town come down, and lords and ladies, too. Ain't that so, ma'am?' He gave another hearty laugh. 'Then my lady doesn't have to rely upon country dwellers like ourselves to fill her drawing room!'

Lady Meon smiled and shook her head at him. 'It is always a pleasure to invite my neighbours here, Mr Lettaford.'

Beneath her drooping lids, Arabella watched the exchange. The bonhomie was slightly forced. She had the impression the local families were not welcome at the Meon House parties and they resented it. She sat up a little and reached for the cup of tea that had been placed on the table at her elbow.

'Goodness, ma'am,' she exclaimed, 'do people come all the way from London for your parties?'

'It is not such a long way, Lady Westray,' replied Mrs Lettaford, bridling in defence of her home. 'There is a good road as far as Plymouth, because of the mail, and the roads around here are not as bad as some in the county. I am sure there would no inconvenience at all in travelling to the capital.'

'Not that we have had any call to make the journey,' added her husband. 'We can find everything we need in Tavistock, or if not there, then in Plymouth.'

Mrs Lettaford glared at him before giving an angry

titter. 'Now, now, sir, Lord and Lady Westray will think we are all rustics living here.'

'I can assure His Lordship that is not the case at all,' purred Lady Meon, quick to soothe the ruffled feathers of her guests. 'And it is true the road from London is a good one. My brother often comes to stay, but I confess we rarely entertain our neighbours when he is here.' She gave a placatory smile. 'He often brings his young friends, you see, who enjoy the break away from the constant social whirl of the capital. This is something of a repairing lease for them. We keep very much to ourselves, nothing very exciting at all.'

Arabella remembered George telling her much the same thing.

'It is only a few close friends, my sweet,' he had said. 'It will be all cards and sport, neither of which interest you. You had much better remain in Lincolnshire, for you would not enjoy their company and there will be no other wives to chatter with. You would be bored within a day. Imagine then how I would feel, knowing you were not happy.'

In vain had she pleaded with him. He had merely pinched her cheek, told her he knew best and gone off, leaving her with his parents at Revesby Hall. If only she had insisted. If only.

She looked up to find the Earl was watching her.

'You look tired,' he murmured. 'If you have finished your tea, my dear, perhaps we should take our leave?'

Arabella suddenly did feel fatigued. She could think of no reason to stay longer and she rose from her chair. When she suggested she would slip upstairs to fetch her cloak, Lady Meon said quickly she would send a servant to fetch it.

'I need to tell my maid what has occurred,' Arabella protested, but the Earl shook his head at her.

'I am sure my lady's footman can explain everything.' He glanced a question at their hostess, who nodded. He continued smoothly, 'You must not exert yourself any more than necessary. As your husband, I must insist, my dear.'

His smile was gentle, but she saw the gleam of laughter in his eyes and fumed in silence until the footman came back with her fur-lined cloak. The Earl took leave of the company, saying all that was proper, and Lady Meon insisted upon accompanying them to the door. As they crossed the hall, she gave a little laugh and touched the Earl's arm.

'My parties here are not *quite* as uneventful as I made out, my lord, I assure you.'

The lady spoke very quietly and Arabella had to strain to hear.

'I would not for the world wish to offend my neighbours,' Lady Meon continued, 'but as you have seen, they are not the sort one would wish to make known to more…er…worldly friends. They would be shocked by our late nights and deep play, so it is best that they do not come. However, if you should be at Beaumount the next time I have house guests, be assured *you* would be most welcome.' Arabella did not miss the slight pause before her final words. 'And your dear lady, of course.'

'I thank you, madam,' he replied easily. 'We should be glad to join you. On our next visit.'

They had reached the door and Arabella could see

a dusty travelling coach waiting on the drive. Another moment and she would be alone with the Earl in that confined, dark interior.

Don't go, Arabella. Say something, now!

There was still time. She might throw herself upon Lady Meon's mercy, but something held her back. The Earl had taken her hand, but his touch was light, supportive rather than keeping her a prisoner. Perhaps it was foolish, but Arabella trusted him far more than she trusted her hostess. She swallowed down her nerves and managed to mutter a word of thanks before he escorted her down the steps and into the waiting carriage.

Arabella pressed herself into one corner, clutching her cloak tightly about her. To her relief, Lord Westray made no attempt to question her, or even to touch her, for the short journey back to Beaumount. They travelled in silence, and when they arrived, he helped her down and pulled her hand firmly on to his arm to guide her up the steps and into the house.

Meavy opened the door and did not appear in the least surprised to see them. He beamed, bowed, and when His Lordship declared they would take refreshments before retiring, he sent a footman running to light the candles in the drawing room and to build up the fire.

To Arabella's stretched nerves, the period since leaving Meon House and arriving at Beaumount had seemed interminable, yet it had not been long enough for her to gather her thoughts. It had been madness to come back here with the Earl. As they made their way to the drawing room, questions raced through her head. What was she going to do? What was she going to tell him?

The servant withdrew, closing the door behind him. Arabella walked across to the fire to warm her hands. The Earl poured a glass of wine and handed it to her.

'Apart from meeting you, madam, I have to say I found nothing untoward at Meon House tonight. The lady's guests appeared to be respectable people.'

'I am sure they are,' she replied. 'It would seem Lady Meon is at pains to keep her neighbours and her house guests apart. No one would admit it outright, of course, but more than one of the ladies gave the impression that they disapproved of the house parties at Meon House.'

'Unsurprising, if they were not invited,' he remarked. 'I suggest you sit down and tell me what this is all about.'

She subsided into a chair. Time to decide what to tell him, and how much.

The Earl sat down facing her and said, as if reading her thoughts, 'It would be best if you told me everything.'

'I did not know you were in England.'

'I arrived in Portsmouth a few days ago. Not many people know yet that I am in the country.'

She was about to ask another question, but he caught her eye, the warning in his own very clear. He would not allow her to digress. She took a deep breath.

'At the end of June, my husband, George, returned from a visit to Devonshire, where he had been staying with friends. He was very ill and he died within weeks. He was in a bad way, raving that he had been ill-used. Robbed and poisoned. I thought at the time that he was delirious, but later, I discovered that he had spent thousands of guineas in a matter of months. You see, the marriage settlement had been drawn up in such a way that upon my husband's death, the money invested in Funds reverted to mc. I knew exactly how much it had been upon our marriage and I was shocked to see how it was depleted.' She took a sip of her wine. 'George was young and…and impressionable. I think he fell in with a bad crowd who tried to take all his money, but I do not know who they are. All I know is that he had been invited to stay at Meon House.'

'One moment.' He stopped her, frowning. 'Why did he not take you with him?'

'We had only just married.'

'I would have thought that all the more reason to be together.'

She blushed, partly out of guilt because she had thought that, too.

'It was only a small party, a few friends meeting up for gambling and a little sport. I should not have enjoyed it.' George had told her as much, had he not? And he knew best; she had never questioned that. She said now, with a touch of defiance, 'He was obliged to go because he had promised his friends, but I *know* he would have preferred to stay at home with me. He told me so.'

What George had *not* told her was that Meon House had no master. It had been an unpleasant surprise for her to discover its mistress was a widow. Even worse that she was a lively and attractive widow.

Arabella had wondered more than once since arriving at Beaumount if jealousy was clouding her judgement of Lady Meon.

The Earl was speaking again and she dragged her thoughts back.

'Do you believe it was these friends who took your husband's money?'

'Someone took it! From what he told me, before he died, Lady Meon lures unwary young gentlemen to her remote house and—and *fleeces* them.' She frowned. 'She most likely drugs them, too, so they know not what they are doing.'

'That is a serious accusation. If it is true.'

'I know. That is why I need to find some proof!'

'And why you set yourself up as Lady Westray.'

'Yes. I had read in the newspaper that the old Earl had died and that his heir was in the Antipodes and not expected to return for some time. By chance I noticed that one of the Earl's properties was near Tavistock. It took only a little further investigation to show it was very close to Meon House.'

'How convenient for you.'

She raised her head and continued with a hint of defiance.

'I was determined to discover the truth and this was the perfect opportunity. Having lived in Lincolnshire my entire life, I thought it would be safe enough to masquerade as someone else. No one would know me.' She added quickly, 'Please do not blame anyone in your household for being taken in by my deception, my lord. I was very convincing.'

'What exactly did you do?'

'I turned up at the door. Told them your letter must

have gone astray and that you would be following me to Devon shortly.'

He gave a shout of laughter. 'The devil you did!'

She lifted her chin higher. 'I gave Meavy a purse when I arrived, to cover any expenses I incurred while staying here, since you had not yet made arrangements with the bank. That helped to convince him I was genuine.'

'I am obliged to you, madam.'

'I assure you my funds are more than sufficient to cover anything I choose to do. I have merely made use of your house and your name.'

'*Merely* made use of them!'

'You were not using them, at the time,' she retorted. 'I had no idea you would choose just this moment to return to England, and even if I *had* known,' she continued, with spirit, 'I would not have expected you to come first to the least important of your properties!'

'And you would still have carried out this charade? By heaven, madam, you are a cool one!'

'I want to discover what happened to my husband! I have explained why I needed to come here. Why should you think it so odd?'

With a hiss of exasperation, he pushed himself to his feet. 'For one thing, it is a hare-brained idea,' he exclaimed, pacing the floor. 'And for another, it is damned dangerous. Was there no one you could talk to about this? Relatives, friends?'

'I have no family of my own. As for friends, there is no one I would trust.'

'Why did you not tell your husband's family?'

'Sir Adam Roffey has a weak heart. Angina. He

was laid low by his son's death and I did not wish to add to his worries.'

He bent a frowning gaze upon her. 'Do the Roffeys have any idea what you are about?'

She shook her head. 'They think I am staying with an old school friend. They will not be anxious because I have Ruth, my maid, with me.'

'The devil you have. Of all the foolish starts! How old are you?'

She put up her chin. 'Two-and-twenty.'

'And you said yourself you have never before been out of Lincolnshire.'

'What has that to say to anything?'

'You can know very little of the world. Whereas I...' he stopped and raked one hand through his hair '... I know too much of it.'

'I am well aware of that!' she flashed back. 'For all your title, you are no less a felon!'

His eyes darkened. She braced herself for a furious response, but he merely shrugged.

'I cannot deny it. But that is all the more reason you should not be here. You should never have embarked upon such a foolhardy scheme, alone and unprotected.'

Arabella suddenly felt exhausted. George had been her world since childhood. Could no one understand that? Tears were not far away and she looked up at him, saying wretchedly, 'What else have I to live for?'

Ran saw those emerald eyes shimmering with tears and thought she must have loved her husband very much. Something clutched at his heart and he turned away to resume his pacing.

He said, 'Have you learned anything that might help you?'

'Very little,' she confessed. 'I want to know who else was at Meon House when George was a guest there. I had hoped, tonight...'

He heard a sniff and glanced around to see her surreptitiously wiping her eyes. He paced a little more, trying to convince himself that the plan in his head was every bit as hare-brained as the one she had described.

'Very well.' He stopped in front of her. 'Let us continue this masquerade for a little longer.'

She stared at him. 'I beg your pardon?'

'I will help you. A short note to Lady Meon tomorrow should repair any damage tonight's little fracas may have caused and we will work on the acquaintance until the lady divulges a little more information.'

'No!' She was on her feet now, staring at him as if he had run mad. 'I cannot stay here.'

'Why not? You have been content to do so thus far.'

'That was different!'

'How was it different?' He uttered the challenge, preferring her anger to the desolation he had heard in that one sniff.

She glared at him. 'You were not here.'

'And now I am.' He smiled. 'Which will make your presence here all the more plausible.' He saw her look of horror and added, 'By Gad, madam, I am not suggesting we should be man and wife in anything other than name, but it will be necessary to live under one roof! I have already ascertained that Beaumount has separate rooms for the Earl and his Countess, so only your maid and my man need be taken into our confidence—'

'But you are a—a *criminal*,' she interrupted him, retreating behind her chair. 'Perhaps even a murderer!'

Ran stopped, all desire to laugh gone.

'You should have considered that before you began this charade,' he threw back at her. 'Let me allay your fears, if I can. My biggest crime was to be a damned young fool! I was sentenced to be transported for fourteen years and, having survived the voyage, I was prepared to serve my time and to make a fresh life for myself on the other side of the world. Circumstances, in the form of a pardon and the death of the old Earl, conspired to bring me back to England.'

'But it cannot be long before people know you are in England,' she argued. 'Word will soon get out that you have no wife.'

'By the time that information reaches Devon I hope we shall be finished here. You will disappear and no one need ever discover your true identity.'

'But what of your staff?' There was a note of desperation in her voice. 'What must be their feelings when they know you have duped them?'

'*I* did not dupe them, my lady! I have merely...' he waved one hand '...not corrected the misapprehension.'

'Now you are playing with words, my lord!'

'Very well,' he said, goaded. 'They will believe you were my mistress. What of it? Is that not the sort of behaviour expected of great lords?' He shrugged. 'I shall no doubt feel obliged to apologise for playing such a trick, but I pay them well enough. The matter will soon be forgotten.'

'Not by me!'

She was staring defiantly at him, her head up, eyes blazing, and suddenly he did not want her to think him the sort of master to disregard the feelings of his staff. He did not want her to think ill of him at all.

He said, 'I do not like this subterfuge any more than you, but what's done is done. We may as well continue with it.'

The words sounded gruff, uncaring, and she continued to stare at him with angry disapproval. Damnation! Did she not realise he was trying to help her? If there had been dark deeds at Meon House then who knew what dangers might await such an innocent if he left her to continue her enquiries alone. He issued his ultimatum.

'So, you must make your choice, madam. You can either accept my help, or you give up your investigation and go home.'

Arabella glared at the Earl. Since leaving Lincolnshire she had been aware of how vulnerable she was, how alone. True, she had Ruth. The loyal maid had been with her since she was a baby, but if there was real danger, then she was putting Ruth at risk, too. Lord Westray might well be able to help her obtain the information she required. If one could forget his past.

It occurred to her that she found it only too easy to ignore the fact that he was a convict, but she was merely being charitable. Wasn't she? All the guests at Meon House had had no difficulty in accepting the new Earl, even with his tainted history. Although *they* were not pretending to be his spouse. She swallowed.

'Very well, sir. I will accept your help.' She hesitated. 'I am very grateful to you.'

Some of his stiffness disappeared and she saw the glimmer of a smile.

'No, you are not at all grateful. You would like to tell me to go to the devil.'

Her own anger seeped away. 'That would be very uncivil, would it not? In your own house.'

'It would indeed.' His smile fully appeared now. 'Off you go to bed. We will discuss this further in the morning.'

She managed a faint smile herself and with a soft 'Goodnight' she left the room, forcing herself not to run.

When she reached her bedchamber, Ruth was pacing up and down.

'Oh, thank heaven!' She took her mistress by the shoulders and turned her towards the light, subjecting her to a close and critical inspection. 'What happened? What has he done to you?'

'Nothing, Ruth. I have come to no harm at all.'

The maid gave a loud sigh and plumped down on a chair. 'I don't mind telling you, when I heard that the Earl of Westray had turned up and was bringing you back here I was that worried! I fear we are undone, Miss Arabella.'

'Nonsense. This is a slight setback, Ruth, nothing more.'

'Has he not exposed you as an impostor?'

A small bubble of laughter fizzed inside her. She said airily, 'On the contrary. He has agreed to help us.'

The maid looked anything but reassured by this news. She frowned.

'And what does His Lordship want in return?'

Arabella could not deny she had asked herself the same question, but she was not prepared to speculate about that just yet.

'I have promised him nothing,' she said at last. 'Now, help me to undress, Ruth. I need to sleep!'

A short time later Arabella was alone in her room, in her bed, with just the bedside candle burning. She lay back against the plump pillows, gazing up at the intricately carved tester as she thought about the new Lord Westray. She did not know what to make of him. He did not appear outraged at her deception, merely amused. Perhaps in comparison to his own dark deeds this pretence was a trifle, but when she had mentioned his past he had flinched as if she had touched an open wound.

She wished she knew just what he had done, that she had made more enquiries into his past, but at the time it had seemed unimportant; the new Earl was half a world away.

How old could he have been when he was convicted? She did not think he was yet thirty, so he would have been almost a boy, one- or two-and-twenty, perhaps. The lines around his eyes and mouth indicated more than mere laughter. Dissipation, perhaps. Or hardship. His hands, she had noted, were not soft, but calloused from tough, physical work.

How had he survived? What deprivation had he suffered? He had received a full pardon for his crimes, but the life he had led for the past six years must have left its scars. And she was in his house, posing as his wife. Strangely the thought did not worry her. She was not afraid of the new Earl, but perhaps she should be.

Arabella slipped out of bed and crossed to the connecting door leading to the Earl's chambers. The key was in the lock and she turned it, giving a little nod when she heard the satisfying click. It was best not to take any chances.

Chapter Four

Randolph woke to the sounds of his man making up the fire in his room to ward off the damp, grey chill of an English November day.

'Good morning, my lord. There's hot water on the stand for you and I can light more candles, if you wish?'

'No, thank you, Joseph. There is sufficient light in here.'

Ran pushed himself up against the bank of pillows and clasped his hands behind his head, his eyes fixed on the dark shape of the connecting door on the far side of the room. He had noticed yesterday that the key was on the other side. He had not tried the door, but he was damned sure if he did, he would find it locked.

As it should be, although he could not deny that knowing Arabella was sleeping in the next room had disturbed his rest. He spent a few moments in agreeable contemplation, allowing his imagination to picture her sleeping, her glorious golden hair spread over the pillows, eyes closed, the long lashes resting on her cheeks, her soft red lips inviting a morning kiss.

Enough! Ran shifted restlessly. It was an agreeable daydream, but he must put it from his mind. He threw back the covers and jumped out of bed. Mrs Arabella Roffey was only recently widowed and still grieving for her husband. Only a heartless rogue would take advantage of the situation.

He was finishing his breakfast when Arabella entered the dining room. She hesitated in the doorway, uncertain and shy. He gave her a reassuring smile.

'Good morning, my lady.'

She was looking particularly fetching in a pale blue morning gown, her shining hair caught up with a matching ribbon, and he fought down an urge to jump up and escort her to her chair. A footman was on hand to do that and a second stood ready to pour her coffee and offer her a freshly baked bread roll.

'I trust you slept well?' he asked her as the servants withdrew from the room.

'Yes. Thank you, my lord.'

'I would much rather you called me Randolph.'

A blush suffused her cheeks. 'I cannot do that!'

'Why not? We are supposed to be man and wife.' He pushed away his empty plate. 'I warn you, I do not intend to call you *my lady* every time I address you. I shall call you Arabella.' His eyes narrowed. 'That *is* your name, is it not?'

Her chin went up. 'Of course. I would not lie to you, my lord.'

'No, it will be much better if we are truthful with one another. What plans do you have for the day?'

'Why, none.' The question appeared to take her by surprise. 'If you had not arrived here, I should have been at Meon House this morning.'

Meavy came in with a fresh pot of coffee and Ran waited until they were alone again before replying.

'Do you blame me for wanting to meet the woman masquerading as my wife?'

'No, of course not.'

'We shall pay a call upon Lady Meon today and I shall apologise for dragging you away so precipitately. Although everyone was most understanding.'

Her cheeks reddened. 'It was mortifying.'

'I am very sorry for it, but I think you deserved to be punished a little, do you not?'

He smiled, to take any sting from the words, but she did not see it. She would not meet his eyes. She had assumed a look of indifference and was studiously applying herself to her breakfast. Ran stifled a sigh. Perhaps it was best she stayed aloof. It was far too tempting to flirt with her.

She said quietly, 'You said you would help me.'

'And I will, but I need to know just what story you have given the people here if we are to carry on with this masquerade.'

'I have told them almost nothing. They could hardly ask me about the reports in the newspapers concerning the new Earl. That is why I thought it would be safe to pretend I was your wife. I merely explained you had returned to England unannounced.'

'Well, that much is true! What reason did you give for your coming to Beaumount alone?'

'I said you had business elsewhere.' She bit her lip. 'I may have given the impression we had quarrelled.'

'A lovers' tiff!' He grinned. 'And your swooning would have done nothing to dispel that idea.' He saw that she was looking uncomfortable and forbore to tease her further. Instead he said, 'Tell me what you expected to achieve at Meon House.'

Arabella paused, considering. 'I hoped to discover what went on there and which of George's particular friends were there with him. He never told me, you see, and I knew so few of his friends. There were only two I recall coming to Revesby Hall. One was George's groomsman at our wedding and the other was Frederick Letchmore. He called upon us soon after George came home that last time. My husband was very excited about his visit and could hardly be still while he waited for him to arrive. He was like a child anticipating a treat.'

'And was that usual for your husband?' asked Ran.

She looked troubled and did not answer immediately.

'His temper had become mercurial in the past year. One moment he was all charming, devil-may-care insouciance, the next he was despairing. Blue-devilled, he called it, but said I must not worry. When Mr Letchmore arrived, George asked me to leave them alone together, to talk. Which I did, but not long after that he sent Mr Letchmore away. He was more angry than I had ever seen him. I clearly remember him saying, *"You have killed me, Freddie. I trusted you to help but you have failed me."* Then Mr Letchmore rushed out and we never saw him again.'

'And did you learn just how he had failed your husband?' asked Ran.

She shook her head. 'George was in a towering

rage following the meeting, almost incoherent and railing against his false friends, as he called them. After his death I wrote to both gentlemen, but I do not think my letters ever reached them, for I had no replies. I discovered Letchmore had left England. I thought it might be to escape any repercussions over George's death. I wondered… I thought perhaps he might be one of those gamblers who exist only to prey on unwary young men and relieve them of their fortune.'

'You think your husband was one of those, er, unwary young men?'

'Yes! Especially after I discovered how much of the marriage settlement he had already spent in just three months. It would explain his anger with Mr Letchmore, too. George would never tell me why he suddenly became so set against him.'

'Sometimes illness can cause people to change,' said Ran, choosing his words carefully. 'Perhaps you could tell me about your husband's last days, if it isn't too painful?'

She pushed aside her plate and sat very still for a moment, her green eyes gazing at nothing.

'He was very disturbed when he came home that last time. I had never seen him like it. He would go for days without sleeping, but sometimes he was almost euphoric, and would talk to me about what we would do when he was well again. At other times the black mood descended and nothing would please him.

'I confess I did not like to be with George when he was in a temper. He would lash out at everyone. He even railed at Dr Philps and complained that everyone was against him. That we all wanted to kill him. The doctor had no remedy for whatever was ailing him. George grew weaker. He was very sick and could keep nothing down. He was very thirsty, too, and confused.'

Ran put his elbows on the table and leaned forward, watching her. 'And what was the cause of this malady?'

She clasped her hands. 'Dr Philps recorded the cause of death as convulsions, but I think that was to avoid any scandal.'

'And what did the doctor say to you, privately?'

'I did not actually speak to him.'

'But you were Roffey's wife. Surely they told you what was wrong with him.'

She looked a little confused. 'Lady Roffey was in charge of the sickroom and dealt with Dr Philps. But when I suggested that George might have been poisoned, she did not disagree.'

Ran turned the coffee cup between his hands. 'You were widowed after only three months of marriage and you told me your husband was away for most of that time. How well did you really know him?'

The worry left her face and she smiled. 'We had known each other all our lives. Our two families have neighbouring lands, you see, and when my parents died Sir Adam and Lady Roffey took me in. I was ten, George a little older. They were all very kind to me and George was like an older brother.' She added simply, 'I worshipped him.'

Ran's fingers tightened around his cup. 'It was a love match, then.'

'Of course. Our parents had always wanted the marriage to unite the two families. But you are not to think we were coerced.' A shadow flickered across her face. 'I would have married him as soon as I left the schoolroom, but George said we should wait. He did not wish to rush me into a marriage. He thought I might change my mind, but I knew I never should.'

'And Lady Roffey brought you out? Why did she not take you to London?'

'It was not necessary. I was happy to live at Revesby Hall.'

'But the society there must be confined. I thought your husband wanted you to be sure of your feelings?'

'He did, but I had always loved him. I lived for the few weeks every year that we spent together at Revesby Hall.'

'He did not live there all the time?'

'He was often away, visiting friends, and he used the family's townhouse when he was in London.'

'While you remained with his parents.'

'You make it sound as if I was a prisoner,' she retorted. 'It was not like that at all.' She gave a huff of impatience. 'Oh, this is ridiculous! It does nothing to help me find out what happened to my husband.'

She made to rise and he said quickly, 'Please, do not go yet. I beg your pardon, but I am trying to understand it all.' She settled back into her seat and he continued. 'This Mr Letchmore. You did not see him again? If he was such a good friend, did he not come to the funeral, even after their falling-out?'

'I told you, he had gone abroad. He sent his condolences, but at the time I was glad he did not come. George had cursed him bitterly during his final days.' She clasped her hands and looked at Ran. 'It was only afterwards, when I learned the state of George's finances, I suspected something had happened at that house party.'

She shook her head when Ran offered her more coffee. He refilled his own cup then said quietly, 'What is it you suspect?'

'Is it not obvious? They tricked him out of his money. You will recall last night that Lady Meon herself said they play deep.'

'It is not against the law to gamble large sums,' he said gently. 'Or to lose them.'

'No, I am aware of that, but George was the kindest, gentlest of men! To see him when he came home that last time, so angry, his health ruined.' She put a hand to her cheek. 'He tried to keep in spirits, for my sake, but often I heard him cursing his ill fortune. And once, when I went into his room, he told me he should never have gone to Meon House, that they were all thieves.' She frowned. 'At least, I *think* that is what he meant. It was very difficult to understand him at the end.'

'You nursed him?'

'No, not as much as I would have liked. Lady Roffey thought I might be carrying his child and said I owed it to my baby to keep away from the sickroom. She feared the shock and distress might be harmful. How could I argue, when Dr Philps agreed with her?' Arabella sighed. 'We had been married such a short time, I suppose it was natural that the doctor should defer to George's parents. Sometimes, I think, if we had lived in our own house, it might have been different.' Her shoulders lifted, then fell again. 'And in the end, I was glad of their support when he…when he died.'

'I am very sorry. It was very hard for you, to lose your husband so soon after the wedding.'

'We were together, as man and wife, for less than a week after the ceremony,' she said, wiping her eyes. 'Then he was obliged to go to London because he had received word from a friend who needed his help. But does that not show you what a good, kind man I had married?' When Ran said nothing, she went on, a hint of defiance in her voice, 'George would much rather have been with me. He told me so.'

'And from town he went directly to Devon?'

'Yes. His visit to Meon House had been planned for months and he could not cry off. His parents were not happy about it, but they, too, had to acknowledge that if he had given his word then he must go. When he came home, he was dying. But you must see now why I want justice for him?' She looked at him, determination in every line of her body and a sparkle in her eyes. 'If someone is responsible for George's death, then they should pay!'

Randolph said nothing. He knew only too well the temptations awaiting any young man with money in his pocket. His gut feeling was that this was a wild goose chase, that she was clutching at any straw rather than face the fact that her husband was a wastrel. But if he did not help her, she would go off alone and into heaven knew what danger. He stirred his coffee, giving himself time to think.

'I have been over and over everything,' she said, a frowning gaze fixed on the table. 'Meon House is the only clue I have to where he was and what he was doing before his death. I *know* there is a link. I am sure of it.'

'Then we must find out more about Lady Meon,' he said. 'But there is little we can do for the moment. As it is such a fine day, I thought I would take a stroll through the gardens and take stock of what I own here. Will you come with me?' The look on her face made him laugh. 'You are not cut out to be a spy, madam. I can read your thoughts quite clearly in your countenance. You want to drive over to Meon House immediately and talk to the lady, do you not? However, I suspect you might find she has not yet left her room. Besides, unless you are prepared to tell her who you are and ask her outright about her house party, I doubt you will discover anything useful by such a direct approach.'

'No, you are right.' She gave him a rueful smile. 'I need to cultivate patience, do I not? Very well, my lord. Allow me time to fetch my shawl and I will join you.'

It was cold, but the sun was shining when they went out of doors and there was the merest scattering of small clouds sailing across the blue sky. After making a tour of the stables, service buildings and kitchen gardens, all of which they agreed were in a relatively good state of repair, they made their way to the pleasure grounds to the south and west.

The ground sloped away from the house and the gardens were laid out over a series of terraces, providing extensive views across fields and wooded hills as far as the Tamar. Winter had not yet tightened its grip and many of the distant trees still retained their red and gold leaves.

They progressed to the lowest level, where a stone

wall separated the formal gardens from the surrounding park. A wide gravel path ran between the lawn and herbaceous borders where a few late-flowering plants still bloomed. Randolph breathed in deeply, realising again how much he had missed the bracing chill of an English autumn.

He had thought conversation might be difficult, given his past and Arabella's reason for being at Beaumount, but within minutes they were chatting away like old friends. He was grateful that she did not ask him about his life in Australia, how he had survived, how he had suffered. Instead she took inspiration from their surroundings and asked him about the landscape and the plants to be found on the other side of the world.

'I attended a talk in Lincoln last year, about Captain Cook's voyages to the southern hemisphere,' she told him. 'England must look and feel very different to you now.'

'It is colder,' he said. 'And the birds are generally smaller and less colourful. Quieter, too. Less raucous. I had forgotten how soothing it is to hear the gentle hoot of an owl or the morning trill of birdsong. And the flowers around Sydney Cove are very different from those in England. They have vibrant colours to match a hot country where the rocks steam after a summer storm.' He waved at the near-empty flower beds. 'Although I am sure these are very pretty in the summer months. But it is the night sky where I notice the change most. The different stars.'

'Do you look at them, too?' she asked, turning her head to smile up at him. 'I used to spend hours at my window at school, looking out, looking for shooting stars, to make a wish.'

'And what did you wish for.'

'Oh…' She waved her hand. 'At first it was unattainable things, such as wishing Mama and Papa had not died of the fever. Later, I wished that a handsome prince would carry me away and marry me.' She laughed. 'And in a way, that wish came true, only it was Sir Adam and Lady Roffey who carried me away when they took me to live with them.'

'And you married their son.'

'Yes. My handsome prince! Not that I needed to wish for that. We had plighted our troth years before, as children. I told you, I'd loved him all my life.'

'People change.'

'Not George,' she said confidently. 'When I finished my schooling and returned to Revesby Hall, we were as much in love as ever. He was at university by then, of course, but I saw him whenever he was home for the vacation. Or if he was rusticated.' She laughed. 'That was a frequent occurrence!'

'He was a wild young man?'

'No more so than any other.' She frowned a little. 'His health suffered whenever he was away, but after a few weeks of fresh air and good food he was quite himself again. His mother and father were always happy to have him at Revesby. He was an only son, you see, and they doted on him.'

'And you married at one-and-twenty?'

'Yes. George had wanted us to wait until he came into his grandfather's inheritance at five-and-twenty before we married, but when I reached my majority I gained control of my own fortune and Sir Adam told him he had better look sharp or some other young man would take my fancy! Not that there was any likelihood of that. I was far too much in love.'

But was he in love with you?

Randolph could not be sure if it was that question or the small cloud passing in front of the sun that made the air suddenly colder. Its shadow also appeared to sober Arabella and the look she cast up at him was more than a little defiant.

'Perhaps you think George did not share my feelings, but you are wrong. He told me often and often how much he loved me. That was the reason we continued to live with his parents, you see. He did not wish to use my fortune to buy a property, even though I had made it all over to him to do with as he wished.'

Arabella stopped. She was chattering on as if she had known Lord Westray for years, telling him details he did not need to know. That he most likely did not want to hear. After all, he did not know George, did not love him as she did. Hot tears stung her eyes. She turned away, hunting for her handkerchief.

'I beg your pardon.' Her voice caught on a sob. 'I did not mean to b-bore you.'

He put his hands on her shoulders. 'Arabella.' His voice was low, quiet. 'You could never bore me.'

She had been struggling alone with her grief for months and it was such a comfort to have him there, strong, protective. Somehow, it lessened the pain of her bereavement.

A footman was hurrying towards them and Arabella quickly pulled away from Randolph, flapping one hand at him.

'I shall be well, my lord, if you give me a moment. I pray you, go and see what your servant wants.'

He walked away and she wiped her eyes. A few deep breaths were all that was required to banish her tears, which surprised her, until she remembered how she had wept when George died. The time for such displays of grief was over. She had set herself a task and must concentrate on that. She gave her eyes a final wipe, blew her nose, and when she heard the Earl's firm step approaching her again, she was ready to turn and look at him. He was smiling.

'There is no need to worry that our sudden departure last night offended Lady Meon. She is even now in the drawing room!'

'Excellent news, my lord.'

She managed an answering smile and he held out his arm. As they turned to make their way back to the house, Arabella noticed a figure on the upper terrace.

She was surprised into a little laugh. 'I believe Lady Meon is coming to find *us*.'

Even as she uttered the words the lady waved and ran lightly down the stone steps.

'I hope you do not mind my coming outside,' she called to them as she reached the next set of steps. 'I should very much like to see the gardens, if I may join you?'

'To see the gardens, at this season?'

Randolph's muttered response made Arabella want to giggle, but she stifled it.

She waved to their visitor and called out politely, 'Of course, madam. We should be delighted to have your company.'

The lady approached, her fur-lined tippet bouncing around her shoulders as she descended the last flight of steps.

'I came to ask after your health, Lady Westray. How relieved I am to see that you have fully recovered from last night's little shock.'

'Thank you. I am perfectly well now.'

It was the first time Arabella had seen the lady out of doors without the face veil she invariably wore when riding. At all their other encounters during daylight hours, Lady Meon had been indoors and at pains to sit with her back to the window. Arabella thought now that candlelight was much kinder to a countenance well past the first bloom of youth. It concealed the lines and faint sagging of the skin that were all too apparent in the pale sunlight.

She caught herself up. Really, she was being most uncharitable! Lady Meon was still a very handsome woman and her excellent figure was shown to advantage in the tawny walking dress trimmed with fur. She was regarding Arabella now with a little frown of concern.

'Are you sure you would not rather go indoors, out of the cold, Lady Westray?'

Arabella batted away the suspicion that the widow would prefer to have Randolph to herself. She said, 'Not at all, I assure you. I am very happy to take another turn around the gardens with you before we go in for refreshments.'

'Thank you. That is very kind.' Lady Meon was all smiles. 'And the path is sufficiently wide that you may give escort to two ladies at once, my lord. How convenient.'

She fell in beside the Earl, laughing up at him

as she took his arm and he, Arabella could not help noticing, was giving the lady the full benefit of his charm. She ground her teeth.

'I regret the gardens are not very amusing at this time of year,' she remarked. 'Mostly lawns and bare branches.'

'But look to the distance,' replied Lady Meon. 'The views are breathtaking.'

'Indeed they are.'

Something in the Earl's tone made Arabella look up. He was smiling at her and the glint in his blue eyes made her cheeks flame. She quickly dragged her eyes away, staring determinedly ahead. He was trying to flirt with her, in all likelihood for their guest's benefit. How dare he?

They proceeded along the path, but although the sun was still shining, Arabella thought the gardens had lost much of their charm. Lady Meon engaged the Earl in conversation, hanging on his sleeve and listening attentively whenever he spoke.

'Your grounds will be beautiful in the warmer months, my lord. I think you will wish to stay here often.'

'Quite possibly,' he murmured.

'The sloping nature of the ground makes it very exposed to the cold winds,' put in Arabella.

'But Devon has very fine weather most of the year,' said Lady Meon.

'I wonder you do not go to town for the winter, madam,' remarked the Earl.

She laughed gently. 'London holds no charms for me, my lord. I go there but rarely. I prefer to have my friends come here.'

'Ah, yes,' he murmured. 'Your legendary house parties.'

Lady Meon shook her head. 'Not *legendary*, sir. I am much more discreet than that! In general, I do not encourage my neighbours to visit, when I have guests, but *you* would be most welcome to call, my lord. Should you be in residence.' She cast a roguish smile up at the Earl. 'I would make sure you did not want for entertainment.'

'That is very kind of you, ma'am.'

He was smiling at the widow and there was a caressing note in his voice. Arabella fought down a wave of irritation. She did not know whether she was most angry with the lady for flirting with Randolph, or with the Earl for responding. She tried to laugh at herself for her foolishness. He was only doing what they had agreed, putting the lady at her ease in order to discover more about her. Only she wished he did not look to be enjoying himself quite so much!

'I do not doubt you are an excellent hostess, Lady Meon.'

Randolph's murmured reply was so low Arabella thought he had not intended her to hear it. Her chin went up and she pinched his arm.

'My dear, it is growing colder,' she said. 'Perhaps we should go indoors and take a glass of wine together.'

Neither Randolph nor Lady Meon made any sign that they noticed Arabella's ill humour. They turned as one and strolled back to the drawing room, where a cheerful fire was burning.

'Ah, Meavy has anticipated us,' remarked the Earl, indicating the refreshments set out on a side table.

Arabella concentrated on handing out the wine and cakes, leaving Ran to respond to Lady Meon's thinly disguised interrogation. After all, the widow clearly preferred his company, so he could make up the details of their marriage!

'But, forgive me!' Lady Meon looked from one to the other, a faint crease on her lightly powdered brow. 'You cannot have been married very long at all, my lord, if you have so recently returned to England. And yet I thought Her Ladyship said it was a matter of months.'

'Did she not tell you? It was a shipboard romance, madam. My lady joined the ship at…er… Rio de Janeiro and the Captain married us.'

Arabella's anger faded as she sipped her wine and listened to the Earl embroidering the tale. It was important she remember the details, in case she needed to repeat them. He caught her eyes once, his own brimming with laughter, and she felt a little bubble of merriment fizz inside her. There was a stab of gratitude, too, knowing he was doing this for her sake.

She could not be sorry when Lady Meon declined a second glass of wine and rose to take her leave, thanking them for their hospitality.

'How pleasant this has been,' she declared. 'I think we are all going to be very good friends. I do hope you will be at Beaumount in May, when I hold my next house party. I invite only a few select guests, the most charming people, I assure you. Our evenings are full of fun and gaiety. We have cards, of course, and dice. Several of my friends enjoy a game of hazard. Do you play, Lady Westray?'

'I play cards, a little.' She added, trying to appear eager, 'I should very much like to become more proficient.'

'That comes with practice, ma'am, but I am sure you would learn very quickly.' Lady Meon leaned forward to touch her hand and Arabella was sorely tempted to snatch it away. Then the lady turned to address the Earl, saying playfully, 'No need to fear we will fleece your lady, Lord Westray. We can play for buttons or penny points and enjoy ourselves just as much as if we were playing for a fortune, I assure you.'

'Oh, I am not worried about my wife losing,' he said cheerfully. 'She has her own fortune and may wager as much as she wants.' He smiled. 'I am not her keeper, nor she mine.'

'I am very glad to hear that, my lord.'

There was a purr in Lady Meon's voice that set the hairs rising on the back of Arabella's neck, and when the widow gave Randolph her hand and he raised it to his lips, she felt again that sharp stab of irritation.

'That went very well,' remarked Randolph, when Lady Meon had been shown out. 'You are frowning. Did you not think so?'

'The lady can be in no doubt that you wish to be friends with her!'

Arabella gathered up the glasses to carry them across to the side table, noting that Randolph had not touched his wine.

'What, because I kissed her fingers?' said Ran,

coming up behind her. 'Why, Arabella, I do believe you are jealous.'

'Not at all,' she said quickly. 'But it is more usual to shake hands these days.'

She busied herself straightening the decanters on the table. He was standing so close behind her she was sure she could feel the heat of him. It sent a trickle of excitement skittering down her spine.

'Ah, then we must blame it on the fact that I have been away from England for six years.' He reached for her hand and she was obliged to turn and face him. 'Do you tell me I should not do this, even to my wife?'

As he spoke he lifted her fingers to his mouth. It was the merest brush of his lips but the effect was shocking. Little darts of fire shot through her and her knees felt weak. She put her free hand on the table to steady herself. She had a sudden urge to throw herself into his arms, but she fought against it.

'I suppose I should be thankful you have any manners at all!' she said crossly. She pulled her hand free and hurried towards the door.

He called after her, 'You are not going?'

'I am.' With half the room separating them she was in control of herself again. 'I promised Mrs Meavy I would discuss the menus with her. It is market day tomorrow and she needs to plan. Which reminds me— is there anything you particularly dislike to eat?'

'No, except perhaps gruel. And thin, watery broth. I like plenty of meat and fish on the table.'

'A typical diet for a lusty male!'

Arabella had made the retort without thinking, but even as the words left her mouth she blushed furiously. Randolph was laughing and she hurriedly whisked herself out of the room. Good heavens, how could she have been so provocative? It was bad enough that she was in this man's house, masquerading as his wife!

A laugh bubbled up. Perhaps she had shown Randolph that Lady Meon was not the only one capable of flirting.

Chapter Five

Arabella busied herself with household duties for the rest of the day and when she met up with Randolph at dinner she expected to feel some awkwardness, but he made no mention of their earlier conversation and treated her with a friendly consideration that soon put her at her ease.

The dining table had been set with the Earl seated at its head and her own place at his right hand, within the glow of the candles burning in the candelabra. At first she suspected the arrangement had been Randolph's idea, but from the fatherly smile Meavy bestowed upon her as she took her seat, she thought perhaps she had misjudged him. She was further reassured when the Earl asked Meavy to bring a jug of water and glasses to the table. Clearly, he did not intend to ply her with drink.

Somehow, they found innocuous subjects for conversation that they could both enjoy—she told him of the little domestic details that had filled her day and he expanded on his plans for the future. Only later, when the covers had been removed, did she remember her reason for being in Devon, and when Randolph made her laugh, she stopped guiltily.

'Oh, dear! How can I sit here and…and be *happy*, when I have yet to avenge my poor husband?' She gave a little huff. 'I should be *doing* something.'

'At this time of night?'

'No, of course not at this minute.' She waved a hand impatiently. 'But it feels wrong to be enjoying myself.'

'Are you? Enjoying yourself, that is.' He smiled at her. 'I am glad of it and I do not think your husband would object. Surely he would not want you to be unhappy.'

'But we are no nearer finding out the truth!'

'Patience,' he told her. 'I have asked Joseph Miller to go into Tavistock tomorrow, to see what he can discover there, and we will call upon Lady Meon. We need to find out who else was present at that last house party. Once we know their names, we can make enquiries.'

She nodded. 'True, but I cannot stay here much longer. Every day brings the chance of discovery a little closer.'

Ran knew she was right. For himself it mattered little. No one would blink an eye at an earl bringing his mistress to Beaumount, but for Arabella it could mean ruin if her identity was discovered. He sipped at his water glass, wondering what madness had induced him to take part in this charade. This was no business of his. He should have sent the woman packing, but her distress had awoken in him some chivalrous impulse to help her. The very idea of it made his mouth twist in self-mockery.

'I beg your pardon,' she muttered. 'You are being very good, when none of this is your concern. Perhaps I should return to Lincolnshire and make my enquiries from there. I might hire someone from Bow Street, perhaps.'

This coincided almost exactly with Ran's thoughts, so he was more than a little surprised to find himself trying to dissuade her.

'You might,' he said slowly, 'but you have come so far, we should at least see if we can learn something. It would be a shame to waste all the effort you have so far expended, would it not?'

He quashed the warning voice in his head that told him he was a fool to become involved in this madcap adventure and watched as she blew her nose and tucked her handkerchief away. She gave him a watery smile.

'Yes, it would. Thank you, my lord.'

Too late to go back now, he thought, and felt a sudden surge of wry amusement. He might as well enjoy himself.

'Randolph,' he reminded her. 'Or Ran, which is what my close friends call me.'

'Thank you, Ran.'

He smiled. 'That's better. Now, it is still early. What say you we play at backgammon, or cards? You did tell Lady Meon you wished to improve your game.'

She chuckled at that. 'May we play backgammon? I fear my skill at cards would sorely test your goodwill, my—Ran!'

They retired to the drawing room, where a small table was soon set up before the fire and they passed a pleasant hour in light-hearted play. The first game was closely fought with Randolph winning by a whisker, and when he suggested another game, Arabella readily agreed.

Together they reset the board, but as Ran put the last of the counters in place, he glanced up and found Arabella watching him.

'Something is puzzling you.' He smiled. 'Well, will you tell me?'

She hesitated. 'You did not drink your wine when Lady Meon was here and you hardly touched it at dinner. It is unusual, I think. Most gentlemen I know—' There was a hint of mischief in her smile this time. 'Not that I am acquainted with so very many! My husband would never drink less than three bottles at a sitting. I wonder, perhaps, if your abstinence is for my benefit?'

'Yes, it is, in a way.' He had been expecting the question, in some form or another, and he had his answer ready. 'Too much wine dulls the wits and I shall need them all if I am to beat you again at this next game.'

She seemed satisfied and he breathed a sigh of relief as he made the first throw of the dice. Arabella would not be here for ever. She did not need to know his secrets.

Two days of torrential rain followed, making it impossible to go out without good reason, and while Arabella fretted at being confined to the house, she knew it would only cause comment to risk overturn-

ing the carriage at a flooded ford for the sake of a social call to Meon House. Joseph, too, had to postpone
his trip to Tavistock.

Not that the days dragged. Forced to remain indoors, Randolph looked out the accounts books and
settled down to study them and familiarise himself
with the running of this small property. Meanwhile,
he gave Arabella carte blanche to play the lady of
the house and sort through rooms and cupboards as
she wished.

'I will make an inventory for you,' she declared,
setting off to find paper and a pencil. 'That is just the
sort of thing a new mistress would do.'

'And the new master would be very grateful,'
agreed Ran, smiling. 'But only if you will not find
it dreadfully dull.'

'Oh, no. I shall enjoy nothing better than playing
housewife. I think.' She stopped, wondering if she
should confide in him. She said in a rush, 'I so wish
George and I had set up our own establishment when
we married, but he said it was not sensible to have
our own household while he was away so much. It
was not to be and I must not repine.'

By dinner time on the second day they were both
feeling very pleased with their progress.

'My land here is in good heart,' Ran told her when
they sat down at the table that evening. 'Although it
is suffering now because the steward retired twelve
months since and has not been replaced. I shall write
to Chislett to attend to it. Can I pour you some wine?'
He looked around for the decanter.

'I told Meavy not to bring wine,' said Arabella. 'I would much rather have water, as you do, since the Beaumount spring is so clear and fresh.'

She was looking a little self-conscious, but Ran did not question her decision. Nothing more was said and the conversation moved on.

They might truly have been a married couple, thought Ran, as the meal progressed. They were at ease with one another, discussing improvements to the gardens and the house, moving on to the arts and even touching on what had been happening in England over the past six years. Arabella teased him for his ignorance and gave him a brief summary of what, for her, had been the main events.

'I was still in the schoolroom when you left the country,' she told him, 'and having lived in Lincolnshire all my life, I fear my memories are coloured by those laws and matters that affect the farmers, rather than foreign policy.'

'You have done well enough sharing this news with me and I thank you for that. I am ashamed to say that before I left England, I was never very interested in anything outside my own enjoyment. However, now I have the Westray estates to administer, I will have to become more knowledgeable about farming.'

'You might leave it all to your steward,' she suggested.

'I might, of course, but I should like to make a success of my new role.'

She studied him for a moment. Then a sudden smile lit up her face.

'I think you will be very good at it.'

Her confidence in him made Ran's spirits soar. He suddenly felt like a giant, capable of anything. It was a heady feeling. Intoxicating. He wanted to shout aloud with happiness. Fighting down the urge to grin like an idiot, he threw down his napkin and pushed back his chair, saying calmly, 'Shall we leave and allow Meavy to clear everything away?'

In the drawing room the candles gleamed and a cheerful fire burned in the hearth. Outside the rain had ceased and ragged clouds chased across the moonlit sky, but the clearer weather brought a drop in temperature and Randolph pulled the curtains to keep out the chill. On previous evenings they had played at backgammon and the board was already set up on a low table, but tonight Arabella hung back.

'I think I would prefer just to sit by the fire, if you do not mind.'

'Not at all.' He dragged one of the wing chairs closer to the hearth. 'You have turned pensive,' he said. 'What are you thinking?'

She fluttered one hand. 'I am feeling a little guilty. I have thought very little about poor George's plight these past two days.'

'That is no bad thing,' he responded promptly. 'Since we could not do anything about it, all you would have done is fret, and that would not be helpful.'

'No.' She clasped her hands and stared into the fire. 'But I must not forget him.'

Ran pulled up another chair and sat down facing her. 'You may talk to me about him, if you wish.'

She gave a nervous laugh. 'What should I tell you? I do not know where to start.'

'At the beginning, perhaps. Your childhood memories.'

Ran folded his arms and sat back, prepared to listen. She began haltingly, but gradually, as she became more engrossed in her story, the words came easier. He schooled his face into an expression of interest, although when she moved from the halcyon days of childhood to more recent times, he was aware of a growing unease. The picture she painted was not of a real, flesh-and-blood young man, but a handsome godlike creature. Kind, generous and totally without fault.

'A paragon of all the virtues,' he said at last.

'Yes, he was.' She beamed at him, unaware of the dry scepticism in his remark. 'Everyone adored him. It was no wonder his mama and papa were inconsolable when he died. They worshipped him. We all did.'

Ran was tempted to say the fellow must have been a saint, but he held back. It was not his place to tell Arabella that no man could be so perfect. She would discover his faults and all too soon, if she continued to look into Roffey's death. Then he berated himself for being a coward. He should say something, warn her, but she was rising from her chair.

'It is late and I should retire,' she said. 'Tomorrow we drive to Meon House, if the dry weather holds, do we not?'

Ran rose. 'I promised we would do so.'

'Thank you.' She held out her hand to him. 'And

thank you for listening to me rattle on tonight. You are a true friend, I think.'

She reached up and kissed his cheek, then walked out of the room, leaving Ran to stare after her.

Arabella hurried down the stairs and across the hall, saying breathlessly, 'I beg your pardon, my lord. I did not mean to keep you waiting.'

It had taken her longer than expected to dress that morning. The green muslin she had chosen last night had suddenly looked too pale, too dull for her visit to Meon House, and she had begged Ruth to seek out her iris-blue walking gown with the muslin ruching around the hem. That, of course, meant changing to the matching bonnet and dainty kid boots and, since the day was chilly, she had looked out the patterned Indian shawl to throw about her shoulders.

The Earl, standing by the door, accepted her apology with a smile.

'It was worth the wait, my lady.'

His words caused a flutter inside Arabella. When she took his arm to accompany him to the waiting carriage, she admitted to herself that she had not changed her apparel to impress Lady Meon. It was Randolph's approval she had been seeking. She pushed the idea aside, unwilling to think too deeply about that now.

As the carriage picked up speed along the country lanes, she asked him if his man had returned from Tavistock.

'Not yet,' he told her. 'A pity, because I had hoped he might be able to tell us something useful. As it is, we shall have to discover what we can about Lady

Meon's house parties. We must find some way to introduce the subject into the conversation.'

In the event, it required no effort at all. Lady Meon was eager to add an earl to her list of conquests and barely had Arabella sat down than the older woman mentioned her plans for her next house party.

'The weather will be much improved by then, I think. It would be a good time for you to return to Beaumount, Lord Westray.'

'As to that, we have yet to decide what we shall do next year.' The Earl was standing beside Arabella's chair. 'Our only fixed plan is to spend the Christmas period in Oxfordshire.'

His words conjured the image of a country retreat for a happily married couple and Arabella fought down a sudden wave of regret. She and George would never share such delights.

Randolph's long fingers rested on her shoulder and their gentle pressure made her wonder if he was aware of her unhappiness. No, how could he read her thoughts? Nevertheless, she was comforted and grateful for his support. She wanted to move her head and rub her cheek against his hand. Impossible of course, but she could not resist reaching up to touch his fingers.

'Westray Priors,' he continued, taking a seat on a sofa, from where he could see both her and Lady Meon. 'It is my principal seat and I have yet to acquaint myself with it.'

'Oxfordshire.' Their hostess gave an elegant moue. 'It would not do for me. If I may say so, the landscape there is very tame compared to Devon. And in the spring the country around here is at its best.'

Arabella could not resist. 'I should have thought it very wet and muddy then.'

'It can be, but we do not mind it.' The lady gave a little laugh and fluttered her eyelashes at the Earl. 'Can I not tempt you to try Devonshire in May, my lord?'

'Perhaps,' he replied. 'If the company is entertaining.'

'Oh, I think I can promise you that.' She waved towards the folded papers on a side table. 'I have already received acceptance from Sir Osgood and Lady Fingell, and Lord Caversfield, too. And I expect to hear any day now from my brother. He always brings one or two of his friends.'

Arabella said casually, 'Are we to understand they are regular visitors to Meon House?'

'Charles, certainly,' replied their hostess. 'The Fingells, too, were here last summer.'

Randolph shook his head. 'Alas, ma'am, I am unacquainted with any of these people.'

'No, of course,' purred Lady Meon. 'You have been…away, have you not, my lord?'

Arabella sat up, alarmed by the inference in the innocent-sounding words. She was surprised at how much she wanted to jump to the Earl's defence.

'I have indeed, ma'am,' he replied easily. 'Sydney Cove was rather lacking in polite society.'

She felt the tension ease from her shoulders. His insouciance showed how little he needed her support. He displayed no remorse for his past indiscretions, no guilt. In all likelihood he was as wicked as their hostess. Set a thief to catch one...

'Are you stopping in town before going on to Oxfordshire?' asked Lady Meon. 'If so, then you should look up my brother. Charles Teddington.'

Arabella caught her breath, but not by the flicker of an eyelid did her expression change. She maintained a look of polite interest while her hostess continued.

'He has rooms in Leicester Street and will be fixed there for the winter, I believe. Look him up and mention my name to him. Town has changed since you were last there, my lord. I am sure he will be delighted to introduce you.'

'Thank you. I shall remember that,' murmured the Earl, inclining his head.

Arabella shifted, impatient to be gone. She glanced at the clock and then at Randolph. He did not disappoint her.

'My dear,' he said, rising, 'it is time we were on our way. We must not take up all of Lady Meon's day.'

Arabella rose like a dutiful wife and said all that was polite. They were soon back in their carriage. As they bowled away along the drive, Randolph turned to Arabella, sitting beside him.

'Now, madam, from the way you were fidgeting, I take it you could not wait to be away.'

'Oh, dear, was it so obvious?'

He laughed and flicked her cheek with a careless finger. 'No, I am teasing you! I doubt our hostess noticed anything amiss, but you *did* recognise some of those names?'

'Only one. Charles Teddington. He was George's groomsman at our wedding.' She frowned. 'George did not tell me of his connection with Meon House. Nor did Mr Teddington mention it when he came to Revesby Hall for the funeral, which is very odd.'

'Dam—dashed suspicious, I would say.'

A chuckle escaped her. 'You need not mind your language on my behalf, Randolph. George never did.' Her smile disappeared. 'As for his friend not talking of Meon House, I wonder if perhaps I missed that. I was overwrought at the funeral, and only spoke a few words to anyone that day.'

'But it does seem odd that your husband did not inform you that Teddington was Lady Meon's brother. However, it gives us something to work on now,' declared Randolph. He reached out and took her hands. 'We shall see what Joseph has discovered in Tavistock and then we can decide just how to proceed.'

He was smiling down at her and it was impossible not to respond, to smile back. Suddenly she wished with all her heart that this was no charade, that she was indeed Lady Westray and they were going into Oxfordshire for Christmas. Together. Man and wife.

The idea rocked Arabella to the core.

They reached Beaumount just as a booted figure was walking from the stables to the house.

'Ah, Miller has returned.' Randolph jumped out of the carriage and held out his hand for Arabella. 'Let us see if he has any news for us.' They waited on the drive for Joseph to come up. 'Well, man, have you learned anything interesting?'

'Oh, I think so, my lord.'

'Good. Let us go in, then.'

They went into the drawing room, Randolph calling for small beer for himself and his man, and a glass of wine for Lady Westray.

'Well, Joseph?'

'It was as I thought, my lord. The rainy days had kept folk at home and today the town was very busy. Lady Meon's carriage horses had been brought in for shoeing and I fell into conversation with her head groom, Stobbing. Seems he don't trust any of the others to see the job's done properly. Which is why I am so late coming back. We got to, er, talking.'

'In the taproom, no doubt.' Randolph smiled wryly. 'What did you find out?'

'Plenty. It seems the lady holds regular parties at Meon House throughout the spring and summer. For gentlemen, in the main.'

'Those that enjoy playing at cards and dice.' Arabella nodded sagely. 'George told me as much.'

'Well, not only—' He broke off when Randolph caught his eye and gave a little shake of his head.

'What could the fellow tell you about these parties?' asked Ran.

'There are always several each year. Very private affairs, apparently. None of the local families are invited to visit while there are guests at the house. The staff are paid well to keep their mouths shut, so very little information gets out to her neighbours, although there are rumours, of course. The guests are very flash with their money, though, when they do go abroad, so the local tradesmen never complain.' He grinned. 'Stobbing told me all this in the strictest confidence, of course, after a couple of tankards of heavy wet.'

'Good man,' murmured Ran.

'Could he name any of the guests?' asked Arabella. 'A Frederick Letchmore, perhaps?'

Miller shook his head. 'No, I don't recall that name.'

'Or Charles Teddington?'

'Aye, he did mention him.' Miller's eyes flickered towards the Earl. 'Nothing I could make sense of, though.'

'Lady Meon said her brother has rooms in town,' put in Randolph. 'It should not be too difficult to track him down.'

He looked across at Arabella, but she was not attending. A tiny frown puckered her brow and it seemed to Ran that it was an effort for her to sweep it aside when he asked her if anything was wrong.

'No, nothing. I must go and change for dinner. Thank you, Mr Miller. I am grateful for your efforts. Truly.'

Randolph waited until Arabella was out of the room before he turned back to his man.

'Now then, Joseph, tell me what you could not say in front of Arabella.'

'To begin with, there's that brother of Lady Meon's. Stobbing was scathing about him. Called him a Leg, a Captain Sharp, who sets out to draw in the pigeons to these little parties, only to my mind, no one's *lured* to Meon House—they are all game to go.' Joseph rubbed his chin. 'I think they are fools with money burning their pockets. Why bother to cheat 'em out of money they're happy enough to lose through reckless play? I gather they are all ripe for a spree and want to kick up a dust but discreet-like, if you get my meaning. Away from their family and any friends who might disapprove.'

Or their innocent young wives.

Ran frowned at the thought. 'Go on.'

'There's drinking and gambling late into the night.' Miller's lip curled. 'Stobbing said they spend very little time out of doors, or out of bed, from what he's heard from the staff inside the house. Females are brought down from town for…er…entertainment and any wives who do come are as free as their husbands. If I understood his nods and winks aright, Lady Meon herself is very partial to handsome young gentlemen.'

Recalling his own encounters with the lady, Ran could believe it. He said, 'The play would be deep, I suppose.'

'Very deep. Cards, dice, the local horse races, the usual things.' Joseph reached for the jug of ale and topped up his glass. 'He did not mention George Roffey by name, my lord, and of course I couldn't ask, but he did tell me the house servants weren't very impressed with my lady's guests at the June party.' He added darkly, 'Opium-eaters.'

Ran frowned. 'That is what I was afraid of. Rich young men with money to spend and no real purpose in their lives.'

'And others very willing to help them spend their money,' said Miller. 'Seems not much has changed in the past six years, my lord.'

'Nor is it likely to, more's the pity,' muttered Randolph. 'But there was no hint of anything illegal going on?'

'No, sir. Stobbing was sanguine about it all. High spirits, he called it, but we know where that can lead.'

Randolph said nothing and the words hung in the silence.

Joseph swirled the last of the ale around in his glass. He said, not looking up, 'If you'll take my advice, sir, you'll not get involved with Lady Meon or her friends.'

'I don't intend to, but I have promised to help Mrs Roffey.' He saw his man was looking at him gravely and shook his head. 'Damn it all, Joseph, returning to England, to society, was always going to be a risk. You know that.'

'Aye, but maybe *this* society is a mite too dangerous for you, my lord.'

He drained his glass and went off, leaving Ran to his thoughts.

'Well, mistress, what did you learn?' Ruth pounced on Arabella as soon as she entered the bedchamber.

'We have made a little progress,' she said carefully.

'And Lady Meon?'

'She holds several parties every year and invites young gentlemen.' Arabella spread her hands. 'I confess I do not like the woman.'

'One can never be sure of the gentry in these out-of-the-way places,' muttered Ruth as she began to help Arabella out of her walking dress. 'Not at all respectable.'

Despite her cares, Arabella giggled at that. 'Revesby Hall is an *out-of-the-way* place, but we know Sir Adam and Lady Roffey are *very* respectable! However, I am quite ready to believe Lady Meon invites gullible young men here to relieve them of their fortune. I also think she is not above feeding them opiates to dull their wits. Only with George she went too far. The problem is, how to prove it. She is hardly likely to tell me as much.'

'Perhaps His Lordship can find out more,' said the maid, shaking out Arabella's gown and laying it over a chair.

'I think perhaps we have imposed enough upon Lord Westray.'

'Never say so, Miss Bella! Why, he hasn't given you the least indication that he wants you to leave, has he?'

'No.' Arabella sat down at the dressing table, staring at her reflection in the glass. 'But I am here under false pretences. Sooner or later I shall be found out.'

'I'd let the Earl worry about that. He'll look out for you, I'm sure.'

Arabella shook her head. How could Ruth be so complaisant? Yet she herself had been happy to live here in the same house as the Earl, pretending to be his wife, sharing everything except his bed.

Until this afternoon in the carriage as they travelled back from Meon House. When he had caught her hands it had come upon her, quite forcibly. The revelation that she was beginning to like the Earl far more than she should. Far more than was safe. From that moment on she had been reconsidering her position.

She had set out to find George's killer and her determination had blinded her to the risks of accepting help from a stranger. Randolph had rescued her from a dire situation, ridden up like a knight in shining armour and quite literally given her the protection of his name. He was kind, gentle and strong. Even handsome, in a rugged, careworn sort of way. Everything a knight should be.

And she found him dangerously attractive.

The thought chilled her. She was ashamed of it, too, since she had been a widow for little more than four months. What she felt for Ran could only be a pale imitation of the all-consuming love she felt for her husband. Why, she had adored George since she was a child. Yet there was no doubt that when Randolph looked at her, teased her, she was in danger of succumbing to his charm. He made her forget her reason for being here. When she was in his company, there were moments, hours, when she even forgot to think about George.

Arabella looked across at the vivid blue walking dress. She could not lie; she had wanted Ran to admire her, to look at her with a warm smile of approval in his eyes. But why? Nothing could come of it. He was dangerous and not just because of his charm. He was a criminal.

Ruth was pulling out the scarlet evening gown from the linen press and Arabella was tempted to tell her to put it back. She would have preferred to wear one of her black gowns, as befitted a widow, but the rest of the staff thought of her as the Countess and she dare not attract comment by suddenly appearing in mourning.

She compromised by arranging a fine lace fichu around her bare shoulders, pinned with the small gold brooch George had given her upon their marriage. If that did not remind her of where her loyalties must lie, then she was beyond redemption.

Chapter Six

Randolph paced the floor of the drawing room, thinking over his conversation with Joseph. There was no evidence at all that George Roffey's death was anything but a tragic accident, brought on by his own excesses. Excesses Ran understood only too well. His man was right—associating with the sort of characters who attended the parties at Meon House held huge risks for him, but there was danger for Arabella, too, albeit of a different sort. He knew how much she idolised her late husband, but he very much feared if she continued with her investigations into his death, she would discover that her god had feet of clay. Even more reason, then, to persuade her to give up her quest. Or at the very least to leave it to someone else to investigate.

The door opened and Arabella entered. She was wearing the red gown again. The scarlet silk clung to every curve of her figure, tapering down to her tiny waist before falling softly over her hips, finishing with the embroidered hem swinging gently about her dainty ankles. A froth of cream lace covered her shoulders, but if she thought that made her any less delectable, she was mistaken. It merely drew attention to the smooth ivory of her complexion and he wanted to push aside its soft folds and kiss every inch of skin as he uncovered it.

She hesitated just inside the room, looking tense and unsure of herself. Ran pulled himself together and smiled at her. He waved one hand towards the hearth.

'Do come closer to the fire and warm yourself.'

'Thank you.'

She crossed the room, not looking at him, and sank into the chair beside the fire. The same chair she had used last night, when she had described her husband in such glowing terms. When she had felt so at home with him that she had kissed his cheek upon parting. For some reason that easy camaraderie had gone. He had done his best to conceal his desire for her, but perhaps she had seen it in his eyes today.

He said lightly, 'We have some names now, including the lady's brother. Are you impatient to go to town and confront them?'

'It will take a little time to hunt them down, I am sure,' she murmured.

He lowered himself into the chair opposite her. 'I have already written to Chislett, asking him to make enquiries. I think we might leave the matter safely in his hands. You can rest assured if there has been foul play, he will discover it and you may take his findings to the magistrate.'

'Thank you, but that will not be necessary. My own lawyer shall find these men.' She looked at him then, her face composed, controlled. 'You have done more than enough, Lord Westray, and I am very grateful.'

'What is this?' He laughed. 'Are you giving me my congé?'

'We can hardly go to town as husband and wife, my lord.'

'No, but that does not mean—'

She rose and began to pace, as he had done. He watched her, noting how pale she was, how determined not to look at him.

'You have helped me immensely, sir, but this matter has nothing to do with you. I cannot embroil you further in my affairs.'

He folded his arms. 'And just what do you intend to do when you find these men?'

'If necessary, I can pay someone to act as my escort.'

Ran felt the first stirrings of anger. 'You would prefer to hire a stranger than accept my help?'

'We took a risk here, my lord, but it would not do to continue the connection anywhere less remote.' She sank down on her chair again and folded her hands in her lap. Only the white knuckles indicated she was not as composed as she would have him believe. 'Your own appearance in town needs to be unfettered by any hint of scandal. The—the circumstances of your past have given rise to a deal of speculation already. There will be any number of gossipmongers ready to delve into your affairs.'

'I know that. I do not deny it, but I promised to help you.'

'And you *have* helped me, sir. I am indebted to you, but I think I must make my own way from here.

I shall go to London as George's widow. It is possible that the gentlemen we seek will feel some sympathy for my situation and talk to me willingly about my husband. If not, then I shall know they have something to hide and act accordingly.'

She was dismissing him!

He said, 'And you have funds for this? You are prepared for the costs?'

'It was never my intention that anyone else should pay. My family's property has passed to the Roffeys, but I still have sufficient money of my own. That is,' she corrected herself, 'I have what is left of the fortune I brought to my marriage. I shall use every penny of it, if necessary, to find George's killer and bring him—or them—to justice.'

'Arabella, your husband is dead,' said Ran gently. 'Nothing you do now will bring him back.'

She sat up very straight. 'I have to do this myself. Do you not see? I cannot rest until I know the truth.'

An iron band tightened around Ran's chest when he saw the anguish in her eyes. He very much feared the truth would only hurt her more, but the stubborn set of her chin told him she would not be swayed.

The butler's entry prevented Ran from responding and he could only admire Arabella's composure as she gave the man a cool smile.

'Is dinner ready for us, Meavy? We shall be there directly.'

Ran pushed himself out of his chair, saying as the butler went out again, 'We shall continue this conversation later, madam.'

'No, there is nothing more to say,' she replied. 'I am decided.'

With that she sailed out of the room. Looking, he thought with a mixture of anger and admiration, every inch a countess.

Dinner was a stilted affair. The presence of the servants prevented Randolph from bringing up the subject he most wanted to discuss, but it was on his mind constantly. If only she could be persuaded that her husband had fallen into bad company, that there was no murderer to be found, she could return to Lincolnshire; they could both leave Devon without anyone ever knowing her true identity. If she continued with her search, there was no knowing where it might lead.

Randolph was not concerned for himself. By the time he came back to Beaumount the scandal of the counterfeit Countess would have died down to a mere whisper, which he could ignore with all the arrogance of the nobility.

He held his peace until they had finished their meal, but when she would have risen to leave him he said, 'Please stay, madam.'

She sank back into her seat and he waved away the servants.

'I have been thinking over everything that has happened here, Arabella. After you left us, Miller told me more that he had learned. Things he did not think suitable for a lady's ears.'

She sat very still. 'Go on, my lord.'

'Your description of your husband's behaviour when he returned from Meon House, the manner of his demise. It was a poison, of sorts, but not administered by anyone else. I believe he was dosing himself with laudanum.'

She shook her head. 'No. That cannot be true. You do not know what you are saying.'

'Alas, I do.' For the first time in many months he wished he had a glass of wine at his elbow. 'I know the effects the drug can have, on the mind as well as the body.' When she would have argued he put up his hand. 'I know it only too well, Bella. I saw it first-hand on the transport ship to Australia.' He barely noticed that he had shortened her name. She was staring at him, her eyes wide with horror. He continued.

'From all we have learned here, I think Lady Meon invites a very dissolute crowd to her parties. Gentlemen of means who wish to drink, gamble and indulge in—in other excesses without restraint. There would have been no difficulty obtaining laudanum, if he wished for it. I do not think your husband was lured there.'

'No. No, I will not believe that! He went because he had promised his friends. He told me so.'

'Then why did he not take you with him?'

'You know why!' She was looking distressed now. 'He…he said I should find it very tedious. He was t-trying to protect me. Oh, you do not understand! George would not lie to me, or to his parents. He was far too good to deceive us. Why, he never gambled at home and he was never in his cups.'

'But how long was he with you at any one time— a week, two at most?'

He read the answer in her eyes, but she would not admit it. She jumped up with such force that her chair toppled backwards and crashed to the floor.

'You want me to think the very worst of George!'

'On the contrary. I am trying to persuade you to go home and mourn him.'

'No, you are trying to turn me against my husband,' she cried. 'I do not know why you should. It can make no difference to my feelings for you.'

'Your feelings!' He reeled back in surprise.

Arabella looked shocked and her cheeks flamed, but she recovered almost instantly.

'I have none!' she shot back. 'I never will have! I am merely furious that you should malign my husband's name in that way.'

'I am merely telling you what I believe to be the truth.'

'But you do not *know*!' She dashed a hand across her eyes.

He said gently, 'I know that too much laudanum plays havoc with the mind, causes periods of euphoria and deepest despair. One becomes very weary and yet restless, unable to lie still in one position for more than a few moments. Only by taking even more laudanum can one find respite. Eventually it will destroy the body as well as the mind.'

'I will not believe George brought about his own death! If—*if*—he was addicted to opium it was because someone had fed it to him.' She leaned on the table, eyes sparkling with anger. 'My husband was an innocent victim. He told me as much. Why would he lie?'

'Because laudanum distorts the mind.' Painful memories surfaced and Ran pushed them back before they could overwhelm him.

'I cannot believe. I *will not* believe it. I shall go to London, find these men and confront them.'

'And if they say the same as I?'

'I shall know they are lying. I shall persist until they tell me the truth.'

Ran was very much afraid they would do just that. Not just about the gambling and the laudanum, but about the women who frequented the parties, too. Roffey might well have been more interested in laudanum than whores, but Arabella wouldn't know that. She would be heartbroken.

'Then at least let me help you.'

'You cannot help me!' Her angry gaze scorched him. 'Your history is already common knowledge, my lord. If it becomes known that I am acquainted with the infamous Lord Westray, it can only harm my reputation.' She straightened, holding up her head proudly. 'I am very grateful for all you have done for me thus far, my lord, but you cannot help me any further.'

She stormed out in a shimmer of scarlet skirts.

Arabella flew up the stairs, scolding herself all the way. How could she, how *could* she have given him any cause to think she cared for him at all? What on earth had made her speak of feelings? She cared nothing for Randolph. Nothing.

At the door to her bedchamber she stopped, breathing deeply to calm herself before she encountered her maid, to no avail. Ruth took one look at her flushed countenance and exclaimed in horror.

'Oh, my dear Lord, what is it? Pray do not tell me the Earl tried to seduce you!'

'No, nothing like that. We quarrelled because I

will no longer accept his assistance.' She put up a hand. 'Pray, do not say anything now, Ruth. I am far too angry to speak!'

The maid's eyes narrowed and she maintained an offended silence while she undressed her mistress and helped her into her nightgown. Arabella then dismissed her, declaring she was exhausted, but once she was alone, instead of sleeping, Arabella paced the floor, trying to work off the agitation of her spirits.

An hour passed. The fire died and her bare feet grew icy as the room became colder, but still she paced, trying to make sense of the emotions churning around inside her. Her love for her husband was as strong, as pure as ever, but there was a darker force at work within her now. She had conceived a passion for Randolph, a frighteningly dark and lustful passion that threatened to overwhelm her.

She stopped and gave a sob, covering her face with her hands. What a pitiful, wanton creature she must be, to forget her sainted husband so quickly.

'Bella?'

She froze when she heard Randolph calling softly to her. She ran to the connecting door. The key was still in the door and it was turned, securely locked.

'Bella, talk to me.'

She placed her hand against the panel, imagining Randolph standing on the other side.

'If I have upset you, I beg your pardon,' he went on. 'It was not my intention.'

She leaned her forehead against the cool wood. 'I know that, my lord.'

He was silent. Then, 'Will you open the door for me?'

'I c-cannot do that.'

'Why not—are you afraid of me?'

'No.' *I am afraid of myself.*

She put her fist to her mouth to stifle a sob.

'You are crying. Bella, let me in! Just let me talk to you.'

'Please, Randolph. Please, go away.' She sank to her knees. 'I l-love my husband. I will not dishonour his memory.'

Silence. She drew a breath.

'I m-must leave here. Tomorrow.'

'As you wish. Is there anything I can do for you?'

'Would you, would you be good enough to inform the staff that urgent family business calls me away? And… I w-would be grateful if you did not tell anyone my true identity.'

'I will not betray your secret, Bella.'

'Thank you.'

'Will I see you at breakfast?'

'No. Ruth and I will break our fast on the road.' The tears that had refused to come earlier welled up and fell, unheeded, over her cheeks. 'I think it best if we do not meet again, my lord. I shall continue to seek my husband's murderer. Alone.'

She waited, steeling herself for his reply, expecting him to argue or to plead, but from the other room came only silence.

The new Lord Westray reached his principal seat in Oxfordshire barely a week before Christmas. Chislett had informed them of the Ninth Earl's arrival in England and the house had been cleaned, staff hired and kitchens prepared in readiness.

Randolph arrived in his new curricle, pulled by a

pair of match bays whose mettle tested his driving skills to the utmost and kept his mind from dwelling on the past weeks. He had left Devonshire only days after Arabella, but he had made no attempt to seek her out when he reached the capital. She had made it perfectly clear she wanted nothing to do with him and, for his part, he thought that was best for both of them. He eschewed all society save that of his lawyer and his man of business and spent the remainder of his time providing himself with the clothes, carriages and horses suitable for his new station.

By the time Randolph was ready to move on to Oxfordshire he had heard nothing of Arabella. There were no reports of her in the newspapers and, although Joseph was making his own discreet enquiries about the widow, there was not even any gossip to be had. He hoped that she had accepted he was right about her husband and was now safely back in Lincolnshire, where she could finish her mourning and get on with her life. As he was going to get on with his.

At the Priors the steward, Foster, was keen to instruct the new lord in his duties, the first of which, Ran knew, was to show himself to his neighbours, which he duly did by attending the Christmas services at the local parish church. After that, when the weather allowed, he spent his days riding over his estate, meeting tenants and listening to their concerns. In the evenings and on inclement days he pored over the accounts, household ledgers and reports from the other estates that comprised his inheritance. Apart from Beaumount and the Priors, he now owned land and houses in Derbyshire and Cheshire. They must be visited, but he would do that in the summer. In the meantime there was plenty to occupy him here.

He decided to reorganise the stables. For a coachman and head groom who had both spent years with little to do and now feared for their livelihoods, the new Earl's interest was invigorating and they set to with a will to carry out his orders. Old carriages that were beyond repair were discarded, horses only fit for farm work were passed on to tenants and the Seventh Earl's aged hack was put out to grass, making way for the new blood Randolph had acquired.

'No sluggards or rips in our stables,' the groom told his cronies proudly when he joined them at the local inn for porter and a steak pie. 'The new Earl's bought himself a rum prancer for hacking about the countryside, plus a couple of gallopers for hunting and as fine a team of carriage horses as you'll find in Oxford. And as for the match bays pulling his curricle,' he ended with a satisfied grin, 'we ain't had nothing as fine as that in the stables for many a long year!'

'I heard he was a scapegallows,' put in one of his audience. 'A hellhound, sent off to t'other side of the world for his crimes.'

'That's as may be, but he was pardoned,' retorted the groom. 'Pardoned for his courageous deeds. He's a man as served his time and come out a hero, so I'll hear no word agin him!'

The indoor staff were equally impressed with their new master, if a little disappointed that he had no interest in entertaining. The squire and the local vicar came to pay their respects, but Cook waited in vain for the summons to produce a sumptuous dinner party, or even fancy cakes for visitors. Hopes rose below stairs at the end of January when it was learned that someone was coming to stay, but it was only one person, for one night, and His Lordship's lawyer at that.

Randolph was out with his steward when Mr Chislett arrived. He had left instructions that his guest should be shown to the best spare bedchamber, and when they met at dinner, the lawyer responded to his host's enquiries by assuring him that he had been given every comfort. Ran then enquired after his family and asked about his journey, and the two men conversed amicably throughout the meal. Afterwards Randolph took his guest into the drawing room, where decanters and glasses were set out on a side table.

'I have brought with me the papers to be signed, my lord, as you required,' said Chislett. He accepted a glass of brandy and sniffed it appreciatively. 'You are sure you want to sell the two Kirkster family properties?'

Ran nodded. 'Perfectly sure.' He had no wish to revisit his childhood home in Liverpool, or to return to the house in Fallbridge. 'I consulted my sister, too. She does not wish for them to remain in the family.'

Too many painful memories, for him and for Deborah. And all of his making.

'Very well, my lord. The local land agents tell me there should be no difficulties disposing of either property.'

'Good. We will deal with the paperwork in the morning.'

'There is another little matter.'

'Oh?' Ran's attention was caught by the lawyer's hesitant tone. 'You had best tell me.'

'You will recall, my lord, you wrote to me from Beaumount, asking me to look into the whereabouts of certain…gentlemen.'

Ran frowned. 'I told you when I was in London that letter had been sent in error. You were to ignore it.'

'Aye, my lord, I understood that and I duly destroyed it, but having read its contents, the names remained in my memory and one of them came to my attention recently. Mr Charles Teddington. I thought, since you had an interest in the gentleman, you might like to know what I have learned.'

Ran wanted to retort that he did not give a damn about the fellow, but it was not quite true. Arabella had said she would seek out Teddington and, try as he might, Randolph could not help wanting to know if she had done so. He glanced at the clock.

'It is early yet,' he drawled with a nonchalance he was far from feeling. 'I suppose it will while away an hour.' He settled back in his chair. 'Carry on, then, Mr Chislett. Amuse me.'

'As to amusement,' said the lawyer heavily, 'I am not sure this little tale will do that, but it might throw some light on the character of the gentleman. I spent Christmas in Bristol, with a cousin who lives there, a solicitor, like myself. As one does, we got talking in the evening. He was distressed by a case that had come his way earlier in the year. A lady wanting redress from a gentleman for breach of promise.'

Ran felt a sudden chill run through him.

'And the lady's name?'

Chislett looked shocked. 'That I could not divulge to you, sir, not without breaking faith with a colleague.'

Ran said carefully, 'Was it, perhaps, Roffey?'

'No, my lord. It was not.'

Ran let his breath go. Of course it was nothing to do with Arabella. If only he did not think of her quite so often.

'The lady's name is immaterial to you,' the lawyer continued. 'However, the accused was one Charles Teddington. I thought this might be of interest to you, since you were so recently enquiring after the gentleman.'

'Of course,' said Ran impatiently. He might as well hear the story out. 'Go on, Mr Chislett.'

'The young lady said she had been courted by Teddington, who then abandoned her, and the unborn child she claimed was his. My cousin was obliged to advise her that she had little chance of winning her case. The defendant had witnesses willing to testify for him, men of some standing, while she had no one. My cousin managed to secure a settlement out of court and the lady retired to the country to have her child. However, somehow the story became public knowledge in Bristol and Mr Teddington left the city rather hurriedly and never returned.

'That was in the spring of last year. When I arrived at my cousin's house in December, he had just learned that the woman and her babe had died.' Mr Chislett cast a rueful glance at the Earl. 'Even lawyers have hearts, Lord Westray. The lady's plight had touched my cousin and he was angry, desperate to share with someone all he had learned about the gentleman.'

The lawyer paused, the corners of his mouth turning down a little. He said gravely, 'If you wish me to continue, I must ask for your discretion, my lord. My cousin has no hard evidence, but he believes what he learned to be the truth.'

'Go on, sir. You may be assured it will go no further.'

The lawyer took another sip from his glass.

'Mr Teddington lives mainly in London, but twelve months ago he removed to Bristol, following the death of his wife. The late Mrs Teddington was an only child from a wealthy family in Staffordshire. Reports say that, at the time of their marriage, his wife was a normal, healthy young woman, but within six months she was an invalid, confined to the house.' Chislett put down his glass. 'It is said—and I must stress, my lord, it is only a rumour—that he plied the lady with laudanum until she was incapable of leaving her bed, and when she died, there was very little left of her considerable fortune.' He steepled his fingers and gazed into the fire. 'If one had a vivid imagination, my lord, one might conclude that the gentleman left London to avoid the gossip arising after his wife's death and went to Bristol to find himself another rich bride. There are any number of wealthy merchants living in the city.'

'And is that your conclusion?' asked Randolph.

'I am a lawyer, Lord Westray. I must deal in facts. In evidence. As does my cousin. It is a fact that Mr Teddington married an heiress. It is a fact that they were almost penniless when she died, less than a year later. Then there is the accusation—case unproven—that he seduced the young lady in Bristol with promises of marriage, only to withdraw when he learned she had no fortune.'

Randolph walked across to the table to pour himself a glass of water. It was possible Teddington had fed George Roffey's appetite for laudanum even if he did not introduce him to the opiate. If the late Mrs Teddington had been taking it, then he would certainly have known its power. And if Teddington was unscrupulous enough to kill, then he would have had no hesitation in taking his share of Roffey's money at the card table.

He returned to his chair, saying, 'Do we know where Teddington is now?'

'He is currently in town. Apart from one or two spells in the country last summer, London appears to be his main abode.' Chislett allowed himself a little smile. 'I made a few enquiries of my own. I thought you might ask, my lord.'

'Did you, now?'

'Yes, I did.' The lawyer was in no wise perturbed by Ran's scowl. 'I ascertained that the gentleman inhabits modest lodgings in a respectable part of town and frequents a number of clubs. If I were one to speculate—'

'Which you are not!'

'Which I am not, I should say he lives by his wits.'

Ran shot him a glance. 'Dangerous to women?'

The old man considered. 'I doubt he is a threat to respectable ladies who can claim the protection of a husband or family, but given his history, I think he might well be an unscrupulous fortune hunter.' He drained his glass. 'Perhaps I am being uncharitable towards the gentleman. I suppose he is not so very

different from any number of bucks you will find
in town, living above their means and looking for a
wealthy wife. Well, well, it behoves us all to be cautious. Now.' He pushed himself out of his chair. 'If it
is all the same to you, sir, I shall be off to my bed.'

The lawyer had to repeat himself before Ran
looked up.

'What? Oh, aye. Off you go, man. Goodnight.'

Long after the door closed behind Mr Chislett, Ran
stared into the fire, deep in thought. Teddington could
well be looking for another wealthy wife, but Arabella
was unlikely to succumb to his charms. She would be
in no danger. Unless she threatened to expose him.

He shifted in his chair. Confound it, that was just
the sort of thing she might try to do, if she thought
he was responsible for her husband's murder. And
the damnable thing was that Teddington could well
be involved.

'Bah!' He jumped up and headed for the door.
'Arabella Roffey is a wealthy widow. She said herself she would hire any help and protection she needs.
And in all probability she is back in Lincolnshire by
now.'

In the hall, he lit a bedroom candle and stood for
a moment, frowning at the yellow flame that danced
and fluttered, reminding him of Arabella's guinea-
gold curls. Uttering a soft curse, he set off up the
stairs.

'She is none of your concern now, man. Let it be.'

But even before his bed was warm, he knew he
could not do that.

Chapter Seven

Randolph arrived in London at the end of a bleak February day when the ground was frozen and a covering of snow glistened on the rooftops. The Westray townhouse had been sold long ago, but Randolph was content to put up at Mivart's Hotel in Brook Street. It was discreet, comfortable and convenient, which was all he asked.

Before leaving the Priors, Ran had sent Joseph into Lincolnshire, but his man had returned with very little information, only that the widowed Mrs Roffey was in London. All Ran had to do now was find her. But it must be done discreetly. Tongues would most certainly wag if anyone thought there was a connection between the disreputable Earl and a demure widow.

Six years ago, as the young Lord Kirkster, Ran had spent very little time in London, certainly none of it in the highest circles. He had no acquaintances in the capital and he wondered how he would fare in society. The Gilmortons always remained in the north for the winter, and although he had toyed with the idea of asking his brother-in-law for letters of introduction, in the end he decided against it.

In the event, Ran was cynically amused to discover that all doors were open to the rich Earl of Westray. True, there were sideways glances and sly references to his past, but he adopted such an air of assurance that no one dared question him outright and he was able to put down any signs of pretension with a haughty stare.

By the end of his second week he was a member of several gentlemen's clubs and, even though town was said to be very thin of company at this time of year, he had more invitations to balls, parties and dinners than he could physically attend. Discreet enquiries had proved effective in tracking down Charles Teddington and he had met the fellow briefly in one or two of his clubs, and even played at cards with him, but of Mrs Arabella Roffey there was no sign.

Glancing at the invitations littering his mantelshelf, Ran picked up one. Lady Aldenham's winter ball. He had met the lady at a card party and recalled being told that she was one of the foremost hostesses in town.

'The world and his wife attend her parties,' he had been told by Sir Arran Eversleigh, a swell of the highest order who had rather taken to the new Earl. 'There is no one she don't know. Just giving you a hint, my boy, if you are wanting to expand your acquaintance in town.'

Ran was sure that, as a widow, Arabella would not attend a ball, but it was possible he might hear something about her. It was worth making the attempt.

* * *

Attired in a new black evening coat, white silk waistcoat and knee breeches in black Florentine silk, Randolph entered Lady Aldenham's crowded salon shortly after the dancing had commenced. Sir Arran was standing near the door and he immediately came up and took his arm.

'So, you came, my boy. Fashionably late, I see, but you are here! Capital, capital. Damned squeeze, ain't it? Our hostess is already on the dance floor, but let me introduce you to a few people you might find it useful to know!'

Ran spent the next hour being paraded about the elegant rooms, renewing acquaintances and making new ones. He knew he would have to dance and was aware that several matrons were already eyeing him as a potential catch for their daughters. He kept smiling, but inwardly he disdained their obsequious attentions. They were all aware that he was a convicted felon—the newspapers had been full of it when he inherited the title—but they were all eager to court his favour without making any effort to ascertain his character or his morals. Title and fortune were all that mattered to them.

It was not his place to quibble. He smiled, said everything that was proper and obligingly requested one young debutante to stand up with him. He engaged her in conversation when the dance allowed, was all polite attention, yet he was constantly watching and listening for any mention of Arabella Roffey. By the end of the dance he had learned nothing

and he hid his impatience as he escorted his partner
back to her friends.

He was just wondering how soon he could take his
leave when the crowd parted and he saw Arabella on
the far side of the room. Ran stood, transfixed. She
was dressed in black velvet, lightened only by the
most delicate of silver embroidery. A length of black
ribbon around the slender column of her neck was
her only ornament, but with her emerald eyes and
guinea-gold locks glowing in the candlelight, she had
no need of jewels. Ran had thought her entrancing in
red. In black, she was magnificent.

He was so engrossed in watching Arabella that he
did not notice Lady Aldenham approaching.

'My dear Lord Westray, you are very welcome! Sir
Arran has been an assiduous deputy for me this evening and I am grateful to him for looking after you.
I do hope you will forgive me for not greeting you in
person when you came in. These affairs are always
such a crush, you see…'

He dragged his attention to his hostess and summoned a smile.

'There is nothing to forgive, madam. I have been
well entertained, I assure you.' He stole another look
across the room.

She followed his glance and laughed. 'You would
like to meet the golden widow? I should have guessed!
She is quite a diamond, is she not? And possessed of a
fortune, I understand.' She laughed. 'No wonder her
late husband's family want to keep her under their
wing.'

'They do?'

'Why else would they open up their townhouse

for her, if it wasn't to keep her within their grasp? They have installed an impoverished cousin as her companion, too, but she is a timid, mouse-like little creature and it is no wonder that the widow prefers to go about without her.' She touched his arm. 'Allow me to present you.'

'No!' Arabella had not yet seen him. He remembered all too clearly the last time he had surprised her. 'No,' he said again, softening the word with a smile. 'Thank you. I recently made the lady's acquaintance and I shall speak to her later. She is engaged at present.'

'Oh. Well, if you are sure, my lord…?'

'Quite sure.' He held out his arm to her. 'There are any number of other ladies here I have yet to meet.'

Arabella was already wishing she had not come. She had not intended to accept, even when Lady Aldenham had been most pressing.

'You have been a widow for more than six months now, my dear. No one will consider it odd that you should be going out a little into society.'

'But not to a ball,' Arabella had objected.

'Even a ball, as long as it is a private affair, and you do not dance.'

As she made her way through the crowded rooms, Arabella thought there was very little that was private about Lady Aldenham's ball and nothing would have tempted her to attend, had she not been led to believe she might learn something of how George had died. She could not ignore that.

She moved unhurriedly from the ballroom into an elegant gilded salon where chairs and tables had been placed for guests to converse at their ease. It was quieter here and cooler. Perhaps she might sit down for a moment. A small group of ladies and gentlemen were seated in one corner, most of whom she recognised, and she went across to join them. She was gratified that Lord Haverford jumped to his feet as soon as he saw her.

'My dear Mrs Roffey, do, pray you, come and sit down with us. Seeking refuge from the music, are you?' He guided Arabella to an empty chair. 'My dear lady was just saying it is all very well for these young people, but when you get to our age, we prefer to hear ourselves think, what?'

'My dear sir, Mrs Roffey is far younger than us and I am sure she does not object to a little noise.' His wife leaned across to pat Arabella's hand. 'Take no notice of him, my dear, but do stay and talk to us. You know Sir Kenelm Prees and his lady and Mrs Darby, I dare say?' She waited until Arabella had nodded before continuing. 'We shall be glad of your company. Haverford, my love, fetch Mrs Roffey a glass of wine. My dear, Sir Kenelm was just telling us about the play last night, *The Fate of Frankenstein*. Have you seen it?'

Arabella shook her head. 'No, but pray, do continue, Sir Kenelm…'

She allowed the conversation to flow around her while she sipped her wine and hid her frustration. This was not what she had wanted, what she had hoped for, this evening.

The gentleman who had promised to meet her here had not yet appeared. Perhaps he had never intended to do so. A glance at the clock told her it was yet early. If he did not appear within the next hour, she would leave.

Her stretched nerves caught a movement by the door. Someone had entered the salon. It was not the man she was expecting, but that did not prevent the breath from hitching in her throat when Lord Westray walked in. Yearning stabbed her, so strong it was like a physical blow. She could not drag her eyes away from his upright form. He walked with a lithe grace, exuding power and confidence. The candle-light gleamed on his mane of fair hair and his skin glowed with the golden tan of a man who had lived in the sun. Not a man, she thought wildly. A god.

A sun god.

She should not feel like this about another man so soon after George's death. A man she had known for barely a sennight. She was racked by guilt, but it made not a jot of difference. Since leaving Devonshire she had tried so hard to convince herself she did not care about Randolph, but now, just seeing him brought on a wave of desire. Oh, how she had missed him!

'Loneliness,' she told herself. 'Loneliness and grief have combined to make you susceptible to the attentions of a charming man. That is all it is.'

Arabella clutched the wineglass with both hands to keep it steady. She was barely aware of the laughter and chatter going on around her.

'…heavens, Sir Kenelm, how dare the theatre put on such a play?' Mrs Darby was fanning herself vigorously. 'It sounds quite terrifying.'

'The monster was more farcical than frightening, madam, I assure you.'

'Just the talk of it has turned our young friend as white as my fichu!' declared Lady Haverford. 'Mrs Roffey…' She reached across and touched Arabella's arm. 'Good heavens, my dear, you really do look quite upset. It is only a play, after all.'

'What? Oh. Oh, yes,' Arabella forced herself to answer. She struggled to remain calm, to remember what they were discussing. Ah, yes, Frankenstein. 'I have read the book and always felt a little sorry for the creature.'

Randolph must have seen her, she was sure of it, but he had walked across to the far wall and was studying a large painting. A servant approached him, offering a glass of wine from a laden tray. The Earl waved him away, but he turned now to look about the room, and when his eyes met Arabella's, he gave a tiny nod of recognition.

'Damme if it isn't the new Earl!' exclaimed Sir Kenelm, raising his quizzing glass. 'And he's coming over. Well, if that don't beat all!'

'And why should it?' demanded Lord Haverford, rising and raising his hand in greeting. 'Servant, Westray!'

'Aye, evening to you, my lord,' put in Sir Kenelm, bowing. 'When we met at Drury Lane last night you wasn't minded to come tonight.'

'Then my thoughts were for the play,' came the smooth reply. 'Tonight, I needed more agreeable entertainment.' He bowed towards the ladies, murmuring each of their names in turn, ending with Arabella. 'Mrs Roffey.'

She was thankful she was sitting, for her bones had turned to water. He was even more handsome than she remembered and heaven knew he had barely been out of her thoughts since she had left Devon. She gave him a cold little nod, reminding herself he was the *reason* she had left Devon.

He was smiling at her, those blue eyes piercing her very soul. The little smile playing about his lips suggested he knew very well what she was thinking.

'You are looking very pale, Mrs Roffey,' the Earl remarked. 'Are you quite well?'

'Perfectly, my lord.'

Mrs Darby laughed. 'We are all of us atremble, my lord. Sir Kenelm has been regaling us with a description of the play last night. *The Fate of Frankenstein!* And now we learn that you were there, too.'

'I was. In my opinion Mrs Shelley's book is far superior.' He turned his attention back to Arabella, his countenance, his manner, all concern. 'Mrs Roffey, perhaps you are in need of a little sustenance. Shall I escort you to the supper room?'

'No, thank you. I want nothing.'

'Are you sure, madam?' Lord Haverford lifted his head. 'Aha, listen! The music has stopped, so I suppose everyone will be going down to supper now. Perhaps we should all join 'em before those young people devour everything!'

'No, no, I assure you I want nothing.'

Arabella's words were almost lost as everyone started to rise. She was about to follow suit when Randolph put his hand on her arm.

'If you are not hungry, then stay where you are, madam. You will recover all the sooner if you remain here, in peace and quiet.'

'I am not ill,' she muttered.

'Of course you are not ill.' He laughed, casting a look about at the rest of the group. 'It is merely that you have no appetite.' He lowered himself into the chair beside her and waved the others away. 'You may safely leave Mrs Roffey to my care while you are all at supper.'

Sir Kenelm gave a hearty chuckle. 'Impudent young dog! You see what he's done, Haverford? Stolen the march on us with a pretty woman.'

'I doubt Mrs Roffey will object to having the Earl keep her company,' put in Mrs Darby, directing a twinkling smile at Arabella. 'We shall return later, my dear, to see how you are.'

Arabella watched them move off, her cheeks burning with mortification.

'I beg your pardon.' The Earl's voice was a nice blend of sympathy and laughter. 'I could not ignore the opportunity to talk to you alone.'

The room was almost empty, save for an elderly gentleman snoring gently in the far corner. Arabella glared at Randolph.

'What are you doing here?'

'I received an invitation from Lady Aldenham.' She almost ground her teeth at his innocent reply and his eyes twinkled with amusement. 'I have been looking for you.'

'Why?'

'I thought you might need my assistance.'

'I do not want your help!'

'You told me so, at our last meeting. I wanted to assure myself that you are well.'

She put up her chin. 'I am very well. Thank you.'

'Truly?' He remained in his chair, seemingly at

ease, but she knew he was watching her closely. 'Tell me where you have been, what you have done since you left Beaumount. Did you come directly to town?'

'No. I returned to Revesby Hall.' She folded her hands in her lap. 'I decided I should tell Sir Adam and Lady Roffey the truth, that I had not been visiting friends but had been to Devon to discover what I could about George's last stay there.' Her eyes flickered briefly to his face. 'I did not tell them quite everything. I thought it best *not* to say I had pretended to be your wife.'

He said nothing and she was grateful he did not tease her or make light of it. After a few moments she continued.

'They were most forbearing and forgave me my deception.' She sat up a little straighter and looked him in the eye. 'I asked Lady Roffey if George took laudanum. If that was the cause of his demise. She denied it, most emphatically. She assured me that was not the case.'

'And did you tell them why you were coming to London?'

'Yes. They tried to dissuade me, but I expected that. In the end they gave their consent, albeit reluctantly.'

'And they allowed you to come here alone?'

'You are incredulous, but why should you be? They do not believe there is any danger.' She frowned. 'Lady Roffey said that if George *was* poisoned it was accidental. Something he had eaten. But that does not make any sense.'

'It does not make sense that they did not accompany you to London!'

'They wanted to do so, but Sir Adam is not well,' she told him. 'They insisted on making all the arrangements. They opened the townhouse and found a companion for me.'

'And how long have you been here?'

'Four weeks. There was a memorial service for George at Christmas and then I remained in Lincolnshire until the end of January.'

Arabella looked down at her folded hands. She had spent much of her time at Revesby Hall alone, in her room or sitting in the little chapel which housed the family vaults. The Roffeys had assumed she was mourning her husband, which was the truth, but only part of it.

She had been trying to forget Randolph, telling herself that grief had made her vulnerable. Convincing herself that he meant nothing to her. She believed she had succeeded. Until he had walked into the room tonight and she had thought she might faint with the desire to throw herself into his arms.

'And what have you learned?' he asked now.

Arabella hesitated. She had discovered woefully little.

'It has been very slow,' she said cautiously. 'But I have met someone who has promised to tell me more about George's visit to Meon House. I am meeting him here, tonight.'

She glanced towards the door, looking for her informant. He had suggested they meet here. Perhaps he had arrived late and was even now in one of the other rooms, looking for her.

'May I ask who?'

She shook her head and rose to her feet. Her limbs

still felt remarkably shaky, but she was determined to get away from Randolph.

'If you will excuse me, I think I should be going.'

She hoped he would remain but he accompanied her. The ballroom was filling up again now, as guests returned from their supper, and she stood by the wall, her eyes searching the crowd. She did not look at Randolph, but she was aware of him beside her, like a magnet pulling her closer. She had only to lean a couple of inches closer and her shoulder would touch his arm. She was sorely tempted to do so, to take advantage of his strength, the protection and comfort she knew he would offer. Perhaps she was wrong. Perhaps, in the months since she had last seen him, he no longer wanted to help her.

The musicians were tuning up again and Arabella had an unexpected and vivid memory of her first ball. It had been at the assembly rooms in Lincoln. She recalled being giddy with excitement, the eager anticipation she had experienced when a gentleman solicited her hand for a dance. If only she was still in those carefree days. Ran might take her hand to lead her out and her heart would sing with the sheer pleasure of being his partner. He would be a good dancer; she was sure of it. He would be both graceful and energetic, and when it ended, she would smile and thank him, and he would reach for her hands, pull her closer and...

'I did not expect to see you here tonight.'

The Earl's voice brought her crashing back to the present. She was not a debutante, but a widow. A widow of less than twelve months. She was not free.

'I came here only to learn more of my husband's death,' she told him. 'My informant has not arrived.'

'And will he come now, at this late hour?'

'I doubt it.' She should leave. Distance herself from this man whose very presence made her tingle with forbidden desires.

'An odd place to exchange information. Are you sure he isn't hoping to persuade you to dance with him?'

Even his voice had the power to distract her. Rich and dark. Smooth as velvet and twice as sensuous.

Stop it, Arabella. You are not a schoolgirl to swoon over a deep voice or a handsome face. How can you forget George so soon?

The rush of guilt brought with it resentment for the man standing beside her.

She gestured to her gown. 'My demi-train indicates I do not dance tonight.'

'Even so, a man might hope.'

She drew herself up and gave him a disdainful look.

'Only a most insensitive creature could think I would dishonour my husband's memory with such frivolity! Goodnight, Lord Westray.'

Arabella turned to walk away, flinging aside her skirts so that the short train slapped against Ran's legs like a rebuke. He cursed silently. He had not meant to insult her. The words had slipped out.

A man might hope.

Inflammatory. Wishful thinking. She was almost at the open doorway to the ballroom as he set off after her, determined to apologise. She had stopped just outside, on the landing leading to the grand staircase, and was looking at something or someone he could not see. Her hand went out and was grasped by a man's gloved fingers. The next moment a man himself came into sight and Randolph stopped abruptly.

Teddington! Was this the man she had arranged to meet? There was no denying, with his handsome face and glossy black whiskers, he was just the sort of fellow to appeal to the ladies. Arabella was smiling at him. Surely she had not fallen under his spell? He felt a sharp stab of anger. She had berated *him* for suggesting she might dance, and yet here she was, allowing Charles Teddington to kiss her fingers. Bah! What did he know of ladies, after all? He had been living a very different life for the past six years.

Teddington did not release that small, dainty hand. He drew it on to his sleeve and turned to escort her back into the ballroom. They were already deep in conversation and did not see Randolph until they were a few steps away. He had had time to school his face to indifference, but it was impossible to smile.

'Ah, Lord Westray. Servant, sir.' Teddington's black brows rose. 'Leaving already, my lord?'

'Yes. It is late.' Ran gave faint but definite emphasis to the last word, but if Arabella noticed she gave no sign. She was gazing straight ahead, her face as cold and indifferent as stone.

'I suppose it is.' Charles Teddington laughed. 'I was just telling Mrs Roffey, got held up at Brooks's. Middle of a game, you see, impossible to withdraw. But I am here now. If you will excuse us, my lord, my fair partner has expressed a wish for a little wine.'

A bow, a smile and he was gone, carrying Arabella

away while Randolph remained frozen to the spot. He had come to London for the sole purpose of warning Arabella about Teddington. He scowled, remembering how the fellow had smirked at her. How she had smiled back. She might think he was helping her, but Ran doubted it, very much. He tried to pull together his thoughts. He had said he was leaving; it would look odd if he turned around and followed them to the refreshment table. He set off down the stairs. Perhaps the fresh air would help him to think clearly.

As he made his way back to his rooms at Mivart's Hotel, he remembered everything Chislett had told him about Charles Teddington. Arabella was still a wealthy woman. Lady Aldenham had confirmed tonight that it was common knowledge. The golden widow. If Teddington was indeed a fortune hunter, he might consider her a prize worth winning, at any cost.

Arabella could not resist a glance over her shoulder as she went back into the ballroom, but Randolph was already out of sight.

'Are you well acquainted with the new Earl, Mrs Roffey?' asked Mr Teddington.

She managed a light, dismissive laugh. 'Well acquainted? No more than with any of the other gentlemen here tonight. This is my first visit to town.'

'Perhaps you have not read his history,' he remarked. 'It is rather unsavoury.'

'His history does not concern me,' she replied. 'I am in town only to discover what I can about my husband. That is the reason I came here tonight,' she reminded him. 'You said you would tell me what you know.'

He laughed softly. 'I did indeed.' He signalled to a passing waiter and scooped two glasses of wine from his tray. 'Shall we find somewhere quiet, a little sitting room, perhaps, where we can talk?'

Arabella had no intention of slipping off alone with him. She said, 'I know the very place.'

She led the way back into the salon where she had first seen Randolph. Mrs Darby, Sir Kenelm and the Haverfords had returned from supper and she gave them a faint smile as she passed them, heading towards a window embrasure with a cushioned window seat. It was not quite as well-lit as the rest of the room, but although no one could overhear their conversation, they were still in full view of the other guests.

She sat down with her back against one of the shutters, making it impossible for him to sit too close.

'This will suffice,' she said.

If Mr Teddington was dismayed at her choice, he gave no sign, but sat down facing her.

'What is it you wish to know, Mrs Roffey?'

'You were with George in Devonshire last summer.' She paused, frowning slightly as if trying to recall some unfamiliar name. 'Meon House, I believe?'

'Ah, yes. My widowed sister's house. What a pity you were not there with George.' He shook his head sadly. 'I begged him to invite you.'

'You did?' She was surprised.

'Of course. But he would not be moved. Poor George was always so protective of you.'

'What would he be protecting me from, Mr Teddington?'

He spread his hands. 'Why, nothing that bad, ma'am, I assure you. My sister is a most considerate hostess. For those who do not like cards or dice there is always the library, or the gardens where one might walk on fine days. We rode out often and even played charades.'

Arabella sipped at her wine and let him continue, listening closely to his reminiscences. It all seemed very harmless.

He ended with a rueful smile. 'The wine and spirits flowed a little freely, perhaps.'

'Are you telling me my husband drank too much, sir?'

He gave a nervous laugh. 'We all drank too much, ma'am, but poor George seemed to feel it more than the rest of us.'

Poor George.

His frequent use of the epithet grated, but she was determined not to do anything that might discourage him from talking.

'Who else was present, Mr Teddington?'

'Oh, I cannot recall…'

'Come now, sir. A month in a house and you cannot remember the other guests?'

He rubbed his brow. 'It is getting late and I fear I am more fatigued than I thought. Perhaps another night.'

But Arabella did not want to spend another night in his company. Something about Charles Teddington disturbed her. She thought she would not have trusted him, even if he had not been Lady Meon's brother.

'Please try to remember, Mr Teddington.' She gave him what she hoped was an encouraging smile. 'I do so want to know.'

He glanced about the room. 'Some of the guests are leaving. It is gone midnight.'

She waved a hand. 'The ball will go on for hours yet, sir.'

'My dear Mrs Roffey, it would give me great pleasure to sit here talking with you until dawn,' he said smoothly. 'However, there is no one else in this room now and I am acutely aware of your situation. I would not compromise you for the world.'

Colour rushed to her face. 'Really, sir, there can be no question of that!'

'A single gentleman, alone with a beautiful woman?' He shook his head. 'Alas, dear lady, tongues will always wag. No, I think we must continue our talk another time. But I can see how impatient you are for news of your beloved, so, shall we meet in the park tomorrow morning at, say, eleven o'clock?'

Curbing her exasperation, Arabella agreed and they parted. She went home feeling dissatisfied with the whole evening. Charles Teddington had told her almost nothing of any relevance and her meeting with the Earl had brought back all the wickedly disturbing feelings she had tried so hard to forget since leaving Devon.

Chapter Eight

It did not take Randolph long to discover that the Roffeys' townhouse was one of the more substantial houses on Park Street.

'Mrs Roffey keeps her own carriage, too,' Joseph informed him, after a productive visit to a local tavern a couple of days later. 'Although word is that the coachman is in the pay of her father-in-law.'

'Thank heavens you did not attempt to bribe him, then,' muttered Ran.

Joseph grinned. 'I got talking to one of the footmen,' he explained. 'He became quite expansive after a drink or two. Told me he and some of his fellows had been sent from Revesby Hall to look after Mrs Roffey. Sir Adam and his lady have cared for their daughter-in-law since she was orphaned as a child and they love her like their own, he told me. They didn't like it above half when she wanted to come to London. He said they'd been anxious enough when she went to stay with friends at the end of last year.'

'When she was in Devon.' Ran nodded, bittersweet memories swirling in his head.

'Aye, sir, *we* know that, but it seems she fooled everyone else. But she did go straight to Revesby Hall when she left Beaumount. The footman told me she was back in good time for Christmas, when they held a special church service in memory of her husband.'

So she had not been lying about that, thought Ran, momentarily relieved.

'Do the servants know *why* Mrs Roffey has come to town?'

'Only that she has come looking for her husband's friends. They think it's quite natural that she should want to talk to them about her husband.' Joseph paused. 'If the footman's to be believed, young George was a bad lot, although his parents wouldn't see it.'

'Hmm.' Ran scowled. 'If the servants know it, why the devil didn't Arabella's maid say something to her? Why did she let her take off into the wilds of Devon and now to come here?'

'It appears Master George had all the ladies wrapped around his little finger. Mrs Arabella wouldn't hear a word against her sainted husband and Lady Roffey had forbidden anyone to talk about it below stairs. Ruth Sawyer might have had her suspicions, but from what I gleaned when we were at Beaumount, she is more than prepared to give the young master the benefit of the doubt.' Joseph shrugged. 'Strange creatures, women. Very loyal.'

'And now the widow is cultivating a friendship with Charles Teddington.'

The thought disturbed Randolph, but he had given his word that he would not pass on what Chislett had told him about Teddington. All he could do was to keep an eye on Arabella, as much as was possible without arousing comment.

Thus, a few days later, he followed her to an Italian concert given by Mrs Beausale. Fortune favoured him and he walked into the drawing room to find Arabella and her companion taking their seats in an otherwise empty row.

Arabella was wearing a gown of black lace over a white slip, perfectly suited to a grieving widow, although the matching lace cap only enhanced the glory of her golden hair and Ran observed that she had already attracted the notice of several gentlemen. He knew he would have to move quickly. With controlled haste but great aplomb, he dodged between the incoming guests, a word here, an apology there, until he had reached his quarry.

Arabella was studying the programme and did not see his approach until it was too late to move away. She greeted him coolly and introduced the frail-looking woman next to her as her companion, Mrs Hatcliffe. Ran nodded affably and settled himself on the empty seat beside Arabella.

'Teddington not escorting you this evening, Mrs Roffey?' She hunched one white shoulder and twisted away, clearly determined to ignore him. He murmured, 'Could not even your charms lure him here tonight? The fellow is a philistine.'

He heard a choke of laughter at that. She turned back in her seat, although she kept her eyes fixed on the programme.

'It is one of the reasons I came,' she murmured.

'He let slip that nothing on earth would persuade him to sit through an evening of Italian songs.'

'Indeed?' His spirits lifted slightly. 'Then he is not worthy of your attention.'

'I wish I could cut the acquaintance.'

'Why don't you?'

'Because he was with George. In Devon.'

Ran bit back his impatience. 'We know that. In fact, you were as suspicious of him as I when you learned of it.'

'I know. But he is, was, George's friend.'

He leaned closer, pretending to look at the programme with her. 'Tell me how you met him.'

'I did what I said I would. I wrote and asked him outright what he knew.'

'You did what?' Ran muttered a curse. 'For heaven's sake, Bella, do you not know the risks you are taking?'

'I do. Of course I do. One of the greatest dangers is to be seen talking to you! And you have no right to call me anything other than Mrs Roffey.'

'What, may I not call you Bella?' He smiled, momentarily distracted. 'I beg your pardon, but it comes readily to my tongue.'

'Well, it should not,' she hissed at him. 'No one calls me that.'

'They should. It suits you.'

He watched the colour steal into her face. She said stiffly, 'We are digressing. I was about to say I do not need your assistance.'

'As you have told me. More than once.'

He straightened, fixing his frowning gaze upon the musicians who were taking their places on a small raised dais in front of the rows of chairs. Damnation, why did he bother with the woman when she was determined to keep him at a distance?

She touched his arm. 'Now I have offended you.'

He was immediately disarmed. She sounded so contrite he wanted to pull her close and kiss her, in full view of everyone. He folded his arms to prevent himself doing anything so outrageous.

She gave a little sigh. 'I *am* aware of the dangers, my lord. I did not come to town with the intention of talking directly to any of George's acquaintances. I asked the Roffey family lawyer to help, to make enquiries, but he was not at all forthcoming. Indeed, he was positively *un*helpful. I think he has had instruction from Sir Adam to keep me from learning anything new.'

His heart went out to her. 'The Roffeys may be afraid you will discover things about your husband that will upset you.'

'And is it better that I should remain in ignorance?'

'Perhaps it is.'

'No. I do not believe it. I knew George better than anyone. He was the kindest man in the world. Honest, too. He would never lie to me. Why should he accuse anyone of killing him if it was not true?'

'And what has Teddington told you about him?'

'He confirmed what I know,' she replied defiantly. 'He says George was the best of men. Although…' her shoulders drooped a little '…he admitted George drank a little too much and was overly fond of gambling.'

'I am sure that is no more than you already knew.'

He watched her wrestling with herself.

'He tells me so little each time,' she said at last. 'He replied to my letter and suggested we meet at Lady Aldenham's ball. The night I saw you.' She blushed a little as she said that. 'Then we arranged to meet in the park the next day, and the next. This morning we met in the circulating library.'

The musicians were tuning up and anyone observing Ran might well think his frown was due to their discordant notes.

'And each time he feeds you snippets,' he said. 'Little morsels to whet your appetite.'

One dainty hand fluttered. 'He is right, of course. To be seen together for too long at any one time could be injurious to my good name and yet we must make sure our conversations are not overheard.' She lifted the programme a little higher and turned it towards the light, as if puzzling over a particular entry. 'Sometimes I think I should invite him to call upon me, but I know that would not answer. The servants are under instruction from my father-in-law, you see. Nothing in the house goes unreported. Ruth is the only one I can trust.' She sighed. 'I know the Roffeys have my best interests at heart, but if they learned I had been meeting a gentleman alone, even a friend of George's, I fear Sir Adam might use the excuse to take me back to Lincolnshire.'

'With some reason,' said Randolph grimly. 'I do not believe Teddington is quite the good friend he pretends to be.'

A hush fell over the room as Mr Beausale moved to the front to introduce the singers and the orchestra. Under cover of the polite applause that followed,

Randolph leaned closer to Arabella and pretended to point at something in the programme.

'You are wise not to meet Teddington privately.'

She put up her chin and gave her attention to the performance. Ran had no idea if she agreed with him, but the stubborn tilt of her chin made him doubt it. It was some small comfort that, at the interval, she continued the conversation.

'Mr Teddington said George was very protective of me. That is why he did not take me to Meon House with him. He thought I would find it tedious.'

'Arabella, do you not think, if he loved you, he would have taken you with him, however boring the company? More to the point, he would never have gone!'

His words caught Arabella on the raw and she scolded herself for not keeping Randolph at a distance, but it was impossible not to respond when he was near. He called to something inside her, as if they were kindred spirits. She knew he meant well, but he was wrong about her husband. He had not known George, not as she had done.

'He *did* love me,' she muttered fiercely. 'And I loved him. I will have justice for my husband, and if that means being friends with Charles Teddington, then so be it!'

She turned to speak to Mrs Hatcliffe and resolutely ignored his presence for the rest of the evening, even though it was like cutting off a limb.

She is playing with fire.
The words echoed around in Ran's head more than

once as the gloomy days of February turned into an equally dark and drear March and London remained thin of company. It was not difficult for him to guess which of the social events a young widow was likely to attend and, with Joseph's help and a readiness to grease palms, he was able to follow her every movement.

Those who observed that the new Earl of Westray preferred musical evenings and poetry recitals to balls put it down to the fact that he had been away from England—indeed, from civilised society!—for so many years. The poor fellow was clearly starved of the arts. He only hoped they would not notice his appearances coincided with those of the golden widow. Much as he wanted to talk to her, he kept his distance, a few words at most, and if she was escorted by Charles Teddington then he gave them no more than a nod in passing. Nothing that could arouse suspicion.

An insipid evening of bad poetry at the house of Sir Kenelm and Lady Prees proved too much for him and broke his resolve not to speak to Arabella. At the interval he begged to be allowed to fetch her a cup of tea. She looked surprised and somewhat suspicious and he spread his hands.

'I have no ulterior motive, madam. I would merely like us to be friends.'

Something flared in her eyes, too quick for him to understand it, but she said quietly, 'I should like that, too. So, yes, my lord, tea would be very welcome.'

With a smile, he headed off to perform this small service for her.

'How can you bear it?' he asked when he returned

and handed her a cup. 'I have never heard such bad verse.'

She chuckled. 'The last young man was particularly bad, was he not? I believe Lady Prees considers herself something of a connoisseur. She is hoping one of her young protégés will turn out to be the next Southey or Wordsworth.'

'Not with poetry like that, they won't.' His vehemence made her giggle and he grinned, enjoying the rare moment of understanding.

'What did you do for entertainment, when you were abroad?' she asked him.

He appreciated her delicacy in mentioning his previous life.

'Nothing like this,' he told her. 'In Airds, where I was granted my one hundred acres, it was mostly settlers, sheep farmers, too busy securing their livelihoods for poetry.'

'That must have been very arduous.'

'It was, but the rewards were good, for those prepared to work. I was fortunate—being an educated man, I was useful to the authorities in Sydney Cove and eventually I became overseer of the Government brickworks.'

'That was after you had saved those poor passengers from the sinking ship.' She chuckled as he stifled a curse. 'You wonder how I know? Joseph Miller told Ruth about you, when we were in Devon. She passed it on to me.'

'The devil she did!'

'Mr Miller's account made it sound very heroic.'

'It was nothing of the kind,' he retorted. 'I organised the boats to row out and fetch the crew and passengers, that is all.'

'He said you rowed out yourself, to pick up the last of the crew, even though you risked your little boat being dragged down with the sinking ship. You acted very nobly.'

She was regarding him over the rim of her teacup and the warm appreciation in her eyes sent a dull flush creeping into his cheeks.

'Fustian,' he growled. 'Did Joseph also say that he was there with me, risking his own life?'

'No, but I can believe it. He is devoted to you. Which I think is why he told Ruth your history. He says your actions that night prompted the authorities to pardon you.'

Ran waved a hand dismissively. 'I was recommended for pardon because we had managed to save most of the valuable cargo, not the people.'

She shook her head. 'I believe you do yourself a disservice, my lord.'

Ran said nothing, but he could not deny the warm glow inside, knowing she thought well of him for that small service, at least. He noticed the change in the room. People were beginning to return to their seats. He had been talking with Bella for a good fifteen minutes. So much for keeping his distance!

He said, 'Our hostess has promised us even more delights when we have drunk our tea. Will you stay?'

'I think I must,' she said seriously. 'Sir Kenelm and Lady Prees have been very kind to me. I should not like to appear ungrateful.'

He drained his cup and set it down.

'I, on the other hand, have no such scruples and do

not intend to sit through any more excruciating sonnets, odes or rhymes. I bid you goodnight, ma'am.'

Ran sought out his hostess and took his leave, assuring her with all the charm he could muster that only a previous engagement could draw him away. He left the house, pausing on the steps to button his greatcoat. He would have stayed, he admitted to himself, if he could have remained at Arabella's side for the rest of the evening, talking with her. Laughing with her. But he had already spent too long in her company tonight.

But as he set off along the street, pulling up his collar against the icy wind, he wished he might have carried her away with him. To his rooms, to her house. Anywhere as long as they might have been together. The ache was so strong he stopped and put one hand on the railings to steady himself. It could not be. It could never be. Had she not said, time and again, how much she loved her husband? His only consolation was the final look she had given him: he had read disappointment in those clear eyes.

She had wanted him to stay.

The thought of it gnawed away at him as he strode away through the darkness, and when he reached the end of the street, he hesitated. It was early yet and he had no wish to retire to Mivart's. Instead he turned his steps in the opposite direction, towards St James's Street and one of the discreet little gambling hells where he knew he would be welcomed.

The card room was comfortably full. He was invited to join a table playing vingt-et-un and sat down, hoping a game or two would relax him, distract him from thoughts of Arabella Roffey. It worked, until Charles Teddington walked in.

Ran had been losing steadily. Not enough to worry him, he knew he was not giving the games his full attention, but he had just risen from the table when Teddington came up.

'Ah, Westray. Well met, sir.'

Ran nodded, disliking the fellow's oily charm.

'What say you to a game of piquet, my lord?'

Ran had been about to take his leave, but instead he accepted. After all, he might learn something of interest. Something that might help Arabella. He followed Teddington to a small table set back in one of the room's alcoves. A servant brought a fresh pack of cards and trimmed the candles while they made themselves comfortable.

'You will drink with me, my lord?'

'Of course.'

'Wine, or would you prefer brandy?'

'Your choice.'

Again, that unctuous smile. 'Brandy, then.'

Teddington nodded to the hovering footman, who hurried away. He won the cut and Randolph watched him as he shuffled the cards and dealt them with practised ease. They played in silence, each deciding upon his discards, weighing up his opponent. The advantage went with the elder hand, as expected, and at the end of the first *partie*, Teddington admitted defeat.

'A few more tricks and I should have beaten you, my lord. Shall we play again?' When Ran hesitated, he gave a soft laugh. 'I should have the opportunity for revenge, I think.'

'Why not?'

'Good.' He picked up the decanter and waved it at Ran, who shook his head. 'What, my lord? You have barely touched your drink.'

'It was a close game and I needed to concentrate.' Not quite true, Ran thought. He had noted Teddington's wild discards, but he would not put it past the fellow to be shamming, drawing him in.

'Well, I shall fill your glass, nevertheless,' said Teddington, suiting the action to the words. 'Don't want to be distracted while we play, what?'

Ran merely smiled. He would not drink it. Over the years he had grown adept at pretending to sip at a glass and disposing of its contents in a flowerpot, an ice bucket, even out of the window. Anywhere but down his throat.

The next two *parties* went predictably, the non-dealer scoring highest. Ran stifled a yawn. His opponent was competent, but he did not like the fellow and he was not in the mood to sit up all night playing at cards with him.

'Talking of distractions,' said Teddington, shuffling the cards for the next round. 'May I ask, are you thinking of matrimony, Lord Westray?'

Randolph was surprised into a laugh. 'Why, no. Not at all.'

'Ah. Then you will not take it amiss if I give you the hint. Concerning a certain lady.'

'Oh?'

'A widow.'

Ran's long fingers played with the stem of his

brandy glass while his opponent dealt the cards. He said coolly, 'There are any number of widows in town.'

'But this one is particularly…tempting. Arabella Roffey.'

'Ah, yes. The golden widow.' Despite his careless drawl and lazy smile, Ran was tense, all his senses alert.

'The same. A veritable diamond.' Teddington glanced up. 'I've seen you watching her.'

Randolph hoped his countenance did not give him away.

'Of course.' He smiled. 'She is a very attractive woman.'

'Damned attractive.' Teddington shot him another glance. 'What do you mean by her, my lord?'

'I? Why, nothing.'

The fellow watched him from under frowning brows. Then he nodded.

'I am relieved to hear that.' He drained his glass and slopped more brandy into it. 'You see, I have an interest there myself.'

Ran cursed silently. The fellow was warning him off!

'Cosy little armful,' Teddington went on. 'A man might do worse for himself, don't you think?'

Ran said carefully, 'She has not been widowed a year, I believe.'

'She's nervous, like a wild bird, but I was a friend of her husband. That gives me the advantage.' He grinned. 'Once the year is up the vultures will be circling, eager to get their talons on her fortune. I am going to make sure of her before anyone else has the chance!'

Randolph shrugged. 'Since I am not one of the, er, vultures, it is no concern of mine.' He picked up his cards. 'Shall we play?'

The next few hands were more closely fought. Teddington gained a pique in the first and won two tricks from a throw-in in the second before Randolph's anger cooled sufficiently for him to concentrate once more on the game. He was in no doubt that he could still win, for his opponent was drinking steadily and Ran's points were mounting. He toyed with the idea of staying for a rematch. He had not touched his brandy and his unclouded brain told him he might ruin Teddington at one sitting, if he so wished. Tempting, but he decided against it. He preferred not to make an enemy of the man, until it was necessary.

'I'm done!' Teddington threw down his cards with a forced laugh. 'That repique in the final *partie* secured your victory, my lord. Shall we play again? I want my revenge!'

'Not tonight.' Randolph pushed back his chair. 'I have an appointment in the morning.'

'Very well, sir. Until the next time.' Teddington picked up his glass and saluted him, saying with a grin, 'Let us hope I am luckier in love than at cards, eh?'

Ran stretched his mouth to a smile and took his leave. He sauntered out to the street, his demeanour that of a man without a care in the world, but his thoughts were very dark. If what Chislett had told him about Teddington was true, the fellow was no mere fortune hunter, but possibly a murderer. The idea of Arabella being his next prey chilled him to the bone.

Chapter Nine

Arabella's black skirts whispered about her as she crossed the hall.

'I wonder if I am right to wear silk?' She stopped to look in the mirror. 'Do you think it too soon, Esther?'

She turned to her companion, who had followed her down the stairs.

'No, no, my dear. You are more than halfway through your year of mourning. I am sure no one can object.'

Arabella cast another glance at her reflection. The soft sheen of the material was very different from the lustreless fabrics she had worn for the past few months and she felt another tremor of doubt, despite her companion's assurance. Dear, timid little Esther Hatcliffe would say whatever she thought was required of her.

The deep chime of the longcase clock sounded just as the footman announced that her carriage was at the door. There was no time to change. She threw her velvet-lined cloak about her shoulders.

'Are you sure you do not wish me to accompany you?' asked Esther, walking with her to the door. 'I have only to fetch my coat.'

'Thank you, but I do not require you tonight. And there is no need for you to wait up for me. I do not intend to remain long at Sweigne House.'

'Oh, but I shall.' Esther smiled at Arabella. 'You know I will not be able to sleep until I have seen you are safely back in the house. And I shall look forward to you telling me all about your evening!'

Arabella walked out to the waiting carriage, leaving her companion standing in the doorway, waving after her. Poor Esther, she thought, as the carriage rattled away along the street. So eager to please, so afraid of offending. Arabella felt quite sorry for her. She was not the companion she would have chosen and quite possibly not the companion Sir Adam had hoped for, when he had insisted she should live with Arabella in London. It was necessary, upon occasion, to take a companion when she went out, but not tonight. Indeed, Esther would be very much in the way.

Lady Sweigne was a hostess of some renown. She was garrulous to the point of absurdity, but her good nature and her fortune were equally boundless. Her routs were famous for the excellence of the refreshments, the elegance of the company and superiority of the entertainment. Even at this time of the year her rooms would be agreeably full. There was no dancing, only skilled musicians whose melodious sounds provided unobtrusive background to the conversation. In the card room, play was not deep; whist, vingt-et-un, cribbage and loo were encouraged, but not piquet. It was all very respectable, which was the reason Arabella had suggested to Charles Teddington that they meet there. She thought it would be a safe rendezvous for what she hoped would be their last meeting.

Sweigne House was aglow with candlelight when Arabella stepped down from her coach, promising a welcome haven from the icy streets, where the blustery wind sent little eddies of snow scudding along the gutters.

She was so busy anticipating the warm rooms that she did not notice the cloaked figure on the flagway until he spoke.

'Good evening, Mrs Roffey.'

She jumped. 'Oh. Lord Westray.'

The heat flooding her cheeks gave away her agitation at seeing him. Not that she could quite *see* him, for his collar was turned up and his hat pulled down, its brim throwing his face into shadow, but there was no mistaking that deep, smooth voice with its hint of teasing laughter.

'Here.' He held out his hand. 'Let me help you up the steps. They may be icy.'

Once over the threshold she released him, but could not bring herself to walk away without a word of thanks.

'My pleasure.' He took off his hat and shook it, sending a small shower of fine snow on to the marble floor. 'A cold night to venture out. You are perhaps meeting friends here?'

The remark seemed innocent enough, but when she looked into his eyes there was no smile in them. She had suspected in the past that he could read her thoughts; now she could read his. He knew she was

meeting Charles Teddington and he did not approve.
She took a deep breath.

'I hope I shall see many friends here, my lord,' she
said, before walking off to the ladies' retiring room.

Arabella entered the drawing room with her head
held high, nodding to acquaintances with a calm assurance that was quite at odds with the nervous flutter inside. Knowing Randolph was present did not
help her anxiety at all. She saw him immediately, on
the far side of the room, talking with Sir Arran Eversleigh. His fair hair gleamed in the candlelight and
he was laughing at something his companion was
saying. The familiar wave of longing swept over her.

As if aware of her gaze, he met her eyes. She
looked away quickly. If she could not ignore his presence, then she must endure it as best she could. She
straightened her shoulders, lifted her head a little
higher and moved on to speak to her hostess, who
greeted her in her slightly breathless, voluble way.

'Ah, Mrs Roffey, you came. I am delighted, delighted. Indeed, I am quite *humbled* that so many
of my friends have turned out on such a cold night
as this to come to my little salon. I see Mrs Darby
and Lady Prees over there by the fire. Shall you join
them? Or in the far corner, Mrs Beausale and her
friends are discussing literature.' She laughed and
leaned closer, putting a hand on Arabella's arm and
saying with a twinkle, 'Novels, I believe, not poetry,
for which we must all be thankful! My dear, the read-
ings at her soirée last week were not quite to my taste,
but then, I know nothing about the finer points of
such matters!'

'Nor I, ma'am.'

A smile and short reply were all that was required of Arabella before her hostess continued.

'Perhaps cards are your pleasure? But here is Mr Teddington approaching. Your especial friend, is he not, ma'am? One can't help but notice! Not that there is anything— That is, no one thinks your behaviour has been anything but irreproachable and he is such a charming gentleman.' She looked relieved to break off as Charles Teddington approached them.

He bowed to Lady Sweigne and, when their hostess turned away to greet more latecomers, turned to Arabella.

'This is not the quiet little party I envisaged, madam.'

'Lady Sweigne's parties are always popular, I believe, but it will suit our purposes.' His brows rose and she added, 'My purpose.'

He glanced around the room. 'I doubt there is anywhere in here we may talk alone together without arousing gossip. Shall we try a hand of cards?'

She inclined her head and he escorted her to the card room, where the air was warmed by a cheerful fire and the glow of candlelight. It was much quieter, only a murmur of voices from the small baize tables that had been set up around the room and one larger table, where a game of loo was in progress. Soft-footed servants circulated with decanters, keeping the guests supplied with drink, sherry for the ladies, port for the gentlemen.

'The table in the corner is free,' he remarked. 'What shall it be, ma'am—cribbage?'

'Anything, as long as we may play alone.'

He gave a soft laugh as he held her chair for her to sit. 'Should I be encouraged by your words?'

'Not really.' She smoothed her skirts while he took his seat opposite and picked up the fresh pack of cards. 'If you know anything more about my husband, you will tell me now, if you please.'

Her blunt words startled him. 'What, here? Madam, I—'

She cut him short. 'Pray open the pack, Mr Teddington. We need to look as if we intend to play. Then no one will interrupt us.'

'You are very severe tonight, Mrs Roffey.'

'With good reason.' She drew a card and waited while he took one. 'Your deal, I think. This will be our last meeting, Mr Teddington. There will be no more walks along deserted paths or tête-à-têtes in shadowed alcoves. It is beginning to cause comment.'

'But we agreed. Discretion was necessary.'

'You have told me very little, almost nothing, in fact, that I could not have guessed. I do not believe you know anything of import.'

There. She had issued the challenge. He continued to deal the cards, but his smile was fixed.

He picked up his hand. 'Let us at least make a pretence of playing,' he muttered. 'There is more I could tell you, but I do not want to upset you.'

'Your procrastination has been much worse!'

'You are impatient for the truth, ma'am, I understand that, but let us proceed cautiously.' When she drew in a breath he added quickly, 'I shall tell you what I know. Names, facts, everything about your husband's death, you have my word, but not here, in front of so many people. What I have to say is too distressing.'

'You must tell me tonight,' she insisted. 'I swear, once I leave this house, I will not meet with you again.'

He was not pleased. His ready smile had disappeared and there was a petulant twist to his mouth.

'Very well. Let us finish our game. Then you must give me a little time to find somewhere we can talk privately.'

'I will not slip off alone with you, Mr Teddington!'

'No, no, a quiet corner, that is all. Believe me, madam, you will not wish to hear what I have to say in full view of everyone.'

She gave a little nod and tried to concentrate on her cards. Could it be so very bad? Surely nothing could be worse than her imaginings.

Every minute dragged for Arabella as they played out their game. At last it was over and Teddington escorted her back to the drawing room before walking off. He had regained his cheerful humour and was all charm as he made his way out of the room, whereas her own face ached with the effort of smiling. She glanced around the room, looking for Randolph, but he was not to be seen. Panic threatened and she immediately beat it back. She did not need his help. Did not want it. Lord and Lady Sweigne were good, kindly people; their guests were respectable. She was in no danger here. As soon as Charles Teddington had told her what he knew she would take her leave.

Arabella joined a group standing beside the fireplace which included Mrs Darby and Lady Prees.

They gave her a welcoming smile and she tried to look interested as the conversation moved back and forth around her. From the corner of her eye she noticed Teddington's return and she waited for him to approach. Before he could do so, supper was announced and the little group around her began to move. It was then that Teddington walked past and slipped a folded piece of paper into her hand.

She hung back. Everyone was making their way out of the drawing room, and when she was sure no one was watching, she opened the note and scanned it quickly. He had scrawled that they would talk in the hall while everyone was at supper. She should meet him by the bust of Aristotle when the clock next struck the hour.

She was reassured by the message. The marble hall was large, but there would be servants posted by the entrance, too far away to overhear, but she would not be alone with Charles Teddington. She threw the paper in the fire and hurried after the crowd.

Arabella followed everyone down to the supper room and, as she descended, she spotted the plinth with its bust of the Greek philosopher. It was almost opposite the supper room, but shielded from view of the big double doors by the sweeping rise of the grand staircase.

An extravagant supper was spread over the white-clothed tables, but Arabella had no appetite. She took a little of the beef and spiced rice, but ignored the pressed tongue and scalloped oysters. There was a fancy ormolu clock on the mantelshelf and she watched the hand making its agonisingly slow progress. The supper room was bustling and noisy and, as the hour approached, she hovered close to the table, as if trying to decide between the selection of small cakes. At last she slipped, unnoticed, from the room, closing the door behind her.

The hall appeared deserted, but as she hurried around the foot of the staircase she saw a solitary footman sitting on a bench by the front door. He was slumped against the wall and appeared to be dozing. There was no one near the bust of Aristotle.

Arabella approached the marble head slowly, making a show of studying the face. She was standing in front of it, gazing into the blind eyes, when the door beside it opened.

'I thought it best not to be found hovering out here,' said Charles Teddington, by way of explanation as he sauntered out.

He had left the door ajar and Arabella could see by the dim candlelight within that it was some sort of sitting room.

She said, 'Tell me everything, then, and quickly.'

He looked at her, his countenance and his voice oozing sympathy when he spoke.

'George was my friend, dear lady. I was very sad to see him…destroyed.'

She clasped her hands tightly together. 'He was m-murdered?'

'Undoubtedly.' His voice broke and he covered his eyes with one hand. 'It was wicked, wicked!'

Arabella stared at him, aghast.

'I beg your pardon,' he said at last. 'I must compose myself.' He stepped back into the sitting room.

Arabella followed him, sick with apprehension as her imagination ran riot with the most horrendous scenes. 'I had no idea, but what happened? If it was so very bad, why were we not informed?'

He shook his head, reaching out to push the door shut behind her.

'The matter was too…delicate.'

'Delicate!' Her initial shock was receding, replaced by anger. 'If there was foul play, then the perpetrators should be brought to justice!'

'It is not quite so simple,' he said sadly.

'Tell me.'

'Laudanum.' He walked across the room and leaned on the back of a chair, his head bowed. 'Poor George was an opium-eater. I had known it for years, but he was deaf to every remonstrance. It was gradually destroying his reason.'

His voice was so low she had to come closer to hear him, but even then his words made no sense.

'Wait, wait, are you saying he was dependent upon it? No, it cannot be. I never saw any sign of it.' She had said as much to Randolph. 'George always seemed so happy.'

'Oh, I am sure he could hide it from you. He would not wish to worry you or his family.'

She frowned. 'George told me he had been betrayed.'

'Did he? That was because we, his friends, would not pander to his habit and refused to provide more laudanum. That month in Devon, we all tried, believe me. We wanted him to get better.'

'Who was there, beside yourself?' she demanded.

'The Fingells, of course, and Lord Caversfield. And Freddie Letchmore.' He sighed. 'All his closest friends.'

'Not all,' she corrected him. 'Someone took advantage of his precarious health to take his money from him.'

'No, no, ma'am, you mistake. You would not understand.'

'I understand only too well, sir. When George returned from Meon House he had lost a vast sum.'

She saw he was about to argue and said quickly, 'I have studied the accounts, Mr Teddington. I know exactly when he withdrew the money and how much.'

He spread his hands. 'Alas, we could not watch him all the time. I suppose he slipped away to the village, or into Tavistock. He would have been able to procure more laudanum there and I don't doubt he found several gambling hells, too.'

Arabella shook her head. 'No. I have it on good authority that the guests rarely left the house.'

'Who told you that?'

'That is not important.' She said stubbornly, 'If he lost his fortune, then it was to the house guests. Unscrupulous persons who would find it a benefit if George's wits were befuddled by drink or...or laudanum.'

'Not I, my dear! I had only George's best interests at heart.' He reached for her hands. 'As I now have yours.'

Startled, she jumped away. 'Do not touch me!'

'You cannot be blind to the fact that I have come to care for you.'

'I do not want your attentions. I want to know who murdered my husband.'

He cursed and said in exasperation, 'No one murdered him. He killed himself by taking too much laudanum. I did not want to tell you, but there you have it. Now let us forget poor George!'

He stepped closer and Arabella quickly retreated behind a chair.

'I cannot forget him,' she said, her voice outraged. 'I am still in mourning!'

He was standing between her and the door, blocking her escape, and she felt her panic rising. She tried an appeal.

'You purport to be my husband's *friend*, sir.'

He put his hand on his heart. 'I was, my dear. I was his best friend. We can grieve for him together.'

'No. Never! If you have any feelings of friendship for George, you will allow me to leave this room now.' When he did not move she added, 'He would not thank you for importuning his wife.'

He said, in a tone of indifference, 'I doubt it would concern him greatly.'

'How dare you!'

He gave her a contemptuous smile. 'Do you think Roffey would ever have married you if you had not been rich?'

'George loved me!'

'I'm afraid not, my dear. I know you thought you were childhood sweethearts, but did you never wonder why it took him so long to make you his wife? He liked his bachelor life, the wine, the women. Once he had run through his own funds, he needed yours. He never really cared for you. I, on the other hand, *do* care. Passionately!' He put out his hand. 'You are overwrought, my dear Arabella. Come and sit down. There is wine on the table over there. Let me pour a glass for you. It will calm your nerves.'

'The only thing I want is never to see you again!' she replied, her voice shaking with anger.

'Ah, how unjust, my fair beauty, when you have led me on. Encouraged me to hope.'

'I have done no such thing!'

He had been edging closer and she saw her chance. She stepped around him and ran for the door. He lunged at her and she jumped aside, but not far enough. His fingers clutched at her shoulder, tearing the neck of her gown and almost ripping off the delicate puff sleeve. Then he caught her arm and dragged her towards him so violently that she collided with his chest. He clamped a hand over her mouth.

'No, no, don't cry out. It is futile. As is resistance. I mean to have you, one way or another.'

He removed his hand, but he was crushing her so tightly she could not draw in the air necessary to scream. He brought his head down to kiss her, his hot breath fumed with wine and brandy. She turned her face away in disgust, crying out as he grabbed at her hair and forced her head back.

'You cannot escape me, madam.'

'This is no way to win my regard!'

'Oh, you will come around, Arabella. You women always do.' He tightened his hold, crushing her to him and making it impossible to breathe. 'In the end.'

Arabella closed her eyes against his triumphant leer, but she could not shut out his savage laugh.

It stopped abruptly and suddenly she was free. She collapsed to the floor, gasping for air. There was a strangled, choking sound, as if Teddington had been hauled away by his collar. Then she heard the crack of bone against bone. When she looked up, her erstwhile assailant was lying on his back, arms raised protectively across his face. Standing over him, fists clenched and looking positively murderous, was Randolph.

Ran breathed deeply, steadying himself, curbing his anger. A red mist had descended when he had entered the room to see Arabella struggling with Teddington. It had been the work of a moment to pull the fellow off and knock him down, but he had to fight the temptation to thrash the cur to within an inch of his life. He stepped back and waved towards the open door.

'Get out.'

Teddington clambered unsteadily to his feet, putting a hand to his nose, to check if it was bleeding, then to his jaw. He glared at Ran, murder in his eyes.

'Damn you for interfering!'

He staggered forward, fists raised. Randolph sidestepped neatly and caught him by the back of his coat.

'I won't brawl with you in front of a lady,' he said, pitching Teddington unceremoniously out of the open door.

Only then did Randolph notice that people were emerging from the supper room, but it was too late. Teddington had stumbled into the hall and landed in an undignified heap on the floor. He dragged himself to his feet, his face almost purple with rage.

'You will meet me for this, Westray!'

'I think not.' Ran's lip curled. 'You are drunk.'

'Drunk, am I? At least I can take my wine, Lord Westray! *I* am not afraid of it!'

Ran stiffened. People were crowding round, hushed and expectant.

He said coldly, 'Taunts will not make me accept a challenge from a drunken sot, Teddington. And as for being able to hold your wine—' his lip curled again '—you cannot even keep your feet.' He threw a disdainful look towards his audience. 'I would be obliged if someone would help this poor wine-sodden fool away.'

Then he stepped back into the sitting room and closed the door behind him.

Arabella stumbled to a chair as Randolph propelled Charles Teddington out of the room. She crossed her arms, trying to stop herself from shaking as she listened to their altercation. From the murmur of voices in the background, she knew the scene was being witnessed by any number of Lady Sweigne's guests. The thought made her shiver even more.

The door closed and she looked up. Ran was frowning at her. It was too much. She gave a sob and buried her face in her hands. In two strides he was across the room and kneeling before her.

'It is all right, Arabella. You are safe now.' He spoke gently, making no attempt to touch her.

She swiped a hand across her wet cheek and he held out a handkerchief.

'Here.'

She took it with a word of thanks. 'I b-beg your pardon. I am not hurt, just…just shocked.'

'Of course. Would you like me to fetch someone? Our hostess, perhaps?'

'Thank you, no. I would rather not see anyone.'

She straightened, one hand holding her ripped bodice in place.

'Then let me order your carriage. You should go home.'

He rose and she said quickly, 'Please do not leave me!'

'Only to speak to a servant.' He smiled. 'I shall not go far beyond the door and will ensure no one disturbs you. I give you my word.'

Within minutes he was back and telling her he had ordered her cloak to be brought in.

'Lady Sweigne asked after you,' he told her. 'She is mortified this has happened under her roof and has promised to do what she can to prevent gossip.'

'If only that were possible!'

'I know, there will be some talk, inevitably. However, the blame is being heaped squarely upon your assailant, where it belongs.'

She shuddered. 'He—he said I had encouraged him.'

'He is so clearly in his cups no one will pay much heed to anything he says.'

'But it does not alter the fact I was here alone with him.'

There was a soft scratching at the door. Randolph opened it just enough to take the garments proffered by the servant.

'Your cloak,' he said, coming back to her. 'And your carriage is at the door. Let us be gone.'

As she rose and reached for her cloak, she noted the greatcoat over his arm.

'You are leaving, too?'

'I am going to escort you home.'

Arabella did not have the strength to argue. She was still trembling and it was as much as she could do to tie her cloak strings. She allowed him to arrange her hood to cover her dishevelled hair, then accompanied him from the room. The hallway was mercifully empty, save for the servant who opened the door for them to step outside. Randolph handed her into the waiting carriage and jumped in.

'There,' he said, sitting beside her. 'You will soon be safe in Park Street.'

Safe. Arabella's hand crept again to her shoulder. The torn bodice was hidden now by her cloak, but Esther Hatcliffe would be waiting for her, wanting to know at least something of her evening. And the servants, too.

'I cannot,' she blurted out. 'I cannot let anyone at the house see me like this, my hair all awry, my gown torn.' She clasped her hands in her lap. 'I sus- pect—nay, I am *sure* the servants report everything back to the Roffeys.' When he muttered angrily she added, 'They are very anxious for me.'

'That does not give them the right to spy upon you.'

'Perhaps not, but it is their house. I saw no harm in them arranging everything, at the time.' She twisted her hands even tighter together. 'There is my compan- ion, Mrs Hatcliffe. She always waits up for me. She is Sir Adam's kinswoman and will undoubtedly tell him what has occurred tonight. I know, once he learns of it, he will order me to return to Lincolnshire.'

'You are of age and a widow, too. They cannot in- sist upon your obedience.'

She sighed. 'You do not understand. The Roffeys

brought me up as their own, took me into their family. They have been very good to me and I care for them a great deal. I cannot turn my back on them.' She shook her head. 'If Esther sees me like this, it will not be possible to make light of any gossip that might follow.'

'And how long will she wait up for you?'

'All night!' She chewed her lip. 'She says if she does not accompany me of an evening then the least she can do is be there to greet me upon my return.'

Arabella had felt a degree of comfort, knowing her household were looking out for her. Until now.

After a moment Ran spoke again, decisively.

'Then we must make you presentable before you see her. We will go back to my hotel. Mivart's has several entrances and we can be very discreet, I promise you. Joseph has needles and thread and is as good as any seamstress. We will return you to your people safely and in good order, never fear.' He glanced out of the window. 'We are turning into Park Street now. I'll tell the coachman you need some air and we will walk from here.'

It was the work of a moment to stop the coach and Arabella alighted, standing beside Randolph on the flagway while he ordered the carriage to return to the stable. As it rattled away he took her arm.

'Come along. It is only a step to Brook Street from here.'

The cold air was bracing and it kept her hurrying along at his side. Her thoughts were in turmoil. She was still trembling and part of her wanted to scream and cry. Instead she clutched Ran's arm as a drowning man would cling to a floating spar. He would take care of her. She trusted him.

Randolph hurried his companion through the darkened streets to enter Mivart's Hotel by a side door. They reached his suite of rooms without meeting anyone in the dim corridors. Joseph was building up the fire when they walked into the sitting room and he could not suppress an exclamation of surprise when he saw Arabella.

'Mrs Roffey!'

Ran explained briefly, 'She has had a narrow escape from that scoundrel Teddington. Her gown suffered a tear and needs a small repair.'

'Of course. I shall see to it immediately.'

Ran grinned in relief. 'Good man, Joseph. I knew we might rely upon you!'

'If you will come with me, ma'am, I will take you to His Lordship's dressing room and we will find you something to wear while I mend your gown.'

Chapter Ten

When Arabella returned to the sitting room, Ran had drawn two chairs close to the fire. He had removed his coat, and his silk waistcoat hugged his lean body, a direct contrast to the white shirtsleeves that billowed out over his shoulders. She wondered if she should be worried by such informality, especially after what had happened at Sweigne House, but a glance at his stockinged feet was strangely reassuring. Surely one could not be afraid of a gentleman who was not wearing his shoes.

He was stirring a pan hung over the fire and the comforting scent of spices filled the air.

'Mulled wine,' he said, waving his spoon towards the chairs. 'Come and sit down.'

'Thank you. Joseph has taken my gown away to his room to mend it.' As she came closer, she saw his brows rise. 'Yes, I am wearing your banyan,' she told him, pulling the heavy folds of the colourful dressing gown more securely around her knees. 'Please do not laugh.'

'I am not tempted to laugh,' he replied, a pronounced glint in his eye. 'I do not think I should tell you what I *am* tempted to do!'

She blushed, but pretended not to hear him. She put her hand up to her curls, which had been returned to some sort of order.

'He also found me a brush and comb to tidy my hair.'

Ran grinned. 'Very resourceful fellow, Joseph.'

'He has been with you a long time, I think.'

'Since I was a boy.' He filled a cup with hot wine and handed it to her. 'Joseph knows all there is to know about me. It is thanks to him I survived transportation.'

She sipped her wine and watched his face as he filled his own cup from the pan. The flames gave his sun-bleached hair a golden glow, but the light also showed the creases about his eyes and the deeper lines beside his mouth. It belied the boyish smile he so often wore.

'That must have been terrible for you.'

He glanced at her.

'Do not be thinking I was wrongly convicted, Arabella. I assisted a counterfeiter and that is a treasonable offence. Men and women have been hanged for merely having a single false coin or note in their possession. At one time there were sacks full of forged notes at my house in Liverpool. The villain I called friend followed me to Fallbridge, when I moved there to live with my sister, Deborah. It was only by the greatest good luck that my actions did not destroy her.'

He stopped and she saw the shadows flicker over

his face, clouding his eyes. It hinted at suffering beyond her comprehension.

'But you did not destroy her,' she said softly. 'I read that she is now Viscountess Gilmorton.'

'Yes, and very happy, thank heaven. But I caused her such distress that I wonder she could ever forgive me. She says I was so besotted with laudanum and wine that I could not help myself, but that is no excuse.'

Arabella cradled the cup in her hands, but even its warmth could not prevent her from shuddering.

'I cannot imagine what it must be like, to be sent away from England, from everything you love. And the journey. All those months at sea.'

'I was too ill to know much about that. Joseph nursed me through it. He kept telling me how fortunate I was to be given another chance of life and eventually I believed him. With his care I avoided the deadly diseases of typhus and cholera that beset many of the convicts on board ship. And once we arrived in Sydney Cove I adapted very well to my new surroundings.'

She sat back in her chair, distracted from her own problems.

'I remember you told me something of it, when we were at Beaumount. How the heavy showers clear quickly and the sun makes the rocks steam.'

'Yes, it is warmer than England, but not at all arid. The winds come in from the sea, too, most of the time, which helps to cool the air. I was fortunate, because I could read and write and keep accounts, I was not put to manual labour like most of the poor wretches. They suffered much more than I from the heat.'

He reached out and took her cup from her to refill it, and a memory stirred.

'What Charles Teddington said tonight. About you being afraid of wine. Is that true?'

'I was wont to drink to excess and I know the harm it can do. I never drink anything other than small beer now.' Her eyes went towards his own cup and he added, 'And the odd cup of mulled wine. I shall not get foxed on this, I promise you.'

She found herself smiling in response. The warmth from the drink and the fire had driven away her chills and fears. She felt safe, comfortable. It could not last, she knew that, so she must enjoy this moment. However, she could not prevent her mind going back over what she had learned that evening. Silently she stared into the fire, lost in her own sombre thoughts until Ran said gently, 'You look troubled, Arabella. Will you tell me?'

'I owe you an apology. You were right. George *was* taking laudanum, only I would not admit it. But tonight, that man—' she could not bring herself to say his name '—he told me much the same as you had done. He—he also said that G-George did not love me.'

'Bella, if your husband was in the grip of laudanum then even the very deepest affection would not help him. I am sure he loved you very much.'

'No, he did not. He could not have loved me.' Unhappiness was lodged in her throat and she had to force the words out. 'He—he said George only m-married me for my money.'

'Teddington is all bluster. He was trying to turn the situation to his advantage.'

Arabella shook her head.

'I think it must be true,' she said sadly. 'You see, there are so many occasions, things George said and did. Things he did *not* do. It all makes sense, now I look back. I do not think he ever truly loved me. Not as a man should love his wife.'

Her voice broke, and although she blinked rapidly, a rogue tear escaped and ran down her cheek.

'Ah, Bella, don't cry!' Ran slipped to his knees in front of her. He took the cup from her shaking fingers and wrapped her hands in a warm, comforting clasp.

She choked back a sob. 'He was all I ever wanted. All I ever dreamed of. But when Teddington said that tonight, I realised it was true. George and I talked of marriage, but for all his honeyed words, he held off. There was always some reason why we could not be wed. And the last few years he spent less and less time at Revesby. T-Teddington said he would never have married me if he had not needed my money and I think he must be right.'

He said fiercely, 'If that is so, then Roffey was a blind fool. He did not deserve you!'

'Oh, pray don't say that.' She pulled her hands free and jumped up. 'He deserved someone far better. I see that now. I was gauche, inexperienced. Until this year I had never left Lincolnshire while he had travelled, made the Grand Tour, lived in the world.' She turned away, not wishing him to see her anguish. 'I quite understand now that he did not want me, that he did not desire me. I m-must have appeared very naive and gawkish compared to the beauties he met in town.'

She felt his hands on her shoulders.

'There is nothing gawkish about you, Bella. You could have all London at your feet if you wished!'

She dashed away her tears and gave a shaky laugh. 'Now you are being foolish, my lord.'

'No, I am not.' Gently but firmly he turned her to face him. 'You have wit, intelligence and beauty.' He smiled down at her. 'A rare combination.'

'But not enough.'

'Hush now.' He put a finger against her lips. 'It is more than enough, I promise you. For the right man.'

Arabella leaned against him, grateful for his kindness. It did a great deal to soothe her distress. But when she looked up, what she saw in his eyes made her heart swell and stopped her breath. Desire.

There had been something similar in Charles Teddington's face, but then it had alarmed and repulsed her. Randolph's sea-blue gaze had quite the opposite effect. It awoke a deep, primal ache inside her. She wanted comfort and tenderness and something more. Something she knew he could give her.

'Kiss me,' she whispered. He hesitated and she placed her hands on his chest. 'Kiss me now, Ran. Please!'

Slowly, slowly, he lowered his head. She turned her face up, eyes half-closed. His lips skimmed her mouth, light as a breeze. She shivered with pleasure. He gathered her in his arms and brought his head down again, capturing her mouth in a long, sensuous kiss that sent chills running down her spine. She pressed against him, her lips parting instinctively to allow his tongue to explore, drawing a response from somewhere deep inside.

Her spirit took flight; she almost swooned as their tongues danced together. It was all new. She had never felt like this before, so beautiful, so *desired*. Her bones were melting beneath the onslaught of their combined need, and when at last he broke off the kiss and raised his head, she remained in his arms, breathless, her head thrown back against his shoulder.

'Ah, Bella, forgive me.'

The words were barely a whisper, his breathing ragged and uneven, but she was too shaken to speak. She put a hand up to his cheek and pulled his head back down, desperate for him to kiss her again. This time there was no gentle prelude. His kiss was urgent, even savage, and when it ended, she gasped for breath while his mouth roamed over her face and neck.

'We should stop now,' he muttered, his lips grazing her face and neck, sending little darts of fire through her skin with every touch.

'No.' She clung to him. Even her voice was shaking with the unexpected passion that was raging through her. 'Take me to your bed, Ran.'

He raised his head then and stared at her. His breathing was ragged and instinct told her he was barely in control of himself. She pushed against him, revelling in the feel of his hard, aroused body. He wanted her, she did not doubt it, but she knew that, even now, she had the power to stop him with a word. Only she did not want to stop. She clutched at his shoulders.

'I am in earnest, Ran. I want you to take me to bed. Now.'

His eyes burned into her, hot blue flames. Resolutely she held his gaze, answering his unspoken question. She was sure she wanted this. More sure than she had ever been of anything in her life.

Finally, without a word, he scooped her into his arms and carried her into the bedroom. No candles burned, the golden glow of the fire providing the only light. He laid her gently on the bed and she watched as he recrossed the room. She heard the soft click of a lock, then a second click as he secured the door to his dressing room.

'Just making sure we are not disturbed,' he murmured.

Bella kept her eyes fixed on Ran as he came back to her, but when he entered the deeper shadows of the bed, for a moment she could not see his face and she felt a sudden panic.

He hesitated, saying gently, 'We need not do this, Bella.'

'No, I want to.' She reached for him, and when he took her hands, she pulled him closer, all doubts forgotten. 'I want this, Ran. Very much.'

He measured his length beside her, kissing, caressing, until her momentary fear had disappeared and once again she forgot everything except the pleasure of his caresses.

His hand slid over her, the touch warm, sensuous, even through the layers of silk and cotton that covered her skin. Then he was pushing the dressing gown from her shoulders and his hand smoothed across her skin to cup one breast, his thumb stroking and teasing until she was gasping with pleasure. He deepened the kiss still further and his roving hand moved on, tugging free the knotted tie at her waist. Then there was only her thin chemise between his hand and her body. She kissed him back eagerly, their tongues dancing while his fingers roamed over her hip, then slowly, slowly moving lower, towards the hot aching core of her desire.

She shifted restlessly against him, wanting more. His palm cupped her and his stroking fingers roused in her an exquisite pleasure she had never known before. Her body was moving now with its own rhythm. Excitement rippled through her, building like a wave. She gasped, tried to speak, but her senses were so disordered all she could do was clutch at the bedcovers, moaning softly while he continued his gentle but inexorable pleasuring.

Her senses were swimming; she was adrift, being carried along on a wave of pure pleasure. It was beyond anything she had known. She thought she might fly away, or drown from sheer delight. She cried out, bucking beneath his hand as the wave crested. Her body was gripped in a shuddering climax and Randolph held her close against him until the ripples faded and she was left exhausted, barely conscious.

Arabella clung to Ran, breathing deeply, drifting away on the smell of his skin, a hint of musk overlaying the clean, spicy fragrance of soap and fresh linen. All too soon he eased himself away from her. She opened her eyes to see him standing beside the bed, a black shadow. He shed his waistcoat, then threw off his shirt. As he discarded it, she saw the flash of firelight on his chest, a rippling landscape of sculpted muscle. Desire stirred again, unfurling within her. She had tasted the delights of his lovemaking and she wanted more. She wanted to feel that naked flesh against her own.

While Ran slipped off his breeches and stockings, she shrugged her arms from the banyan and quickly dragged off her chemise. When she would have removed her stockings, he stopped her.

'No.' He placed a hand on her knee. 'Let me.'

His voice was low, rich, and she shivered with anticipation. She lay back on the bed, watching from half-closed eyes as he slowly untied the ribbon garters. He rolled down the stockings, one at a time, stopping to plant a kiss on every inch of newly exposed flesh. Arabella's mouth dried. Every touch reverberated through her until her whole body was singing. He kissed her toes, the inside of her ankle. Then his mouth began a slow exploration up to the knee. And onwards.

She closed her eyes and reached for him, wanting him to stop. Wanting him to go on. She tangled her fingers in his hair as he knelt between her legs and began to kiss her. Where earlier his fingers had worked to such devastating effect, now his tongue roused her to new heights. The wave was building again. She was losing control. He slid his naked chest up over her until they were breast to breast. Her hips lifted instinctively, offering herself up to him. He eased himself into her and she gave a cry, but the little pain was forgotten as he began to move, slowly at first, but gradually increasing the pace.

She matched each thrust, her fingers clutching at his shoulders. She could not think, could not speak as wave after wave of bone-melting pleasure rolled through her. Her spirits were soaring, flying. Ran-

dolph gave a shout of triumph and held her fast, tee-
tering on a pinnacle for one brief, heart-stopping
instant. She clung to him, felt his body hard and rigid
in her arms, every muscle straining. Then it was over.
He relaxed with a sigh and dropped beside her, drawing her close, wrapping himself around her, warm
and protective.

Stunned, Arabella lay in the darkness, listening to
Ran's now-steady breathing. She had never felt like
this before. So complete. She heard a clock chime
in the next room and wonder became tinged with
anxiety.

'It grows late,' she murmured, sitting up. 'I should
go.'

'Not yet.' He pulled her down beside him again.
'Sleep with me for a while.'

She did not have the willpower to refuse. He
helped her beneath the covers, and the banyan, which
had been lying beneath them, slid to the floor with
a whisper.

Arabella opened her eyes. By the light of the single bedside candle, she looked about the unfamiliar room and memory flooded back. Randolph was
sitting, naked, on the edge of the bed. Smiling, she
reached out to touch his broad shoulders and run her
fingers down his shadowed back. He straightened,
but did not look around at her.

'Why did you not tell me you were a virgin?'

Chapter Eleven

The bedside candle flickered as Arabella raised herself on one elbow. Ran turned towards her, holding up the dressing gown.

'There is blood on here, from our first coupling.'

'Oh.' She sat up, clutching the sheet to her. His face was in shadow, but she knew he was watching her.

'Did it not cross your mind to tell me you were a maid?'

Yes, it had crossed her mind, but by then her body was crying out for him, so much that she had shut it out. As she had shut out all the horrors of the evening. For a short time she had allowed herself to forget everything, even her grief at the loss of her beloved husband. Now she was filled with remorse.

'It was foolish, irresponsible.' She hung her head. 'I am very sorry, Ran.'

'So, too, am I.'

His voice was hard, cold, and her misery increased. She felt herself shrinking inside. The glorious euphoria of their union was gone.

'You are angry with me,' she whispered. 'I did

not mean to deceive you, truly. I did not *think*. I only knew that I w-wanted you to take me to bed.'

He exhaled softly. 'I am not angry, Bella. Not with you.'

He slipped off the bed and went over to the hearth, where he stirred up the fire with the poker and added more coals to the hot embers.

'Stay under the covers while I dress,' he ordered. 'I will fetch your gown. Heaven knows, Joseph has had long enough to finish it by now.'

Feeling quite wretched, she huddled in the bed while he threw on his clothes. If he was not angry with her, then he must be disappointed. Suddenly his good opinion mattered to her. Very much.

She heard him walk out of the room, returning a few minutes later with her gown over his arm.

'Here.' He laid it carefully across the chair by the fire. 'Joseph has mended it well enough to pass all but the closest inspection. When you are dressed, I will escort you home.' He turned his head to look at her and his tone softened. 'It is not so very late. Certainly not late enough to cause comment.'

'Thank you.'

He walked across to the bed and sat down, reaching for her hand.

'Do not despair, Arabella. We have made a mull of this, but we will resolve it, I promise you.'

His grasp was warm, comforting, but she shook her head at him. 'It is not for you to resolve *anything*.'

'Oh, I think it is.'

'No,' she whispered, her cheeks burning. 'I *wanted* you to take me to bed.'

She must tell him the truth, shameful as it was.

Arabella kept her eyes fixed resolutely on their clasped hands, drawing strength from the connection.

'My husband n-never did so. We n-never shared a bed. He always had some excuse why he would not c-consummate the marriage. That is why I *know* that man was telling the truth tonight, when he said George did not love me.'

'There may be other reasons why Roffey acted as he did,' Ran suggested, but Arabella shook her head.

'His parents were eager for our marriage. There was no reason why we could not have been wed much earlier, if George had wanted it. If he had wanted *me*. You said yourself, if he had loved me, he would not have gone to Meon House alone. No, I must face the truth. George married me for my money, then left me at Revesby Hall while he continued his life very much as he had done as a single man.'

Ran's silence only added to the pain. She bowed her head, a little tremor of sadness running through her. His grip on her hand tightened.

'Oh, Bella, I am so sorry.'

His voice was full of compassion, full of sympathy, and for a moment she wished he would take her in his arms again. He would do it, out of kindness, but that would only make the inevitable parting even harder. She gently pulled her hand away. It was time to be strong, to show that she had learned something from her time away from Lincolnshire. She did not want any man to pity her. Especially Randolph.

She said, 'George did not love me enough to—to show me the pleasures of the marriage bed, but you have done that now, Ran.' She wanted to smile at him, but could not bring herself to meet his eyes. Thankfully, her voice was under control and she continued without a tremor. 'I shall always be grateful to you for that, but be assured I shall not ask any more of you. I understand that tonight was…a singular occurrence.'

There, she had said it. She had been calm, composed. A woman of the world.

'I am glad I could be of service, madam.' There was something about his tone that made her think she had angered him, but before she could find the courage to look into his face he said lightly, 'We should not tarry any longer. We must get you back to Park Street.'

I was wrong, she thought. *He is not angry. He is relieved that I am being so reasonable.*

The idea made her feel even more miserable.

He rose to his feet. 'Now, in the absence of your maid, I had best help you to dress!'

He was teasing her, trying to ease her embarrassment. The time for intimacy was over and once again he was Randolph, her friend. That was some small comfort. She replied in the same light manner.

'It is fortunate for me that you are so familiar with the intricacies of female dress, my lord.'

'Not that familiar,' he muttered, picking up her corset and turning it this way and that. 'Which way up does this dashed thing go?'

Arabella laughed and the last shreds of awkwardness between them disappeared.

'Here,' she said, slipping out of bed. 'Let me show you!'

Once Ran had fastened her stays, he left Arabella to finish dressing and returned to the sitting room.

She did not tarry, and when she joined him, he cast a critical eye over her. She was pale, but composed. The hectic flush had died from her cheeks. There was no outward sign that she had enjoyed a most satisfying bout of lovemaking and he felt a stab of disappointment. What a conceited dog he was to expect that!

He said, 'Hmm, you will do. I think you might well convince your companion you had been attending a sad crush where you were jostled by the crowd.'

'That is what I shall tell her.' Her hand went up to her shoulder. 'Joseph's repair of my gown is unnoticeable, unless one looks closely, and the only person to do that will be Ruth, my maid.'

'And she is in your confidence,' said Ran, putting her cloak about her shoulders. 'I am glad you have at least one person in your household you can trust.'

'Sir Adam is paying the servants well to look after me,' she replied with a sigh. 'I know I should be grateful for their care, but I feel…stifled by it. Despite what—what happened at Lady Sweigne's tonight, I do not need anyone to look after me!'

'That's as may be, but I am still going to escort you back,' declared Ran, shrugging himself into his greatcoat.

'But there is no need, truly,' she assured him. 'Joseph could escort me.'

'Joseph has gone to bed and I will not let you ride alone at this time of night,' came the decisive response. 'Come along now. I sent a runner to fetch a cab and it should be waiting for us at the door.'

They slipped quietly through the dark, empty passages of the hotel and emerged into the icy night. The wind had dropped, and above the black line of the housetops, the moon was shining brightly from the clear sky. Arabella would dearly have liked to walk all the way to Park Street, to spend as long as possible with Ran, because it would be the last time they would meet. But she knew how it would look if she arrived at the door with the Earl as her escort.

Randolph hurried her towards the cab standing a few yards along the street and handed her in. A word to the driver and he jumped in beside her.

'What will you do now?' he asked as they rumbled through the moon-washed streets.

'I do not think there is anything to gain from looking further for George's murderer. He was living wildly and paid the ultimate price for it. Much as I do not wish to believe anything I heard tonight about my husband, I am forced to conclude it must be so. There is nothing for me now but to return to Lincolnshire.'

'I see. When will you go?'

'In a few weeks. Lady Roffey wrote to tell me she has ordered a new lilac gown and wishes me to collect it, and buy her gloves and so on to match. The least I can do, after all her kindness to me, is to carry out the commission and take it all back with me.'

'But what will you *do* there?' he pressed her. 'How will you live?'

'I shall finish my mourning for George, which is what I should have done from the beginning, only I was so sure there was a case to be answered.'

'And if there are…consequences from what we did tonight?'

She did not pretend to misunderstand him.

'You may be sure I shall inform you, my lord.'

He reached out and caught her hand.

'Promise me you will do so, Arabella. If I am no longer in town, a note to Chislett and Partners in Burlington Street will find me. If there is a child then it shall be my heir. We must wed, for the child's sake.'

For the child's sake.

'Of course.'

She withdrew her hand and turned to look out of the window. An iron band had tightened itself around her heart. Ran did not love her, any more than George had done, but he would marry her. For the sake of the child. What a cruel trick that would be, she thought bitterly, for fate to rescue him from exile, raise him to a peerage, then consign him to life tied to a woman he did not love.

The hired carriage drew up at the house in Park Street, the golden glow from the fanlight above the door indicating that lamps were still burning. Her return would not go unnoticed. Arabella gathered her cloak about her and prepared to alight.

'I hope we do not need to meet again, my lord, but I thank you—sincerely—for all you have done for me. Goodbye. God bless you.'

Ran would have liked to hand her out of the carriage, to kiss her fingers one last time, but all he could do was to watch from the shadowed interior as she was admitted into the house. He waited until the door closed again behind her before ordering the driver to take him back to Brook Street.

I hope we do not meet again.

Could she have made it any clearer? Of course

she did not care for him. Tonight had been no more than a distraction for her. A brief moment of comfort, something to assuage her loneliness and grief at the loss of a most beloved husband. She was wearing the willow for Roffey, even though the fellow had treated her abominably.

From all she had said, Ran suspected Sir Adam had always had an eye to her fortune. It was not uncommon for neighbouring families to use marriage to unite their lands. Arabella had been put into their care when she became an orphan and the Roffeys had kept her in that damned isolated place. She had not been given a Season, either in Lincoln or London, so was it any wonder she had fallen in love with the only young man within her orbit?

He hunched himself further into the corner. She had said goodbye to him, but he would remain in town until she had left for Lincolnshire, just to ensure Teddington made no further attempts to seduce her. Then he would return to Westray Priors and forget all about Arabella Roffey.

Unless, of course, their lovemaking resulted in a child. Then he would do the honourable thing and marry her.

Ran had to admit the idea was not repugnant. Not repugnant at all.

For the next two weeks, Randolph busied himself with his own affairs. When he met with his man of business, it was inevitable that Chislett would ask him about Charles Teddington, and Ran gave him a brief outline of their meeting at Sweigne House.

'The more I learn about the fellow, the less he deserves to be called a gentleman,' remarked Mr Chislett, looking very grave. 'My, ah, sources tell me he is very low on funds. Very low indeed. Deep play,' he said darkly. 'Apparently he is running on tick, as they say.'

'Thank heaven I have put a spoke in his wheel where Mrs Roffey is concerned,' said Ran. 'She is no longer blind to his faults and, after our little contretemps, his reputation in town has taken a further knock. I hope it may save other young women from succumbing to his charms.'

'I wish it might be so, my lord, but such fellows have a way of bouncing back. How is Mrs Roffey?'

Ran pushed back his chair and got up. 'She returns to Lincolnshire soon, I believe. I do not expect us to meet again.'

Not after the note he had received that morning, a short missive written in a sloping hand as feminine and elegant as the lady herself.

You will be as relieved as I am, my lord, to know there are no consequences following Lady Sweigne's rout.

He had not known what he hoped for when he had opened the note, but its contents had winded him. The tiny seed of hope he had been germinating inside was killed off.

Completely.

Charles Teddington was smarting. His public humiliation at Sweigne House had led to him receiving the cut direct from several high sticklers in town

and he had noticed that parents of eligible young ladies kept their offspring well out of his way. That
would not have worried him unduly—the *ton* was no-
toriously fickle and, once the gossip died down, his
charming manners and elegant address would ensure
he was soon welcomed back into society.

However, he had recently been told, politely, and
with deep regret, that he was no longer welcome at
more than one well-established gentlemen's club. He
was not turned away from the hells, of course, where
no one questioned his appearance, as long as he paid
his dues, but his livelihood depended upon making
friends with young gentlemen of means, and that required a certain aura of respectability.

Damn Westray for showing him up like that and
then refusing to meet him. And damn Arabella Roffey for being the cause of it all! He would not deny
he lusted after her, which had made the prospect of
marriage all the more alluring. And with her money
he could have lived very comfortably. But now doors
were closing against him, and if his fortunes did not
turn around soon, he would be obliged to leave town
and try his luck in one of the smaller cities, as he had
done before. The only bright spot on his horizon was
a letter from his sister. She was making a rare visit to
London and had asked him to secure rooms for her
at Grillon's Hotel.

Mr Teddington was zealous in his arrangements
for Lady Meon's comfort and was on hand to greet her
when she eventually arrived at the hotel in Albemarle
Street. He was anxious not to miss her and kicked his
heels in the elegant public sitting room overlooking

the street for the whole morning. A few coins pressed
into the hands of one of the lackeys paid dividends.
When the lady finally walked into the hotel shortly
after noon, he was just emerging from the sitting
room and gave a start of surprise.

'Ursula, what a pleasure. I had just come to assure myself that everything is in readiness for you.'

She gave him her hand and a smile.

'How thoughtful, Charles. Pray, come upstairs
with me. We will enjoy a glass of something while
my bags are unpacked.'

She took his arm and allowed him to escort her to
her rooms. He enquired after her health, her journey,
and discussed the state of the roads until they were
seated on each side of a cheerful fire in her drawing room with a glass of sherry. Outside the door the
servants bustled about, but they were undisturbed.

'What brings you to town, my dear, if I might en-
quire? Your letter did not tell me.'

Lady Meon waved one languid hand. 'I was in desperate need of amusement, Charles. Devon is so quiet
at this time of year. The isolation is ideal for our little
parties, but I have felt an unusual degree of ennui this
winter. I toyed with the idea of Bath, or Tonbridge, for
the waters, but decided a little town shopping would
revive me better. I shall buy new gowns for our first
party in May, I think.'

'An excellent idea. The modistes will be delighted
to have your custom so early in the Season, I am sure.
I am very happy to escort you, if you wish.'

'That is what I like about you, Charles. You are
so very obliging.' She held out her glass for him to

fill up again. 'If you are not too busy, I should be delighted to have your company.'

'Not busy at all, actually.' He was unable to keep the bitter note from his laugh. 'I have had, shall we say, a little setback.' He could not help noticing that his sister's manner cooled somewhat and he hurried to continue, 'Oh, 'tis nothing I cannot manage and London is very empty of company, so the damage is not irreparable, but still. It is annoying.'

'Tell me.'

'George Roffey's widow.'

'What of her?' Lady Meon's eyes were wary.

'She approached me in town, wanted me to tell her anything I knew of his death.'

'And what did you say?'

'I fobbed her off, of course, but I was hoping I might secure her for myself. She is quite a beauty.' He savoured his wine, his eyes narrowing in pleasure as he thought of the golden widow. 'Not only that, but the fortune she brought to the marriage reverted to her, and her alone, upon Roffey's death. Even after his lavish spending in Devonshire there must still be twenty thousand pounds invested in the funds and no damned trusts to worry about.'

'You tried to woo her.' She sat back, regarding him with a slight, cynical smile. 'She turned you down, is that it, Charles?'

'No. I swear she was responding, only she was determined to know more about her husband's death, so I was obliged to tell her something of it. Oh, nothing very much, merely about his liking for laudanum.'

'And what happened?'

'She insisted on having more information. I ended

by telling her he had killed himself with his excesses.' His mouth twisted. 'I should have left it there, given her time to come to terms with the thought, but I rushed my fences.'

'Good heavens, Charles, that is not like you.'

'I know, but I could not help myself. She is such a beauty, Ursula. Golden hair, eyes a man could drown in. And a delectable body, too! I had managed to get her alone and determined I would have her before the night was out.' He scowled. 'I would have succeeded, too, if we had not been interrupted.'

'Unfortunate.'

'Aye. What was even more unfortunate was that it turned into a damned brawl, in front of a dozen or more guests.'

'Then word will have spread around the town almost before the night was done,' she remarked. 'Foolish, Charles.'

'I know it.' He added, trying to sound more confident than he felt, 'But my standing will recover.'

'I hope it does,' she said coldly. 'You are no use to me if you cannot supply me with the right sort of guests for my parties.'

'No need to worry, Ursula. We have more than enough time for that. Town will be filling up soon and this little slip will be forgotten. What irks me most is that the Earl refused my challenge. 'Fore Gad, madam, you'd think even a convicted felon would know that's not the way to behave in polite society.'

Lady Meon sat up in her chair. 'Do you mean the new Lord Westray?'

'Aye, the very same. Why, do you know him?'

She sat back again, smiling. 'Oh, yes. He visited

the neighbourhood at the end of the year and called upon me once or twice. I am not unhopeful that he will call again, the next time that he is in Devon.' Her eyes narrowed and a little smile played around her mouth. 'I found him quite…charming. If he is in town, I shall look forward to renewing our acquaintance.'

'Well, I don't want to meet him again. Damned impudent fellow. And he spoiled my chances with the widow.'

Lady Meon only laughed softly. 'Oh, do stop scowling, Charles. You have handled the whole thing very badly, but if that particular bird has flown then put it behind you. Come, I want no sour faces around me. Take another glass of sherry while I go and change. Then you can escort me to Bond Street.'

'What, now? Are you not fatigued from your journey, ma'am?'

'Not a bit of it. I travelled in easy stages and I am not at all tired. Nothing that a little shopping will not dispel!'

Arabella knew she was not carrying Randolph's child. The signs were irrefutable and they caused her a surprising amount of disappointment. She was tempted to visit him to tell him the news, but held back. It was hard enough to see him in public, when they would exchange the briefest of greetings. To meet with him and talk to him about something so intimate and yet keep her distance would be sheer torture.

It was not as if anything could come of their friendship. And she did not wish anything to come of it, she told herself. George might not have loved her, but she had loved *him*, and whatever it was she felt for Randolph could be nothing more than infatuation. And lust, she thought sadly. She could not deny that she had enjoyed his lovemaking. Or that she wanted more.

After that one memorable night with the Earl, she would have liked to pack up and leave London immediately, but having written to her mother-in-law and told her she would come home with her gown and accessories, she knew it would cause no little speculation if she abandoned her plans and arrived early. Besides, there were engagements that could not be ignored without alienating her new acquaintances. She had received a great deal of kindness in town and she had made several friendships that she hoped she could maintain now with correspondence, but for all that, when she finally heard that Lady Roffey's lilac gown was ready, she thought she would always remember the past two weeks as the longest of her life.

Arabella received word from the modiste in the morning and decided she would go and collect it at once. She could then spend the rest of the day trailing up and down Bond Street to find gloves, shoes and other little trinkets to match. It had turned into a bright day and she would enjoy being out of doors in the sunshine.

With a footman accompanying her and carrying the gown in its distinctive box, she made her way from one end of Bond Street to the other, looking in every shop for suitable accessories. A pair of lilac-kid gloves were soon purchased, but a suitable reticule proved much more elusive, in Arabella's opinion the ones on offer being either too small or too gaudy for her mother-in-law. She would have to cross the road and make her way along the other side.

The cold March day was drawing to a close and the temperature was dropping when Lady Meon made the last of her purchases and told Charles they could now return to the carriage. He gave her his arm, but any hope he had that they might make haste was soon dashed, for my lady wished to prolong her outing and stopped to look into every shop window they passed, even though they had already visited most of them. With the daylight fading, the lamps and candles burning inside made it easier to see what was going on and my lady delighted in observing the bustling scenes through each window.

They were halfway along Bond Street, when Lady Meon stopped to look into the haberdasher's window. Her escort glanced in and gave a grunt.

'That lady by the counter, it is Arabella Roffey. Now you can see for yourself what a piece of perfection she is.'

His sister turned quickly to look up at him, then peered more closely into the lighted interior of the shop.

'Do you mean the one choosing ribbons, with her footman hovering at her side? *That* is Arabella Roffey? Are you sure?'

'Of course I am sure!' He hunched a shoulder and turned away. 'Not that it matters to me any longer. Can we move? Dawdling in this dashed cold wind is chilling me to the bone!'

'But I know her,' said Lady Meon, as they walked on. 'I met her in Devon.'

He laughed. 'Impossible. George made very sure she stayed in Lincolnshire, with his parents.'

'Her husband may well have done so, but she has been to Devon since his death, believe me. She even came to Meon House. Masquerading as Lady Westray.'

He stopped and looked down at his sister in amazement. She smiled.

'Close your mouth, Charles, and let us continue to my carriage. Then I will tell you everything.'

'Westray's mistress, eh?' he said, when she had finished. 'That explains a great deal. No wonder the Earl reacted like a dog in danger of losing a bone when I tried to kiss her.' He grinned. 'So, she is not the virtuous little widow she would have us believe! But she gave me no sign that she had ever heard of you, or Meon House, when she approached me a few weeks ago.'

'But how could she do so, without giving herself away?'

His eyes narrowed. 'The scheming minx. She inveigled her way into the Earl's bed and persuaded him to take her to Devon. You are convinced it was not pure chance that brought them there?'

'Of course not. With the death of the old Earl, the Westray inheritance was discussed in great detail in the newspapers. She would have known about Beaumount and persuaded him that it was remote enough for them to live there as man and wife with impunity.'

She laughed. 'And all the time she was trying to discover what had happened to her husband.'

'Westray could not have known about that,' he told her. 'His reaction when I tried to kiss her was mightily possessive. He is not the sort to share his woman with anyone, even a dead man.' He laughed. 'Perhaps I should have held out. She might have traded her favours for information about Roffey's death.'

'When she had caught herself an earl? Do be sensible, Charles.'

He said emphatically, 'She ain't *caught* him at all. He will never marry her. But it could be good news for me, though.'

'I am pleased for you, Charles, truly. I thought you would be disappointed to find your goddess so mightily flawed.'

'On the contrary. I see now how I may use it to my advantage!'

Chapter Twelve

Having entered London society, Randolph could not withdraw completely without comment, but he did cut down his social engagements to a bare minimum. He saw Arabella occasionally but she was always accompanied by Mrs Hatcliffe. At most, on such occasions, they would acknowledge one another with no more than a common bow in passing. As if they were almost strangers.

However, when they met at Mrs Darby's soirée, shortly after he had received her note, conversation could not be avoided. There was a crush of guests proceeding down the stairs to supper. Ran was talking with Sir Arran Eversleigh and did not notice Arabella until he found himself beside her. Something must be said.

He gave her a nod and a smile. 'Our hostess will be delighted with the attendance this evening.'

'Yes.'

She looked uncomfortable, but there was no help for it. They were hemmed in by the crowd and progress was slow as they filed into the supper room.

'Your companion is not with you tonight?'

'Yes, she is following.'

Ran glanced back and nodded in a friendly fashion towards Mrs Hatcliffe, just visible behind several more guests waiting behind them.

'I thought you would have returned to Oxfordshire by now,' remarked Arabella.

'Not for a few weeks yet.' He lowered his voice. 'I want to see you safely away from town first.'

'I pray you will not prolong your stay here on my account. I am perfectly safe now. I do not need a protector.'

'I am glad to hear it.' They had reached the supper room and were no longer confined by the crowd. Randolph wanted to lead her to one of the little tables and sit down together, but it was impossible. However much he wanted to choose the daintiest morsels and feed them to her, to laugh with her about the amusing things they had seen or heard this evening, he could not. Instead he gave her a polite smile, a friendly nod before he turned one way and she went the other.

When Arabella learned that Lord Westray had departed, the life went out of the gathering. The ladies exhibiting their talents at the pianoforte lacked charm, the singing of one of them was most definitely flat and even the pianoforte sounded sadly out of tune. She managed to endure another half-hour before she, too, took her leave of Mrs Darby and went home.

She wished she might return to Lincolnshire and never see London or Lord Westray again. His presence confused her. She could not regret asking him to take her to bed, it had done much to dispel the heartache and loneliness she had been feeling, but it also swamped her with guilt, because for a short time she had forgotten her grief. Forgotten everything save the pleasure of a man's caresses. An illicit pleasure she had no right to enjoy.

It did no good to argue that George had never loved her, had never shared her bed. She had loved him. Worshipped him. Married him. How was it she could forget him so quickly? She concluded sadly that her heart must be very shallow.

The sooner she returned to Revesby Hall the better, but it could not be immediately. True, she had collected her mother-in-law's new gown that day, but a pair of kid slippers had not yet been dyed to match it, she still had to buy a reticule and the jeweller commissioned to make a jet mourning brooch for Lady Roffey was so busy he could not complete the order for a full week yet. She thought of the line of invitations sitting on her mantelshelf in Park Street. Perhaps she would pretend she was ill and cry off from them all.

But Arabella knew she would not do that. Despite the gnawing guilt, the possibility of seeing Randolph again, even if they did not speak, was too great a temptation. It hurt her almost unbearably to see him and know that they could never be more to each other than distant acquaintances. But that, she told herself, was her punishment.

Thus it was that the next night, attired once more in the black velvet with its silver embroidery, Arabella set off for the house of Sir Kenelm and Lady Prees with Esther Hatcliffe as her companion. Their hostess had described the evening to her as a little musical gathering for a few friends, but when they arrived, the rooms were bursting with guests. It was hot and noisy, and when she learned from Sir Kenelm that the Earl of Westray had cried off, Arabella was tempted to go home.

She would claim to have a headache. Esther would not argue at her sudden change of heart, because earlier that evening she had told Arabella how pale she was. Arabella was about to make her excuses to her host and hostess when Sir Kenelm looked past her.

He exclaimed in his hearty tones, 'It is Freddie Letchmore, as I live and breathe! I thought he was on the Continent.'

Arabella's head came up immediately. She looked towards the door and observed a pale, thin young man with a sulky mouth sauntering into the room. With a word to Esther that she should sit down and enjoy the music, Arabella slipped past Sir Kenelm and stepped into the gentleman's path.

'Mr Letchmore.'

The rather protuberant eyes stared at her for a moment. Then he bowed.

'Mrs Roffey.' He took her hand briefly in a limp grasp that felt clammy, even through her gloves.

'I believe you have been abroad,' she remarked.

'Yes. For my health, you know. I only arrived back a week ago.' He dropped his voice. 'I am so sorry I could not be there for George's funeral.'

'Yes, it was a pity,' she answered. 'He had so few friends there to mourn him at the end.'

He looked uncomfortable at that. She put a hand on his arm.

'I wonder, sir, if I might have a word with you.

About George. You came to see him, just before he died.' He looked startled and she added quickly, 'It will not take long, Mr Letchmore, but it would mean a great deal to me.'

'Of course, ma'am. Anything to oblige.' He did not sound at all obliging, but Arabella was not deterred, not while there was the faintest hope that she might yet learn something new about her husband's demise. She led him across to a small window embrasure, where they might talk without being jostled by the crowd.

'I believe you were with George in Devonshire,' she began. 'At Meon House. I wonder if anything untoward happened there.'

'Why, nothing out of the ordinary, ma'am, I assure you. It was the usual type of party. Fun and games, you know, but perfectly innocent. A little gambling, plenty of country pursuits. Hunting, shooting, you know.'

She said, 'I remember, when you called at Revesby Hall to see him that last time, he said, *"You have killed me."*' She clasped her fan and fixed her eyes on his pallid face. 'What did he mean by that, Mr Letchmore?'

'Why, why, nothing, ma'am.' His eyes darted about the room before fixing on her again. 'Poor George was raving, the day I saw him. He was not himself. Laudanum,' he added. 'Devilish stuff and he couldn't get enough of it.'

Her heart sank. It was just as Charles Teddington had told her.

'Aye.' He was shaking his head at her. 'We tried to help him, but he would have none of it. He was convinced we were all in some plot against him, which was nonsense, of course.'

'I see. Then, there were no quarrels, nothing I should know?'

He laughed, 'Good lord, no, ma'am. Nothing like that at all. We'd all been the best of friends for years, don't you know. It was just unfortunate that poor George was taken ill like that and dashed off. We wanted him to stay and see Lady Meon's doctor, but he would not. I fear that was his undoing. The long journey from Devon to Lincolnshire would have tested the strongest constitution.' He gave a sigh. 'A sad business, but nothing to be done, I'm afraid. I hope that helps you, Mrs Roffey?'

'Yes, thank you.' She wanted to ask more, but he was already moving away, saying there was someone he must see, and she let him go.

Arabella found an empty chair in a corner and pretended to listen intently to the string quartet hired by Lady Prees to entertain her guests, while her thoughts went over everything Freddie Letchmore had said. Had she really been hoping that there had been dark deeds afoot, that George had been duped, robbed of his money? How sad that she could not accept the fact that he was weak-willed and unhappy. That he had succumbed to a narcotic to escape his troubles.

By the time the music stopped for an interval she had had enough. She would go home. There was nothing new to discover here. She looked for Esther Hatcliffe, but could not see her. Perhaps she had slipped away to the retiring room. That would suit Arabella very well as they might collect their cloaks and leave without further delay. She made her way across the room, a word here, a smile there. As she was approaching the door she stopped to make way for her hostess, who was coming into the salon with Mr Letchmore and a voluptuous brunette.

Lady Meon! Arabella's heart stopped. It was impossible to melt into the crowd, but she looked away, hoping she might avoid attention. That hope that died when Lady Meon saw her and paused, a wide smile on her face.

'Ah, I am not entirely without acquaintances in town, you see, Lady Prees.' She looked directly at Arabella and swept a curtsy. 'Good evening, ma'am. How delightful to meet you again.'

Freddie Letchmore looked startled. 'You *know* Mrs Roffey?'

Arabella froze, waiting for Lady Meon to look confused and declare that she knew her as Lady Westray. She would have to assert that the lady was mistaken, but she knew in her heart that she would not be able to do it. The lie would not pass her lips.

In the event, it was not necessary. Lady Meon did not look at all confused. She merely smiled.

'Oh, yes, we have met,' she said softly. She took Arabella's arm. 'My dear, you look shocked. I know, I told you, did I not, that I rarely come to town? This occasion was merely a whim, but I am so very glad now that I decided to make the journey. Already, I am vastly enjoying myself. Come, ma'am, let us take a turn about the room and you may tell me all that you have been about since we last met.'

Obedient to the pressure on her arm, Arabella moved like an automaton while her mind was almost bursting with worry and conjecture. Lady Meon had not exposed her. Yet. The lady was speaking again and she forced herself to concentrate.

'I am so pleased you are here tonight, Mrs Roffey. It saves me the trouble of seeking you out.'

'Indeed?' Arabella was already planning how quickly she could leave London. She must let Ran know, too. The lady's revelations would affect him very little, compared to the harm it would do to her own reputation, but she could warn him.

Lady Meon guided her to the side of the room and they sat down a little apart from the rest of the guests. Not that anyone was paying them any heed, for the quartet in the far corner of the room had begun to play again and the audience was giving them their attention. Nevertheless, Lady Meon spread her fan and lifted it to cover her mouth.

'How unfortunate for you, Mrs Roffey, that I should discover your outrageous deception. I could ruin you, you know.'

Arabella was mute. What was there to say?

'However,' Lady Meon's honeyed tones continued, 'I might choose not to do so. If you show a little… kindness towards my brother. You are acquainted with him, I believe?'

'I am.' She must be cautious and give nothing away.

'Such a charming man, do you not agree? I should like to see him happily settled. With a good wife and a comfortable fortune. Oh, my dear, was that a shudder?'

'You are suggesting I marry a man I barely know

for…for a business arrangement,' Arabella retorted coldly. 'The very idea is repugnant to me.'

'I do not know why it should be. After all, you have already had one such marriage, have you not? And, unlike poor George, Charles is both willing and able to fulfil his duties in the marital bed.'

Arabella's face flamed. 'How dare you,' she said. 'You know nothing about it!'

'Ah, but I do, you see.' She gave Arabella a look full of spurious sympathy. 'Poor George confessed everything to me, the last time he was in Devon. That he had never been able to bring himself to…' She trailed off delicately. 'It is no wonder that you succumbed to Lord Westray's charms. After all, he is a very attractive man, but what will your parents-in-law think of it? They brought you up as a daughter, I understand. Think how wounded they would be by such an insult to their beloved son's memory.'

Arabella jumped up. 'You have said quite enough. Excuse me.'

Lady Meon caught her arm. 'The Earl will never make you his Countess, my dear, if that is what you hope for. A man does not marry his mistress, you know.' She was smiling, but the menace in her eyes was unmistakable. 'Think about what I have said, Mrs Roffey. I have a great fondness for Charles. Marry him and I shall keep silent about your scandalous liaison. It will save everyone a great deal of unpleasantness.'

Only by exerting all her willpower did Arabella manage to walk away without attracting unwanted attention. She kept her head high as she crossed the room, pausing only to find Mrs Hatcliffe and to make her excuses to her hostess. This she was able to do with perfect sincerity, for she did indeed have a headache now. The pain throbbed at the back of her eyes as she waited in the hall while her companion collected their cloaks.

By the time they were in the carriage and driving back to Park Street Arabella was already making plans. She would return to Revesby Hall in the morning. Esther could close up the house and complete her commissions for her mother-in-law. The thought of confessing everything to the Roffeys sent a wave of nausea flooding through her. She had no doubt that if she fled London Lady Meon would waste no time in revealing her scandalous behaviour.

Even if she could persuade them that she had been Lady Westray in name only, in order to discover more information about George's death, Sir Adam and his wife would be outraged. They might even cast her off and she must be prepared for that. Thankfully she had funds, she could set herself up in a quiet cottage somewhere until the fuss had died down, but it would be hard to bear the loss of the family she had thought of as her own since her parents' sad demise, almost as hard as never seeing Randolph again.

She twisted her hands together. She had discovered all she needed to know here, in town, so it had been both foolish and unnecessary to go to Devon. If she had not done so, she would not now be fleeing from London with her reputation in tatters. She would never have met Lord Westray. She would never have lost her heart to him.

In the darkness of the carriage, she acknowledged

the truth to herself. She had always known that what she felt for Ran was very different from the love she had felt for her husband. Now she knew that her feelings for George had been illusory. Hero worship, based on childish affection and her own imaginings, not on the real, flesh-and-blood person he had been. It was clear to her now that she had never really known George. She had loved a dream, a creature so perfect he could never exist in reality. The more she learned of her husband the more distant he became. She could not love him. She could only pity him.

Whereas she had always known Ran was no saint, but it made no difference. She loved him.

'And he must never know.'

She did not realise she had spoken aloud until Esther stirred in her corner.

'Oh, I'm afraid I was dozing, ma'am. Did you say something?'

'No,' murmured Arabella. Dashing away a tear. 'Nothing at all important.'

Ran glanced at his watch. Eleven o'clock. He was bored with Sir Arran's card party, but he felt restless and did not want to go back yet to his rooms at Mivart's. He recalled the two other invitations he had received for tonight, a musical evening, that Lady Prees had told him would be a small, intimate affair, and Lady Aldenham's supper party. He needed to decide which one was Arabella most likely to attend and he would look in at the other. Not that he wanted to avoid Arabella. On the contrary. He wanted to see her too much for his own peace of mind, but she had made it plain she did not want him watching over her all the time.

He guessed Arabella would prefer a quiet evening listening to music, and thus, once he had collected his coat, he made his way to Aldenham House.

As he had expected, the rooms were crowded, and he sought out those acquaintances who would be entertaining and agreeable company at supper. Afterwards he followed the crowd drifting back to the salon, thinking that he had done his duty and could now leave.

'Lord Westray, good evening to you!'

The voice was as cheerful as it was unwelcome.

'Teddington.' He turned, his face a mask of indifference as the man approached him.

'Still at odds with me, my lord?' Charles Teddington laughed. 'I hoped we might put that little incident behind us. After all, we are both men of the world, what?'

The hairs on the back of Randolph's neck began to prickle. Teddington waved towards a couple of armchairs in the bay window. 'Shall we sit down?'

Ran shrugged and lowered himself into one of the chairs, every nerve-end tingling with suspicion. The fellow was up to something; he would swear to it. Teddington took his time sitting down, crossing one leg over the other and smiling in a way that made Ran want to throttle him.

'I did not realise you were acquainted with my sister,' murmured Teddington. 'Lady Meon has come up from Devon and asked to be remembered to you.' He paused, a sly smile on his lips. 'And to *Lady* Westray.'

Inwardly, Randolph cursed the bad luck of it. Another few weeks and Arabella would have been safely out of London. Teddington sat forward in his chair.

He said, his tone confidential, 'Thing is, my lord, we both know you ain't married, but I was with my sister earlier today when she saw your...er... Countess in Bond Street.' He grinned. 'Damme if it wasn't the golden widow. Ursula was only too eager to tell me of your visits to Meon House. You and your... er...*wife*.'

Someone had begun playing on the pianoforte. A jolly piece that Ran did not recognise. It jarred his nerves.

'What do you want?'

Charles Teddington looked pained. 'Want, my lord? No, no, it ain't what you can do for me. It's the other way around, in fact.' He sat back and studied his nails. 'Perhaps I should give you the hint, your having been out of England for so long. You see, it ain't the thing to pass your mistress off as your wife. The *ton* don't like it. The two of you have been very careful to keep your distance in town, but it's plain as a pikestaff that you are still lovers. Why else would you have come so quickly to her defence at Lady Sweigne's?' He rubbed his jaw, as if remembering the punishing blow Ran had inflicted. 'For all your discretion, the lady will be ruined when this little story gets out. But I can help you there, my lord. I have some influence with Lady Meon and I am sure I can persuade her to be discreet about this.'

'Then you should do so,' Ran told him. 'It would be best for everyone.'

Teddington laughed softly. 'Oh, I don't think you

are in any position to threaten me this time, Lord Westray. The golden widow would be irrevocably tarnished by this juicy bit of gossip, would she not?'

It took every ounce of willpower for Ran to keep his seat and not deliver another crashing blow into that gloating face.

He said coolly, 'What do you propose?'

'Let me have her. You are never going to marry her, are you? If that had been your intention you would not have behaved in such a hole-and-corner fashion.' Teddington quickly threw up a hand as Randolph straightened in his chair. 'Pray, my lord, let us put aside our differences. I am offering you a way out of a difficult situation. A clinging female can be the very devil, you know. I will take her off your hands.'

Ran shrugged and said, with a fine show of indifference, 'The lady is free to bestow her favours as she pleases.'

'But there's the rub, my lord. She sees you as her protector. As you have demonstrated only too clearly!' He touched his jaw again. 'I need you to withdraw from the lists and leave me free to try my luck with the widow. I think she will not be so unwilling once she knows there is nothing more to come from you.'

'She has already spurned your advances once,' Randolph said coldly. 'And let me remind you that the lady has an independent fortune. She does not need to marry anyone.'

'You think not? Society will forgive us our peccadilloes, my lord, but a woman's reputation can only be lost once. When my sister makes known the facts of your little adventure in Devon, Mrs Roffey will become a pariah, despite her fortune. No respectable door will be open to her. I can prevent that. I will ensure Lady Meon's silence and give Arabella Roffey the protection of my name.'

'In exchange for her fortune.'

'Of course.'

Randolph willed his hands not to curl into fists. He rose.

'Thank you for informing me of the matter, Teddington. Let me tell you straight that Mrs Roffey will remain under my protection and I would advise you to use what influence you have with your sister to prevent her spreading these scurrilous stories.'

With a bow, he turned and strode away. He needed to think. He might challenge the fellow and discredit him, but Lady Meon was a different matter.

He had no idea what influence she had in town, but any gossip about the new Earl of Westray, from whatever source, would be bound to cause a stir. Damn him, Teddington was right. As he'd always feared, a man's reputation was rarely damaged by the knowledge that he kept a mistress, but it was different for a lady. Bella's good name would be ruined.

Arabella was at breakfast with her companion when she received word that Randolph was in the morning room.

'Lord Westray!' exclaimed Esther, her face alive with speculation. 'Well, this is an honour, my dear, and no mistake. Do you wish me to come with you?'

'There is no need.' Arabella was surprised at how calm she sounded. She even managed a smile. 'Finish your breakfast, Esther, while I see the Earl.'

Randolph was staring out of the window when she

went in, his broad frame blocking the light. He turned and regarded her silently until she had closed the door.

'I came to warn you,' he said. 'Lady Meon is in town.'

'I know.' She clasped her hands together. 'I was going to write to you. I met her last night and it was clear she knew...'

'She and her brother were in Bond Street yesterday. She recognised you.' He came closer. 'Teddington wants you to buy his silence.'

Arabella put her hands to her cheeks. 'Lady Meon hinted as much.'

'I think he might call later today to put his proposition to you.' He went on roughly, 'He will ask you to marry him. He will protect your reputation in exchange for your fortune.'

She shuddered. 'I can think of nothing worse than to be his wife! I would never marry any man merely to save my reputation.'

There. If Ran had any plans to be idiotically honourable and suggest they should wed, she had destroyed them! But he had no such plans. He was frowning, disappointed that she would not accept Teddington's offer and save them both from scandal.

'Then what will you do?'

How close he was, she thought, distracted. If she reached out she would be able to touch him. She could cling to him and beg him to look after her. His innate chivalry would not allow him to refuse, even though he would regret it, in the end. She could not, would not bind him into a loveless marriage.

Turning away was like tearing off a layer of skin, but she managed it and began to pace about the room.

'Let them say what they will.' She threw a glance at him. 'I am sorry if it makes things awkward for you.'

His mouth quirked. He said wryly, 'A little more scandal to add to the rest? It will not worry me unduly. It is your reputation that concerns me.'

'Then pray, do not let it do so. I mean to quit town as soon as I am able.' A few more steps took her to the window, and she stood as Randolph had done, looking out at the street. She said slowly, 'Freddie Letchmore was at Lady Prees's soirée last night. I asked him about George and he confirmed what I had learned from Charles Teddington. He swore that the parties at Meon House were perfectly respectable.'

'And you believe him?'

She shook her head. 'No, not entirely. But I do believe George destroyed himself.' There was so much she did not know. So much she did not understand. She burst out, 'What I cannot believe is that George's parents knew nothing of his dissolute habits.'

'Perhaps they were trying to shield you.'

'I wondered about that. I need to talk to them again.'

'Another reason, then, to return to Lincolnshire,' he said. 'Today, if possible.'

'That was my plan, but unfortunately I cannot. I had word this morning that Sir Adam and Lady Roffey are even now on their way to London. They will be here this evening.' She clasped her hands tightly together. 'I intend to tell them everything, because I will not give in to Charles Teddington's demands. I know he will carry out his threat. He and Lady Meon will take great delight in exposing me.'

'And will the Roffeys believe you?'

She shrugged. 'They have always treated me like a daughter. I hope they know I would not lie to them.'

'I think the fact that you are still in possession of a fortune will weigh greatly in your favour.'

'No! Why should they care about that? G-George may not have loved me, but I think, I hope his parents care enough for me that they will not cast me off entirely.'

'If they do, then I will marry you. I will not have your ruin on my conscience!'

Arabella flushed. He clearly considered it a duty that must be done.

'I am sure your…your conscience will recover,' she retorted. His eyes narrowed and she added quickly, 'It is quite unnecessary for either of us to make such a sacrifice, my lord.'

Sacrifice!

Ran felt as if she had slapped him.

'I shall come back this evening,' he said. 'I want to be here when the Roffeys arrive. To support you.'

'No! You cannot do that. How would it look?'

Ran tightened his jaw to prevent uttering the words that came to his tongue. He did not care a damn how it looked. She needed him and that was all that mattered.

'Please, Ran.' She looked at him with sad, imploring eyes. 'It is not only my current predicament to be explained, but there is George, too. They will not wish to discuss their son with anyone outside the family.'

She was right, he knew it, although capitulating did nothing for his temper.

'Very well. Inform Sir Adam and Lady Roffey that

I will call upon them tomorrow. In the meantime, I advise you to remain in the house and tell your staff you are not receiving any callers. I will relieve you of my presence now. Do not ring for a servant. I will see myself out.'

He strode out, banging the door behind him. Hell and damnation! She was so stubborn, so dashed independent! Could she not see he only wanted to help her?

'Ran, wait!'

Arabella had followed him into the hall. 'Pray do not be angry with me.'

She clasped her hands before her, as if afraid one might reach out for him if she did not hold it back.

She said in a rush, 'I don't regret it. I don't regret a single moment with you, my lord. I am grateful for all you have done for me. For…everything.'

With that she went back into the room and closed the door.

Chapter Thirteen

Arabella spent the rest of the day trying to keep busy. She received word that Sir Adam and Lady Roffey would dine on the road and, after a solitary meal where she could do no more than pick at her food, Arabella went upstairs to make sure that their rooms were prepared. She had done the same thing at least twice before during the day and knew it was unnecessary, for the excellent housekeeper needed no reminding of her duties, but she went up anyway.

After assuring herself that the fires were banked up and the beds aired, Arabella made her way back towards the stairs, but her steps slowed beside the door that led into her husband's room. Picking up the lamp from the side table, she went in. When she had first arrived in London she had searched this room, looking for something, anything that might give her a clue about his demise, but there was nothing. The room had been cleaned and cleared of any personal items.

She lifted the lamp and looked around at the dark, heavy furniture, the huge tester bed with its velvet hangings, imagining George bringing his mistresses here. He might not have loved her, but she did not doubt now that he had had mistresses. Everything she had heard from his two closest friends pointed to a life of excess and dissipation. Not that it helped, nor did it make her own position any less shameful. She had no doubt that by the end of the week everyone in town would believe she had been Westray's mistress. She shivered, suddenly feeling the chill of the cold, unheated room. She must go below and join Esther in the drawing room. She must prepare herself to confess everything to her parents-in-law.

In the event, Sir Adam and Lady Roffey were kindness itself on their arrival. They entered the house in a flurry of cold air and hugged Arabella with unreserved affection before they went upstairs to remove their outdoor clothes. It was not until they were all seated around the fire and glasses of Madeira had been served that Arabella had an opportunity to begin her confession.

'Now we are alone there is something you should know.' She stopped, wondering how best to phrase it. 'I am afraid I did not tell you the whole truth, about my visit to Devon, but now it has become necessary.'

'Oh, dear.' Esther Hatcliffe fluttered a nervous hand. 'Perhaps you would like to be alone?'

'No, no, Esther, you should stay. You will hear it soon enough, if you remain in town, so it is best you know the truth.'

Haltingly, and with many interruptions from her auditors, Arabella told her story. The only thing she did not tell them was about the night she had spent with Randolph in his rooms at Mivart's Hotel. That was too special to share with anyone.

By the end of her recital, Sir Adam was pacing the floor, his usually cheerful countenance sober.

'You pretended to be the Earl's wife? And when he discovered you living in his house, he *continued* the masquerade? By heaven, I have never heard the like!' He stopped and bent a frowning glare upon Arabella. 'What did he ask of you in return?'

'Nothing. You may ask Ruth. She was with me the whole time. Lord Westray was most honourable. I had told him why I was there and he wanted to help me.'

'An honourable man would have sent you packing! It is all of a piece with the fellow, I suppose. I read the reports in the newspapers, when he succeeded to the title. A criminal! By heaven, I have a mind to call him out, the scoundrel!'

Lady Roffey reached out and touched his arm. 'Pray, my dear, do not work yourself into a rage,' she beseeched him. 'To challenge the Earl would only add to the scandal.'

'Hmmph, I suppose you are right. But, by heaven, I should like to give him a piece of my mind!'

'Lord Westray has said he will call upon you tomorrow,' Arabella informed them. 'I am sure, once you have met him, talked with him, you will realise he is a good man.'

'A good man!' Sir Adam spluttered with indignation. 'The fellow should never have allowed such goings-on, and when he comes here tomorrow, I shall take him to task over this, and make no mistake!'

'The blame is mine, sir,' said Arabella. 'I went

searching for the truth about George's death. In the end, I found it here, in town, from those he called his friends. They told me about his—his need for laudanum.' She fixed her eyes upon Lady Roffey. 'Why did *you* not tell me?'

'What's this?' Sir Adam stopped his pacing. 'Laudanum? Nonsense. George did not have need of such stuff!'

Lady Roffey flushed and looked for a moment as if she would deny everything, but then her eyes filled with tears.

'I am afraid he did, sir.' She hunted for her handkerchief. 'It was evident, when he came home for that last time. You were recovering from another bout of angina and Dr Philps and I thought it best not to distress you with the information.'

'But why did you not tell *me*?' Arabella asked her. 'I was not ill and I was his wife.'

Lady Roffey gave her a pitying look. 'Oh, my dear, I wanted to spare you the pain of it. And the humiliation.'

She wiped her eyes and Sir Adam came across to drop a clumsy hand on her shoulder.

'There, there, my dear. It is all over now. Nothing can bring our beloved boy back to us. 'Tis a pity poor George couldn't father a child before he died, but there we are.'

Arabella knew they intended to be kind, but her father-in-law's words brought a fresh wave of guilt.

She had lain in the marital bed, waiting for George, but there had always been some excuse why he would not share it. Now she knew the truth. He had married her for her money, but he had never loved her enough to lie with her and truly make her his wife. She thought sadly that she must be very unattractive after all, if he could not even bring himself to consummate their marriage.

Her thoughts drifted to Randolph, how he had responded when she begged him to take her to bed. She remembered how wonderful she had felt when he made love to her. Beautiful. Cherished. She felt even more grateful for what he had done for her.

When Ran paid his morning visit to the Roffeys' townhouse, he was shown directly into the drawing room. His eyes went immediately to Arabella. She was pale but composed, sitting close to Lady Roffey on a small sofa. Her hair was hidden by a white lace cap and she wore a demure gown of soft dove-grey. The only colourful thing about her was her eyes. Even in her sorrow they gleamed, green as a cat's. It was an effort to look away, but he managed it and glanced about him. Sir Adam and his wife and daughter-in-law were in the room, but there was no sign of Mrs Hatcliffe, the companion, which suggested the family wanted to talk privately.

Ran's neckcloth suddenly felt a little tight. Civilities were exchanged; the Earl was invited to sit down while refreshments were brought in and served. Once the servants had withdrawn the mood changed.

'Well, my lord,' barked Sir Adam, 'I believe we are about to be embroiled in a scandal.'

'I fear so, sir. Lady Meon plans to tell the world that Mrs Roffey was my mistress while we were together in Devon. I assure you, it was not the case.'

'Salacious gossip,' exclaimed Lady Roffey. 'How can people believe such lies?'

'But we know it is not a complete lie,' said her husband, his voice grave. 'Our daughter-in-law *was* masquerading as Lady Westray and living with the Earl *in his house*. That alone is enough to damn her.' He turned on Ran. 'And let us be clear on this, my lord. It is Arabella's good name that will be destroyed.'

'I am aware.' Ran met his angry eyes steadily. 'I will do whatever I can to put that right.'

Arabella gave a little hiss of displeasure.

'If you mean by marrying me, Lord Westray, then you have already had my answer. It is no.'

Shocked, Lady Roffey looked at Ran, her brows raised. In response to her unspoken question he nodded.

'It is true, madam. Mrs Roffey has refused me.'

'Indeed?' She turned back to Arabella. 'If Lord Westray is offering you his hand, with all the status and protection that would bring, then you should consider carefully, my dear.'

'I *have* considered carefully,' Arabella replied, not looking at him. 'I do not think a marriage of convenience would make either of us happy.'

Ran opened his mouth to object, but Sir Adam cut him off.

'I will not have my daughter-in-law bullied or browbeaten into anything, my lord. She and my son were sweethearts from childhood. Such deep affection is not easily replaced.'

Arabella's head was bowed and she was clinging to Lady Roffey's hand. Ran had come to Park Street prepared to dislike the Roffeys. From all he had heard, all he knew, he had thought their affection for Arabella was based upon greed and the fact that she was still a wealthy woman, but perhaps he was wrong. He sensed there was genuine fondness between them all.

They would look after her, which was all he wanted, wasn't it? To be assured of her safety. He should go, his presence here unnecessary. Arabella did not want him here.

He was about to take his leave when Lady Roffey spoke.

'There is also the matter of your own character,' she said, choosing her words carefully. 'Your…history, my lord.'

'Madam, no!' Arabella's whispered protest went unheeded by all but Randolph.

He said stiffly, 'I am aware, madam, that my past is far from unblemished. There is no excuse for what I did in my youth, but I was pardoned and given an opportunity to prove myself. I have come back determined to fulfil my duties as Earl of Westray.'

Sir Adam coughed. 'If I may say so, my lord, you ain't begun on a very good note, have you? You have not been in the country six months and already you are involved in a scandal.'

'The Earl is not to blame for that!' Arabella's quick defence warmed Ran's heart. 'I will not allow you to take all the blame, my lord. I was in the wrong to go to Devon, to trick my way into your house, pretending to be your Countess. This is all my fault.'

Sir Adam gave a growl of exasperation. 'For heaven's sake, girl, he is a *murderer*!'

The words rang around the room and hung there, resonating like the chimes of a death knell.

'I was in London at the time of the trial,' Sir Adam went on. 'I remember it well. It caused a sensation, a young lord killing a counterfeiter.'

Ran saw dawning horror in Arabella's eyes, but there was nothing he could do about it. Perhaps it was best. He had known from the start she could never be his.

He said quietly, 'Not a day goes by that I do not regret my past, most bitterly.' He waved a hand. 'But that is by the bye. The immediate problem is how best to protect Mrs Roffey's good name.'

Lady Roffey looked up. 'We shall say, if anyone has the audacity to ask us about this matter, that our daughter-in-law was too grief-stricken to know what she was about. As for the wider society, well, little said is soonest mended. There is always another scandal just around the corner.' She turned to Randolph. 'Thank you for your candour, my lord, and for your concern. We will take care of Arabella now.'

He was dismissed. Arabella was surreptitiously wiping away a tear and Lady Roffey was comforting her. There was nothing more for him to do but give a little bow, assure Arabella that he was hers to command, now and always, and to take his leave.

Miller was waiting to relieve him of his coat, hat and gloves when he returned to his rooms.

'Well, my lord, how were you received by the Roffeys?'

Ran threw himself down into a chair by the fire.

'Arabella is safe, Joseph, which is all that matters.'

'Is it, though?' He eased off the first of Ran's boots

and shot him a look from under his brows. 'What do we do now?'

'We go to Oxfordshire.' He gave a savage laugh. 'I was dismissed, Joseph. For all the world as if I was a suitor!'

Joseph pulled off the second boot.

'Well, are you not?' He held up the pair of Hessians and studied them, turning them this way and that, looking for scratches. 'You and Mrs Roffey make a handsome couple, my lord.'

'What's that got to say to anything?'

'Only that anyone seeing you together could be forgiven for thinking you was besotted with the lady.'

Joseph turned to carry away the boots, but as he reached the door Ran called out to him.

'Is that what you think, Joseph?'

His man looked at him and a slow smile spread over his craggy features.

'I've known you since before you was breeched, Master Ran. I don't think it. I *know*!'

'I heard the front door,' remarked Ruth, when Arabella went up to change out of her morning gown.

'Yes. Lord Westray has gone.'

'Oh? I thought you might have invited him to stay for dinner.'

'It was not my place to do so.'

'Did Lady Roffey not ask him?'

'No.' Arabella turned so that Ruth could unbutton her gown.

'But he confirmed that I had chaperoned you all the time you were in Devon? And you told them how he has looked out for you since you have been in town, how he saved you from Charles Teddington's unwanted advances?'

'I merely told them I was the cause of their quarrel.' She tried to keep her voice light. 'There were so many witnesses they were bound to hear something of it.'

'Hmmph. From the state of your gown you were lucky to escape with your virtue intact,' replied Ruth, alarmingly forthright.

Remembering what had followed in the Earl's rooms brought a hot blush to Arabella's face and she was glad she had her back to the maid, who was far too observant at times. She sought to change the subject and quickly.

'You had best start packing up my clothes, Ruth. Esther is to return to her own house in the morning. Poor thing, I believe she is very relieved that she need no longer feel responsible for me! Sir Adam says we shall return to Lincolnshire within the next few days. We shall live quietly at Revesby Hall until the scandal has died down. He and Lady Roffey were most shocked by my behaviour and, in all honesty, I cannot blame them. I do not know what prompted me to embark upon such a madcap scheme.'

'Because you heard Mr George's ravings and believed him,' retorted Ruth. She sniffed and added more quietly, 'As I believed the poor young master. That, together with the amount he spent in his last months, was of great concern to you and no wonder.'

'Yes.' Arabella sighed. 'I thought at the time George's parents were too grief-stricken to act, but I know now that Lady Roffey knew something of the life he was leading. She knew he was not blameless.

If I had not been so set on justice, if I had listened to her, I could have saved everyone a great deal of pain and trouble.'

'And what of Lord Westray?'

'We—we decided it would be best not to meet again.'

'I see.' Ruth twitched the grey muslin up and over her head. 'When you say "we", does that mean you and His Lordship agreed it between you?'

'Why, yes.'

'I did not think the Earl would be so happy to abandon you.'

'He has not *abandoned* me! I have Sir Adam and Lady Roffey. I no longer need him.'

She shivered and pulled on her wrap. Randolph had not argued when she had declared she would not marry him. Then Lady Roffey had brought up his own history and she had learned that he had killed a man.

He had said he regretted it and she believed him. She did not doubt there was a very good reason for what he had done, but it had made her realise that they could never marry. With such a thing in his past, it was imperative that his bride was a woman of spotless reputation. Someone from his own rank to provide him with heirs. Not a disgraced widow.

'You might no longer need him, madam,' remarked Ruth, breaking into her thoughts. 'But do you *want* him?'

Arabella sat down at her dressing table and began to pull the pins from her hair, taking refuge in anger.

'Let me remind you, Ruth, that I am still mourning my husband. A husband I loved very much.'

'Oh, I ain't saying you didn't love Mr George, in a childish, infatuated sort of way, but if you pardon me for saying so, I think you've outgrown that now.'

'I will *not* pardon you!' Arabella's fingers shook so badly that it was as much as she could do to remove the final pins and pull off her cap. 'That is absurd. I still love George!'

'That's not what it's looked like to me these past weeks, Miss Arabella, the way you talk about the Earl when you return from an evening's entertainment. Even when we were in Devon, I saw how you looked at him. How your eyes followed him whenever he was in the room.' Ruth began to brush out Arabella's gleaming curls. 'No one watching you could doubt you was a fair way to falling in love. Of course, I can't say the same for the Earl, not knowing him as I do you, but I've a strong feeling he is in the same case. After all, he was the one to come to your aid when that wicked Mr Teddington attacked you. And then to get Joseph to mend your gown and to bring you home with no one the wiser. That ain't the actions of someone who don't care about you.'

The memory of that night brought the colour rushing to Arabella's cheeks.

'You are quite, quite mistaken,' she replied, her voice faltering. 'We were friends, nothing more.'

Arabella looked at her reflection. The colour had ebbed away, leaving her face pale and wan. Aye, that was the rub, she thought miserably. Randolph felt nothing more for her than friendship. True, he had taken her to his bed, but he had said nothing, shown no desire to do so again.

She could only conclude that he had discovered what George had known years ago. That she was unlovable.

Chapter Fourteen

Long after he had finished his dinner Randolph sat in the little parlour, alone, staring into the fire. Several times he was tempted to ring the bell and call for a bottle of brandy to be sent up, but he never stirred from his chair. He would not go back to those dark days of living a half-life, his mind permanently fogged by drink or opium. But he could not deny that part of him would have welcomed the blessed oblivion, to shut out the memories of Arabella. Living with her. Laughing with her. He had not realised how much he had enjoyed her company, until now, when he knew it was over. Irrevocably.

Strong spirits might provide some relief from the nagging ache of unhappiness within him, but it would only be temporary. He had learned from experience that keeping busy was the best way to keep the cravings at bay. He must look to the future. There was plenty of work to keep him occupied on the Westray estates. He glanced at the invitation cards littering his mantelshelf. To quit town precipitately could cause gossip and no little offence. He would stay another week or so, honour his obligations, but then he would leave London. He would return to Oxfordshire and forget Arabella.

Joseph's words kept ringing in his head, taunting him. Had he fallen in love with her and never known it? Was that why he had such an ache inside him, why he felt that leaving town would be like leaving a part of himself behind?

Not that it mattered now. She had loved her husband deeply, even worshipped him. He might have hoped, once she had recovered a little from her grief, that she could come to love him. But even if she could forgive him for contributing to her ruin, she now knew the truth about his past. He had seen the horror and revulsion in her eyes when she learned that he had killed a man.

There was no way back from that.

'Mr Charles Teddington, my lady.'

The servant's announcement caused Arabella to drop her embroidery frame. Lady Roffey smiled at her.

'Do not look so anxious, my dear. I shall not leave you alone with him.'

'I wish you would deny him.'

'But how can we do that? He was George's friend, after all. And who knows, perhaps he has come to tell us he has dissuaded his sister from spreading rumours about you.' She rose from her seat in readiness to greet their visitor. 'Ah, Mr Teddington. This is a surprise. Do come and sit down, sir. You will take a glass of wine, I am sure? Sir Adam will join us shortly.'

'Lady Roffey, delighted, ma'am. I did not know you were in town. When Mrs Roffey did not appear at the recital last evening I was concerned and called to assure myself that she is well. However, I think your arrival explains her absence.'

He turned and bowed to Arabella, all smiles.

She gave him a cold stare. 'I am perfectly well and all the better now I have Sir Adam and Lady Roffey with me.'

She picked up her embroidery and continued to set her stitches, allowing Lady Roffey to carry on a conversation with their guest. It was only a few moments until Sir Adam joined them, followed quickly by a footman with refreshments. All the while Charles Teddington continued to chatter.

She marvelled at his effrontery. He was charm itself, taking a seat opposite Lady Roffey and talking about George, recalling many harmless and amusing anecdotes of times they had spent together. It was a performance designed to appeal to grieving parents and after a while Arabella felt obliged to speak.

'Since you were clearly so fond of my husband, Mr Teddington, I am surprised you did nothing to prevent him destroying himself.'

'Ah, ma'am, as I told you, Letchmore and I tried to help him. We pleaded with him to refrain from his excesses but, alas, the last time we saw him, at Meon House, I felt there was some deep-seated unhappiness in the poor fellow. Looking back, I can see he was growing a trifle…unstable.'

'And you did not think plying him with strong spirits and laudanum was making his situation worse?' Arabella challenged him.

'My dear Mrs Roffey, no one *plied* poor George with anything. He was his own master and he seemed perfectly well when he left us. His death was a shock to us all and a great loss. I am only sorry, now, that his name will be brought into disrepute.'

Arabella froze.

'Oh?' Sir Adam lifted an enquiring eyebrow.

Teddington's face was solemn, a picture of concern. 'You may not be aware of it, having so recently arrived in town, but a storm is about to break.'

'Oh, we are aware, Mr Teddington,' replied Lady Roffey coolly. 'Arabella informed us of it the moment we arrived.'

Teddington looked taken aback, but he quickly recovered.

'You will know, then, that my sister has made one of her rare appearances in town. She was quite shocked to discover the lady she had met, calling herself Countess of Westray, was no such thing.'

'As well she might be,' growled Sir Adam. 'The thing is, what does she propose to do?'

'I have for the moment persuaded her not to say anything about the unfortunate episode,' came the smooth reply. 'Not that I hold any regard for the Earl, you understand, but I would not wish to see Mrs Roffey's name dragged through the mud.'

'Good of you,' grunted Sir Adam.

'No,' Teddington continued, sitting back at his ease, a glass of Sir Adam's finest sherry cradled in one hand. 'My sister holds family ties very dear. I think she might forget the matter entirely, if I could assure her that Mrs Roffey was soon to be her sister-in-law.'

'Never!' declared Arabella, sitting up very straight.

Sir Adam waved to her to be quiet. 'And if such an assurance is not possible?'

'Then I regret the whole unfortunate incident is certain to become known.'

Lady Roffey leaned forward and said earnestly, 'Mr Teddington, if you were so very fond of George, surely you would not want his widow to be disgraced in this way?'

'Of course not, ma'am, but my sister has been tricked. Deceived by Mrs Roffey and Lord Westray. Such outrageous behaviour cannot be concealed. It *should* not be!'

'So, I must marry you to buy your sister's silence,' put in Arabella.

Teddington inclined his head. 'Precisely.'

'Outrageous,' declared Sir Adam.

'I am glad you agree with me,' replied the gentleman.

'I am not talking about Lord Westray, or my daughter-in-law, although their behaviour was reprehensible.' Sir Adam jumped to his feet, his voice shaking with barely repressed anger. 'I am talking about your coming here today. Why, 'tis not only outrageous—it is despicable! We will not be swayed by your threats, sirrah!'

'Indeed not,' Lady Roffey agreed. 'Arabella has explained why she was in Devon and, although she was misguided, we shall stand by her.'

Teddington shook his head and said sadly, 'You are making a mistake, ma'am.'

'The mistake I made was not telling Arabella the truth about our son's illness,' she retorted. 'If she had known his ravings were the consequence of taking too much laudanum, she would have accepted his death more readily. As we have done. We will not force her into a distasteful marriage.'

'Distasteful! I can assure you I have a great deal of regard for your daughter-in-law.'

'A great deal of regard for her money!' snapped Sir Adam. 'Get out. You are beneath contempt.'

Teddington was on his feet, a dull flush darkening the cheeks beneath his whiskers.

'The truth will be all over London within a sennight.'

'Do your worst. We shall refute it and we shall make sure your part in this whole sorry episode is made known, too,' exclaimed Sir Adam, his face alarmingly red. 'We are returning to Lincolnshire in the morning. I doubt it will cause much of a stir there.' He stalked to the door and threw it open. 'Now leave, before I call the servants to throw you out!'

The air was charged with anger. Arabella held her breath until Charles Teddington had picked up his hat and strode out of the room.

'Damned scoundrel,' muttered Sir Adam, closing the door behind him. 'How dare he threaten me!' He stood still, rubbing at his chest with one hand. 'Fetch me a glass of brandy, Arabella. There's a good girl.'

Lady Roffey was already on her feet. 'My dear, you are unwell. I shall send for the doctor.'

'No need for any damned sawbones,' he said testily. 'That rascal put me in a taking, that is all. But we saw him off. Now do not fuss!'

But this the ladies could not do. Arabella flew across the room to the decanter while Lady Roffey helped her husband to his chair and hovered about him, bringing him an extra cushion and putting a stool beneath his feet. She sent a footman to summon Dr Locke, then sat down beside Sir Adam, rubbing his hand. After a few moments his laboured breathing eased.

'There,' he said, 'I told you not to fuss. I am very well again now.'

'You are not at all well,' declared Lady Roffey. 'Come along, we must get you upstairs and into bed.'

Arabella knew it was a sign of how ill Sir Adam felt that he did not object. She helped Lady Roffey to pull him to his feet and they set off to escort him up the stairs.

'There's no need for all this,' declared Sir Adam irritably, when they reached his bedchamber. 'A lot of fuss over nothing!'

'Yes, of course it is,' replied his lady calmly. 'But you will go to bed, nevertheless.'

Having left Sir Adam in the hands of his wife and his valet, Arabella made her way to her own room, where she threw herself down on the bed and indulged in a hearty bout of tears. She remained there for the rest of the day, praying she would not have to add Sir Adam's demise to her already burdened conscience.

Charles Teddington was still raging over his treatment in Park Street when he made his way to Grillon's Hotel to dine with his sister that evening. He was shown directly into the private parlour, where the table was already set, but although Ursula might guess from his demeanour that things had not gone well, it could not be discussed until the servants had withdrawn. Only then could he tell her in a few short sentences that his proposal had been rejected.

'So, Charles, they threw you out.' Lady Meon regarded her brother over the dining table, a faint, malicious smile on her lips. 'I am not surprised.'

Teddington glanced towards the door to make sure it was securely closed.

'You were right' was his grudging admission. 'The Roffeys are standing by their daughter-in-law, even in the face of scandal.'

'Of course. She is a wealthy woman.'

'Hah! Why should that matter to them? They do not need her money, whereas I—'

'Yes, we could make good use of a fortune, could we not?'

'It's imperative that I get some funds soon, or at least the promise of them, if I am to hold off my creditors,' he muttered.

'Do not look to me to bail you out,' she retorted. 'I rely upon you to bring at least a couple of affluent guests to my next house party.' She gestured to him to refill their glasses. 'My own funds are running low, so your marrying well would be advantageous to both of us. And there is no doubt that Arabella Roffey would do very nicely for you, since her fortune is still her own.'

Teddington's eyes narrowed. 'It's not just the money, Ursula. She is a bewitching creature. If I must marry, then I'd as lief have her in my bed as any other!'

'Even though she was Westray's whore?'

'Why, yes.' His lip curled. 'Cringing virgins have

never been my style and Arabella Roffey has enough spirit to make the bedding of her...interesting.'

Lady Meon eyed the dish of sweetmeats in the centre of the table. 'Very well, then. We must make sure you have her.'

'And how do we do that?' he snarled. 'Do you propose to abduct the chit? You may be sure they will not allow the wench to step out of the house unaccompanied. There is no chance of stealing her away.'

'I have no intention of abducting her. I have a much better plan.' She selected a sugared almond and sat back in her chair, smiling at him across the table. 'Arabella Roffey will come to you of her own free will.'

Chapter Fifteen

Sir Adam was advised to keep to his bed for the rest of the week, which he accepted with a bad grace. Esther Hatcliffe offered to postpone her departure to help nurse him, but since her birdlike nervousness irritated Sir Adam beyond bearing, Lady Roffey insisted she should continue with her plans, saying she and Arabella would look after the patient. They put aside their own plans to return to Revesby Hall and spent their hours keeping him company, amusing him with books, card games and backgammon until, after five days, Dr Locke allowed him to leave his bedchamber and come downstairs. He also said one or two close friends might be allowed to visit the patient, but always with his wife in attendance. So anxious was Lady Roffey to keep her husband from exerting himself that she asked Arabella to manage the household.

'I shall spend every waking hour with him,' she said, once her husband was comfortably settled on a daybed in the drawing room. 'You know as well as I what needs to be done around the house, the accounts, the correspondence and so on. After all, you have been dealing with it yourself for the past several weeks. You also know the sort of food Sir Adam needs to tempt him back to health.'

'I do and I shall speak to Cook about it,' said Arabella, delighted to be able to help.

With the threat of her escapade in Devon becoming common knowledge, they had agreed she must retire completely from society and she was only too pleased to have an excuse to decline every invitation that arrived. She also wrote to several hostesses to express her apologies for any parties they had already missed.

Rather than disturb the family by using the elegant little writing desk in the drawing room, Arabella retired to the back room that served as the household office. Here she kept the accounts ledgers up to date, talked to the housekeeper and consulted with Cook over menus suitable for the convalescent in the coming days.

She was in the office, tidying the desk, when her mother-in-law came in, her countenance unusually grave.

'I thought you should see this.' She waved a newssheet. 'Lady Meon has clearly been gossiping.'

'Oh, dear.' Arabella's hand crept to her cheek.

'Yes.' Lady Roffey referred to the newspaper, which she had folded to the relevant page. 'It begins innocently enough. The writer wishes Sir Adam a speedy recovery "from the unfortunate illness which has caused the family to cancel all engagements". But it continues: "However, they will surely be distressed by reports that the widow of the late Mr G— R—

was seen in Devonshire recently, in the company of the new Earl of W—and *posing as his wife*." It's what we anticipated, but the audacity of it!' She broke off, her cheeks pink with indignation. 'It goes on to say that the Earl has made no comment on the reports.'

'What can he say,' whispered Arabella, 'other than admit it is true? He must hate me for dragging his name into the gutter. And yours, too. Oh, ma'am, I am so very sorry to have brought this upon you.'

'I am sure you are,' came the brisk reply. 'But there is nothing to be done about that now. We must make the best of it. I would like to take you back to Lincolnshire immediately, but I cannot leave Sir Adam, and I will not allow you to go alone.'

'When do you think he will be well enough to travel?'

'Doctor Locke is calling here again tomorrow, so perhaps we shall know better then. In the meantime, we shall deny all visitors save Sir Adam's closest friends, those who can be relied upon to support him.' She managed a smile. 'Do not look so downhearted, Arabella. We shall get through this.'

'Thank you, ma'am.' Arabella blinked rapidly. 'I do not deserve such kindness.'

'Nonsense. You have always been like a daughter to us. The daughter we never had. We shall not abandon you.'

Lady Roffey kissed her cheek and went out, leaving her feeling even more unworthy of such kindness.

Arabella was crossing the landing the following day just as Dr Locke left Sir Adam's room. Lady Roffey was with him, but when she saw her daughter-in-law, she called to her.

'Arabella, would you be so good as to see Dr Locke out, my dear? I should like to stay with my husband. He is a little fractious this morning.'

The doctor laughed. 'That is because I have told him I will not countenance his travelling for another sennight at least.' He held out his hand. 'Good day to you, Lady Roffey. Send for me if you need me. If I do not hear from you, I shall call again in a week.'

He accompanied Arabella down the stairs, chatting amicably. She was heartened to perceive that he was a sensible man with a cheerful air and he soon put her at her ease.

'And you are young Roffey's widow,' he said. 'I have heard a great deal about you, ma'am.'

Arabella's step faltered. Was her perfidy already so widely known in town?

'Oh, f-from whom?' she managed to ask.

'Your late husband, of course. The family has always come to me, when they are in town, which is why I am surprised we have not met before.' He chuckled as they continued down the stairs. 'Pray do not think I shall be offended if you tell me you employ the services of another practitioner when you are in town, madam. There is more than enough business for all of us! Most likely you are attended by Dr Archer. I believe many of the younger married ladies call on him.'

'No, I am not attended by any doctor.' She managed a faint smile. 'I have never visited London before and I am in excellent health.'

'Are you indeed?' He looked a little surprised, then

said gravely, 'I heard of your husband's death, ma'am. A sad business, to be taken so young. Please accept my condolences.'

They had reached the door. Arabella waited while he collected his hat and gloves from the footman, and when he stepped out of the door, she followed him.

'You say my husband spoke of me,' she said quickly. 'Do I take it you treated him, shortly before he died?'

Dr Locke paused on the flagway. 'Aye, ma'am, I did. I saw him quite frequently, whenever he was in town. The last time would have been, let me see, April. Yes, about a year ago.'

'Just before our marriage.'

'Yes. Roffey told me he was about to take a bride.' He nodded. 'He told me you had remained in Lincolnshire, preferring the country to the town, which most likely explains your good health, ma'am. I hope it continues that way for a long time to come!' He smiled, touched his hat and strode away along the street, leaving Arabella staring after him.

She made her way to the little office, deep in thought. Closing the door, she looked at the leatherbound books lined up on a shelf. Household accounts going back decades. She reached for one. Not the ledger currently in use, but the one beside it, which detailed every transaction for the previous year. There was a small fire burning, so she pulled a chair close and sat down with the book on her knees. Slowly she began to turn the pages.

It did not take her long to find what she was looking for. Entries made last spring, when George had been in town. Among the payments for candles, salt and wine were several to the apothecary. She read the entries again, carefully, then closed the book and returned it to the shelf.

The weather continued cold and a grey blanket of cloud hung low over the houses as Arabella and her maid hurried back to Park Street.

'So much for March going out like a lamb,' muttered Ruth, trotting along beside her mistress. 'This north wind is biting. I have just felt a spot of rain, too. We should have taken the carriage.'

'To carry us barely half a mile? I think not,' said Arabella. 'Besides, I did not want Sir Adam or Lady Roffey to know where I had gone, in case it was a fool's errand.'

Ruth's response was no more than a sniff, but it clearly conveyed her disapproval. Arabella ignored her. She pushed her hands more firmly into her fur muff and lengthened her stride. By the time she walked around the corner into Park Street she was some way ahead of her maid.

She had not gone many yards when a man crossed the road in front of her. He touched his hat as she approached.

'Mrs Roffey?'

Arabella stopped. He was dressed respectably enough in a plain dark coat with a muffler wrapped about his neck, but she regarded him with suspicion. He held out a small bundle, tied with string and sealed.

'I was instructed to give this to you.'

Cautiously she held out her hand, and as the man

gave her the package, he said, 'You are to read the enclosed note when you are alone. Tell no one.'

He touched his hat again and went on his way.

'Who was that, madam?' Ruth came up beside her mistress, breathing heavily from the exertion. 'What has he given you?'

Arabella shook her head and tucked the package into her muff.

'We will open it when we are indoors.'

They continued to the house in silence and made their way to Arabella's room, where Ruth banked up the fire while her mistress took out the small bundle, placed it on the dressing table and stared at it for a long time.

'Well,' said the maid, 'are you going to open it?'

'I think we must.'

Arabella carefully broke the seal and unfolded the heavy paper. Inside was a gold ring, wrapped about with a sheet of notepaper. As she studied the ring a chill ran down her back. She felt the blood draining from her face.

'It is Randolph's,' she whispered, her throat drying with fear.

With trembling fingers she flattened the paper and read the black writing sprawled across it. Ruth hurried across and tried to peer over her shoulder.

'What does it say?'

Arabella handed the paper to her maid, who scanned it silently, her lips moving as she read the words. When she had finished, she looked up slowly.

'But I do not understand.'

Arabella looked again at the ring. 'It is very simple.' Surely it was not her voice speaking. It sounded far too calm for the churning fear inside her. 'A carriage will be waiting for me at the corner of the street tonight at eleven o'clock. To take me to Ran. If I do not go, if I tell anyone of this, he will be killed.'

Ruth stared at her mistress. 'We should tell someone, immediately.'

'But who?' Arabella spread her hands. 'Sir Adam is too ill, and the only other man in town that I trust...' Her voice caught on a sob. 'My only friend here is Randolph.'

'Bow Street, then. Let us inform the magistrate!'

'What can they do? We have no idea where the Earl may be.'

'They could follow you. *I* could follow you!'

She shook her head. 'You have read the letter, Ruth. It says quite clearly that if there is any reason to suspect I am not alone, the Earl will die immediately.'

'And you believe that?'

'I cannot afford to take the risk.' She began to pace the room, the ring clasped between her hands, pressing into the palms. 'If, as I suspect, Charles Teddington is behind this, he hates Ran enough to dispose of him without a qualm.'

'How do we know he has not already done so?'

Arabella stopped.

'I dare not think of that,' she whispered.

The maid closed her eyes as if uttering a silent prayer.

'What will you do?' she said at last.

'I must go and find out what they want with me. Although I think I know that, already.'

'Miss Arabella, I cannot let you do this.'

'I have no choice.'

'I shall tell Lady Roffey!'

'You will do no such thing.' Arabella caught Ruth's arms and gave her a little shake. 'You will tell no one in this house. No one, do you understand me? Not while there is a possibility of rescuing the Earl alive.'

'Oh, Miss Bella, I won't stand by while you go off heaven knows where! Let me come with you!'

'No, I think you will be more use to me if you stay here,' said Arabella. She fixed her eyes on Ruth. 'You must promise to do exactly as I say!'

Chapter Sixteen

The sonorous toll from a nearby clock tower had already begun to proclaim the hour when Arabella slipped out of the house. Wrapped in a black cloak and with the hood pulled well over her face, she was nothing but a shadow moving silently along the dark street. Ahead of her, near the junction with Upper Brook Street, stood a coach, its driver huddled into his greatcoat and his hat pulled low. As she approached, a figure detached itself from the shadow of the carriage, and in the dim light of the streetlamp she recognised him as the messenger who had accosted her earlier that day.

'Mrs Roffey?'

'Yes.'

'Put back your hood, madam. I need to be sure.'

With shaking hands she lifted the heavy material back from her face. The man peered at her for a moment, then nodded, apparently satisfied. He opened the door of the carriage, but made no effort to help her ascend the steps. She paused.

'Where are you taking me?'

'Get in.'

Her heart thudding, Arabella climbed into the black interior, her eyes straining in the darkness to see if there was anyone else in the coach. To her relief, she was alone. She sat down in one corner and looked out through the glass as the coach moved off. She kept a careful watch, noting when they swung around at the corner of Hyde Park, then on again, past Green Park and the Queen's gardens. They were going south, towards the river, and her mind was turning over so many frightening scenarios she could hardly breathe. Pressing her face close to the window, she could see no sign of anyone following the same route, and she could not decide whether that was a matter for hope or despair.

At last the carriage turned into a side street and stopped at a terrace of houses. Arabella stepped out and stared up at the line of buildings. There were no streetlamps, but from the light of the half-moon she could see it had once been a row of substantial houses, although they had now fallen into disrepair. There were boards across many of the windows, and as she descended from the carriage, she noticed a general smell of decay in the air.

The door directly in front of her was open slightly and lamplight glimmered from the narrow passage. It was the only sign of life in the whole row. The man she had come to think of as the messenger touched her elbow.

'This way.'

She shook off his hand and trod briskly up the steps. Pushing open the door, she stopped.

'Where is the Earl?'

The man waved her on.

'Top of the stairs,' he said, following her up the steps and into the passage. 'First door.'

Arabella picked up her skirts and climbed the dark, unlit stairs. The air felt damp against her skin and beneath her feet the treads were gritty with dust. A bead of light gleamed under the door at the top of the stairs, and she reached for the handle, her hand trembling. Taking a steadying breath, she opened the door and stepped inside. From the light of the single lamp on an upturned crate she could see a figure lying on the bare boards, his hands and feet shackled. Her heart jumped and she felt a jolt of confusion. It was not the Earl.

By the next heartbeat she had realised her mistake. Blood had darkened his blond hair and streaked his face, but it was definitely Randolph. With a cry she ran forward, dropping to her knees beside him. His eyes were closed, but he was breathing. She felt faint with relief to know he was alive.

'Ran! What have they done to you?'

'Don't worry, he will live. For now.' A black shape rose from a chair in the shadowed corner of the room. Charles Teddington.

Arabella turned to glare at him. 'What have you done to him?'

'Ursula said you would come, if you thought Westray was in danger. No need to fret because he is in irons. He will be used to that, as a convict. We have things to discuss, Mrs Roffey.'

'I will discuss nothing until I have ascertained how badly he is hurt. I must bathe his face. Fetch me some water, now.'

She feared he might refuse her imperious demand, but he shrugged and walked to the door, shouting orders to someone below.

'He has sustained a beating, nothing worse. It would not accord with my plans for him to be killed. Yet.'

'Your plans?'

'To make you my wife, of course.'

She had picked up Randolph's hand, staring at the grazed and bloody knuckles. He had fought back, but it had not been enough and had probably resulted in more injury. Arabella felt quite sick at the thought, but pushed it away. She must be strong, for both of them.

She said, with withering scorn, 'You think doing this to him will persuade me to marry you?'

'No,' replied Teddington. 'It is the thought of what I *might* do to him that will persuade you.'

The messenger came in carrying a washbowl and jug and over his arm was a ragged piece of material. As he put everything down beside Arabella, she ordered him to bring some drinking water.

'Or tea. Tea would be better.' She added scornfully, 'I doubt the water in this place is fit to drink.'

The man hesitated and looked towards his master.

'There is no tea and the water is perfectly drinkable,' Teddington snapped. He turned to the messenger. 'Bring wine, Barnes. And brandy. I am sure the lady needs something to revive her, do you not, madam?'

Arabella ignored him. She set to work cleaning Ran's face with the wet cloth, gently wiping the blood from his cheek and his brow. It was impossible to clean the hair thoroughly, but closer inspection showed the head wound was not as bad as she had first thought and thankfully it had stopped bleeding.

There was a scrap of worn blanket beside the Earl. She folded it and tenderly lifted his head to place it on the improvised pillow. She raged inwardly, but held her tongue as the man named Barnes came back in with a tray bearing glasses, bottles and a jug of water.

'How dare you do this,' she muttered angrily, when Barnes had departed again.

'Oh, I dare,' replied Teddington, sneering. 'I dare a great deal to win the woman I love.'

'Love! You do not love me. It is my money that you want.' She stood, refusing to beg on her knees. 'I will give it to you, all of it. You have my word. I will sign everything over to you, only let me take the Earl away with me now.'

'Do you think I will believe that?' His lip curled. 'Do you think the Roffeys would allow you to give away your fortune? No, Arabella, I want you for my wife. George never appreciated what a little beauty he had in his possession, but I intend to enjoy your money *and* your charms, madam.' He smiled and her blood ran cold.

There was a groan and she quickly turned back to kneel beside Randolph, who was trying to sit up. He fell back, his breath coming in painful, ragged gasps.

'Be easy,' she murmured, wiping beads of sweat from his brow.

His eyelids flickered, the long, thick lashes lifted. At first his blue eyes looked dazed, vacant. Then he recognised her and her heart swelled when he murmured her name.

'Yes, Ran,' she said softly. 'I am with you.'

'Here,' said Teddington. 'Give him this.'

Without thinking, Arabella took the glass from him and held it to Ran's lips, but he pushed it away.

'No. No wine.'

'No, of course,' she murmured. 'I beg your pardon.'

Teddington snorted. 'What sort of man is he if he is afraid to drink a glass of claret?' He sneered. 'Damned Methodist!'

'He is more of a man than you will ever be!' cried Arabella, turning on him.

'He has a title, madam, and I suppose that is what attracts you, ain't it? He's a damned killer, but you will overlook that to make yourself a countess.'

'I would no more marry for a title than I would for money!' She took a deep breath, trying to calm herself. She needed to keep her wits about her. 'Why are you doing this? I have already refused you. Surely you do not want an unwilling wife.'

'Once we are married you will come around. You will soon learn to appreciate my attentions.' She shivered in horror when he bared his teeth. He did not see it, for he was already looking away, brushing dust from his sleeve. 'But I need you to come to the altar willingly. I cannot risk your friends and family forcing an annulment.' He patted his coat. 'I have a licence in my pocket. Everything is arranged. In the morning we shall drive to St Anne's and be married at eleven o'clock. Everything will be carried out with the strictest propriety. And once I have made sure of you…' again, that lecherous smile '… I will give orders to release Lord Westray.'

Ran lifted his manacled hands and plucked at her

sleeve. 'Do not believe him.' His voice rasped painfully. 'I could inform upon him. He cannot. He cannot let me live.'

Arabella covered Ran's fingers with her own, knowing he spoke the truth. She held up her head and spoke with a confidence she was far from feeling.

'You should forget this nonsense, Mr Teddington. I will not make a pretence of wanting to marry you. You should allow me to leave now and to take the Earl with me.'

Teddington laughed and folded his arms.

'Why should I do that, my dear? There is only one bargain to be struck here. Your hand in exchange for the Earl's life. If you refuse to cooperate, then his body will be found in the Thames and yours may follow, when I have finished with you. So, you see, you *will* marry me, if you want your lover to live.'

Ran had slipped back into unconsciousness and she could only be thankful he had not heard Teddington's words. They hung over her like a threatening cloud. All she could do was to play for time.

'And if I agree, tell me what will happen to the Earl.'

'He will be put into the care of the Captain of a certain transport ship, bound for the Americas.'

'No!'

'Why are you so horrified, my dear? His Lordship is accustomed to long sea voyages. He has survived two and it is possible he will survive a third.' That horrid smile grew. 'Only this time I have taken steps to ensure he will never find his way back to England.'

Arabella could not speak. She was filled with a sickening combination of fear and horror. Not at the prospect of her own fate, but the idea that Ran might perish at sea or, at best, face another lonely exile. It was too much to be borne.

Teddington looked at his watch. 'It grows late and I need your decision. Now, madam.'

'It seems I have no choice.'

He nodded. 'Very wise. There is a pencil and paper by the lamp. I need you to write to the Roffeys, saying you are staying with friends this evening. Do it now and make it convincing, or I shall have to dictate it for you.'

Slowly she complied. He picked up the note and read it before folding it and placing it in his pocket. 'Good. Now let us get out of here.'

She ignored his outstretched hand.

'I want to stay. With Lord Westray.' She was shaking, but anger gave her the strength to look Teddington in the face. 'I have promised to give you the remainder of my life. Surely you can allow me this one last night.'

She saw the flash of triumph in his eyes as he took her words as an acceptance of his plan. He nodded.

'Very well. You may stay here. Sleep on the floor with your lover, if you wish.' His lip curled. 'I do not think he is capable of pleasuring you tonight! I shall be back at dawn to take you to Lady Meon. She will ensure you are dressed appropriately for your wedding day.'

He picked up the lamp from the makeshift table.

'I almost forgot. I have this for the Earl.' He pulled a small bottle from his pocket and put it down where the lamp had been. 'You might want to give that to him. It will help with the pain.'

He went out and shut the door, plunging the room into darkness. She heard the key turn in the lock, footsteps descending the stairs, the thud of the door. Then there was silence. The moon shone in through the window, and as Arabella's eyes grew accustomed to the gloom, the pale light was enough to see all but the darkest corners of the room. She looked down at Randolph, lying unconscious on the floor.

Lover.

He had taken her to bed but once—did that make them lovers? She thought not. She had been distraught, needing comfort, and he had given her a glorious night which would live in her memory for ever. In return, she had dragged him into disaster. She squeezed her eyes, but could not prevent a tear trickling down her cheek. She dashed it away angrily.

'Don't cry, love.'

Ran's gentle voice brought even more tears. She sniffed and dragged out her handkerchief.

'I beg your pardon. This is no time for weakness.' She wiped her eyes. 'What happened, Ran—how long have you been here?'

'I was set upon this morning. I thought it was foot-pads, but I know now they were Teddington's hirelings. They clubbed me unconscious and brought me here.' He tried to get up and fell back, wincing. 'I don't think anything is broken, save perhaps a rib or two, but it hurts like the very devil.'

'Then lie still and rest.'

'Arabella, I am so sorry that I have brought you to this.'

'No, no, this is not your fault. It is mine,' she told him earnestly. 'But never mind that now.' She reached for the bottle Teddington had left. 'Here. At least he had the goodness to leave this for you.'

'No.' He turned his head away as she held the phial to his lips. 'It is laudanum. I. Cannot. Take. Laudanum.'

'What do you mean?' She sat back on her heels, frowning at him.

'Teddington forced some down my throat earlier. If I take more, I may not be able to stop. I was addicted to it, years ago. It addles one's brain, Arabella. One will do almost anything to get it.'

His eyes were closed and for a moment she thought he was unconscious. Then he began to speak again. His voice quiet with fatigue.

'I spent six months on the transport ship. Prisoners are not allowed laudanum. I was denied it, no matter how much I begged and pleaded. It was a simple choice: to survive or perish. Thankfully I had Joseph to look after me. With his care I did survive the voyage, heaven knows how. When at last we reached Sydney Cove I was assigned to Joseph—as a free man he made himself responsible for me. Over the years, with his help, I thrived. The cravings for opium and for strong drink eased, although they have never disappeared completely. I can never let down my guard where those temptations are concerned.' He exhaled slowly. 'There, you know my weakness now. Despise me if you wish.'

'I do not despise you,' she said softly. 'I admire your fortitude.'

She picked up the bottles and the glass of wine that Teddington had left and carried them to the corner of the room, where she emptied everything into the chamber pot.

'You do not want the wine for yourself?' he asked her.

She came back to kneel beside him. 'If you cannot drink it, then neither shall I. We have water, if we are thirsty.' She took off her cloak and threw it over him. 'You should try to rest.'

'What about you?'

'I shall keep watch. I told Ruth to take your ring and Teddington's note to Joseph Miller. I hoped he might be able to follow us.'

Ran nodded. 'If anyone can find us, it is Joseph.'

He sounded weary, and when he closed his eyes, Arabella rose and went to the window. The moon was no longer visible and a handful of stars twinkled. She remembered talking with Ran at Beaumount, discussing the night sky. She had told him how, as a child, she had wished on a shooting star, if she saw one. Her eyes searched the velvet blackness, but there was no sudden streak of light, nothing to wish upon tonight. She looked down into the deserted street. Her hopes of rescue were fading. She had been so sure Joseph and Ruth would have followed them. Perhaps they had tried. Perhaps they had been turned back, or had lost sight of the carriage. Whatever the reason, there was no one in the street below.

Arabella kept her lonely vigil for an hour or so until the chill in the room grew too much and she could not prevent a shiver. Ran stirred.

'You are cold.'

'I thought you were asleep.'

'I was, for a little while. Come and lie with me. Let me warm you.'

She glanced out the window again. Apart from a stray dog running through the shadows, it was empty. Surely if help was coming it would have arrived by now. She went back to Randolph and stretched herself out on the floor beside him, arranging the cloak over them both.

'I had hoped the next time we lay down together it would be a softer bed than this,' he murmured.

His attempt to lighten the moment brought a lump to her throat.

She said, 'Is your shoulder bruised or may I put my head on it?'

'I have no idea. You will have to try it.'

She gently rested her cheek on the soft wool of his coat. 'Does that hurt?'

'Not at all.'

She measured her length against him, allowing his warmth to drive away the chill from her bones.

'Bella?'

'Yes?'

'I am so sorry. I never meant for it to end like this. I wanted only to help you. Instead of that I have made things infinitely worse.'

'Hush now.' She put a hand over his, trying to ignore the cold unyielding manacle that shackled his wrists. 'Do not give up hope just yet. There is still time for someone to find us.'

Ran wished he could share her confidence. Joseph would have been looking for him from the moment he realised Ran was missing. It could take him days to discover what had happened and by then it would be too late. At least for him. The best he could hope for was that they might rescue Arabella from a forced marriage.

He squeezed her hand, saying bitterly, 'I should never have interfered. As soon as I found you at Beaumount I should have sent you back to the Roffeys.'

'No, I needed to find out about my husband.'

'But even that has brought you nothing but pain.'

'It was painful, yes, but it has made me understand George better.'

'To discover that he had used you!'

'Yes, perhaps, but I have learned a great deal more in the past few days. I know now that he did love me, in his way.'

She snuggled closer and he clenched his jaw not to cry out. He would bear the pain as she pressed against his bruised and battered body. It was a small price to pay to have her lying beside him. But now she was going to tell him about her husband and that hurt would be much harder for him to bear. Her breath caressed his cheek as she spoke, adding to his torment.

'I learned from Charles Teddington that George was weak-willed and prone to wild living. He had spent the independence he inherited from his grandfather and he was living on a small allowance Sir Adam made him. Then, last year, his father told him he would no longer fund his excesses. That was when he married me. He had no option.'

Ran took a breath to speak, but she quickly placed her fingers on his lips.

'I know. I know you would argue that an honourable man would not have done so, but I believe George was already a slave to laudanum and…and other desires.' She sighed. 'He suffered so much before he died. When he came back to Revesby Hall, he asked me to get him some juice of the poppy, for the pain. I begged Lady Roffey to let me send out to the apothecary, but she said Dr Philps had advised against it. That it would only make matters worse. Now I realise he was so near death that it would have done him little harm. It might even have eased his suffering.'

'And the Roffeys did not tell you of his liking for laudanum?'

'Sir Adam did not know. George had confided in his mother, but she had never spoken of it. To anyone, until I asked her about it.' She paused, then continued in a whisper. 'But it was not only laudanum. When the Roffeys' London doctor called at Park Street a few days ago, he told me that he had treated George, just before his death. Then I found some entries in the accounts. Bills from the apothecary for calomel and something called *liquor swietenii*. I went to see Dr Locke and I… I asked him about them.'

She stopped again and Ran did not press her. He merely held her hand, trying to comfort her as best he could. Eventually she continued.

'Doctor Locke was treating George for the pox. *That* was why he did not consummate our marriage. Why he refused to share the marriage bed. He did not wish to pass on the infection.' Her voice broke. 'So you see, he d-did love me, in a way.'

It was an effort, but Ran managed to put his shackled hands around Arabella, and he held her while she cried. When at last she fell asleep, he kept his arms about her and stared up at the ceiling, the aches of his body as nothing compared to the pain in his heart. She saw George Roffey as a martyr and he could never compete with that.

Chapter Seventeen

Ran woke just as the first grey streaks of dawn were lighting the room. He felt stiff from sleeping on the floor all night, but when he moved, he was relieved to find the pain had lessened considerably. Arabella was already awake and standing by the window.

As if aware of his gaze, she turned.

'Good morning.' She filled a glass with water and brought it over to him. 'You are moving a little easier, I think,' she said, helping him to sit up.

He held up both hands to take the glass and she saw the red marks where the iron shackles had rubbed his wrists.

She said fiercely, 'I will not let them send you to America! When Teddington returns, I will insist he releases you before the marriage.'

He shook his head. 'He will never agree to that. You must save yourself, Bella. Play along with him, at least until you get to the church, then throw yourself upon the mercy of the priest.' He saw the stubborn set to her mouth and added quietly, 'It is the only way.'

'No.' Her voice shook. 'I will not let him kill you!'

Her distress pained Ran more than his bruised body. He railed silently against his feeble state. Shackled as he was, he could not even hold her. She was wiping her eyes, trying to be brave, and he gave a hiss of frustration.

'If I could just remove these chains, we might try to get out of here!'

'I have been attempting to open the lock with this.' She held up a bent and twisted hairpin. 'To no avail, alas.'

'It is too weak.' He struggled to his feet, putting his hands against the wall to steady himself. Just as *he* was too weak to save her, he thought bitterly. Confound it, he was as feeble as a newborn babe!

'I have looked about the room and there is nothing else to use,' she said. 'I even considered climbing from the window, but we are too high.'

He forced his aching limbs to move so he might stand beside her at the window.

'You are right, Bella. It would most likely result in broken legs, if not worse.'

The air in the room shifted as the front door opened and thudded shut. There was a rumble of voices below.

'They have come for you.' Ran cupped her face with his hands, sweeping his thumbs across her wet cheeks. 'Even if you are forced to go through with this marriage, you do not have to stay in it. Escape from Teddington as soon as you are able.' There was the sound of heavy feet on the stairs. Time was short. He said urgently, 'Promise me!'

The door opened and Teddington came in with two men. Ran thought it likely they were part of the gang that had attacked him, a suspicion strengthened by the fact that one of them was sporting a black eye and split lip.

'A farewell kiss,' Teddington scoffed. 'How touching. But you won't pine long for your lover, madam. I shall soon make you forget him.'

It was a blatant taunt and anger flared in Ran. Bella caught his hands. He saw the tiny shake of her head and he fought down the urge to throw himself at his enemy. She smiled up at him.

'I shall never forget,' she said softly.

Ran's heart leapt as he read the message in her eyes, clear and unequivocal. She cared. Perhaps not as much as she had loved her husband, but she cared.

Teddington strode forward. 'Fine words, my dear, but it is time to complete our bargain.'

'Not yet,' she said quickly. 'It cannot be more than seven o'clock.'

'It is in fact some minutes past the hour,' he corrected her. 'We must dress you as befits a bride and that will take time. Come.'

Teddington grasped her wrist. Instinctively Ran moved to protest, only to be felled by a blow from one of the henchmen.

'Ran!'

Arabella cried out in horror as Randolph collapsed, his face twisting in pain. She struggled to free herself, but Teddington's grip on her arm only tightened.

'If you fight me, I'll order them to stay here and kick him senseless,' growled her tormentor. 'Believe me, they would be only too happy to oblige.'

She could not stop her voice from wavering as she pleaded with them not to hurt him further.

'He shall have every care,' replied Teddington. 'As

long as you behave yourself.' He was pulling her towards the door. Ran was on his knees, coughing. He looked up at her.

'I will find you, Bella,' he gasped. 'I promise you I will survive this.'

'Of course you will,' mocked Teddington.

He stopped, pulling Arabella out of the way as Barnes came into the room carrying a number of bottles, which he placed on the upturned crate.

'You see, I have catered for your every comfort, my lord. Barnes has brought you more wine and brandy, so you may toast our nuptials. And believe me, I intend to enjoy my new bride. I shall tell you all about it tomorrow, when I come to see you on your way. Oh, there is another full bottle of laudanum, too. You see, I understand only too well what it is you need, my lord. Enjoy them all. They will help you to endure what is to come.'

'You devil!' Arabella gasped. 'You know what laudanum can do! You saw what happened to my husband.'

'Aye, poor Roffey could not get enough. When we were in Devon, I could barely keep up with his demands for it.'

'So you did not try to help him,' she said, twisting in his grasp. 'You killed him.'

'He killed himself! As will your precious Earl, no doubt.' He turned to Barnes and barked out an order. 'Take away the water. If His Lordship is thirsty he can avail himself of the bottles.'

Arabella managed one last look at Randolph before she was dragged out of the house and to the waiting coach.

* * *

Randolph remained on his knees until they had all left the room. Then he staggered to the window. He was in time to see Bella climbing into a closed carriage followed by Teddington, Barnes and one of the henchmen. Then the door was shut and the carriage rattled away along the street. Only one man came back into the house and Ran heard and felt the dull thud of the door being closed. He waited, listening, but there was no sound of booted feet on the stairs.

So, he was not to be murdered just yet. He had thought Teddington might have given orders for him to be dispatched as soon as Bella was out of the way. Then his eyes moved towards the bottles standing on the upturned crate. His mouth twisted. Of course. He was expected to do the job himself.

Ran picked up Bella's cloak, which was still lying on the ground. He bundled it up and sat down in the corner with it in his arms. He was damned if he would destroy himself. He would do his best to escape, but first his aching body screamed out for rest. He buried his face in the cloak, breathing in the faint trace of Bella's perfume and ignoring the siren call of the wine and laudanum on the far side of the room.

He must have fallen asleep. A loud crash roused him, followed by the rumble of voices, then shouts and swift feet on the stairs. He heard the scrape of the key. The door burst open and Miller entered, his usually neat appearance somewhat ruffled. He strode towards his master, his face creased with anxiety.

'Joseph!' Ran hid his relief behind a growl that he

knew would alleviate the worst of his man's fears. 'What kept you?'

The anxious look faded. 'I beg your pardon, my lord. I would have been here last night, only they were obviously expecting someone to follow Mrs Roffey and a group of ruffians held us off. They bundled us away so we had no idea of your direction. It has taken us all night and a great deal of palm-greasing to find you. How are you, sir?'

'Bruised and bloodied, but it could be worse.' Ran saw Joseph's eyes move to the upturned crate and his lip curled. 'Our friend was considerate enough to leave those bottles for me. I haven't touched them, although if I had been here much longer, I might have had to empty them into the necessary in the corner.'

As Bella had done. Just the thought of her brought back the gut-wrenching urgency he had been trying to conceal.

He glanced to the window. 'Teddington took Arabella away at sunrise. What's the time now, Joseph? Those curs took my watch and ring.'

'As to the ring, my lord, Mrs Roffey's maid brought that to me, but I am very much afraid we shall have to buy you a new timepiece.'

He noted Ran's look of impatience and became serious again.

'It is gone eight, sir. We cannot be more than an hour behind them.'

'Good.' Ran struggled to his feet. 'Teddington intends to marry her at eleven. At St Anne's. The problem is I have no idea *which* St Anne's church! We must—'

Miller interrupted him. 'I know a few reliable men

below who can help, my lord.' He frowned down at
Randolph's wrists. 'First of all, though, we need to
find you a blacksmith.'

Chapter Eighteen

The image of Randolph, bruised and on his knees, remained with Arabella throughout the morning, and it numbed her to her own plight. When they reached Grillon's Hotel, her escort explained away her dishevelled appearance to the startled staff by saying she had been taken ill. She was hurried up to Lady Meon's suite, where she permitted herself to be bathed and gowned in sprigged white satin.

Lady Meon herself fixed the white veil over her golden curls and invited Arabella to view herself in the long mirror.

'There,' she purred, standing with Arabella before the glass. 'As pretty as a picture. What do you say, Charles?'

Her brother approached, a glass of wine in one hand.

'Quite ravishing,' he declared. 'By Gad, I think I will kiss the bride now!'

Arabella recoiled as he came towards her, but Lady Meon held him off, laughing.

'No, Charles. If you spill wine on that white dress,

you will undo all my good work. Off you go to the church. Leave me to follow with Mrs Roffey.'

'Very well.' He drained his glass and picked up his hat. 'Barnes will accompany you, to make sure there are no mishaps on the way. I do not wish my bride to change her mind at this late stage.'

It was an effort, but Arabella lifted her head and replied coldly, 'I have given you my word to go through with this.'

'Aye, so you have.' He leered at her. 'But you must smile, my dear. If you bring that sad face to the church, I promise you Lord Westray will not live out the day.'

Arabella was silent. The thought of Randolph made her want to weep, but while there was a chance he might live she must be strong.

At the appointed hour she left the hotel with Lady Meon for a short carriage journey along Piccadilly and into Soho. As she stepped down on to the pavement, Arabella peered out through the heavy lace of the veil, hoping there might be a familiar face close by, some sign that help was at hand, but there was no one. She wished she had put a plea for help in her note to the Roffeys last night, but with Teddington watching her so carefully she had not dared.

Gazing up at the looming bell tower of the church, she was seized by panic. She considered picking up her skirts and fleeing, but Barnes was standing at her elbow. He would catch her immediately and, if she drew attention to herself in public, she had no doubt they would carry out the threat to kill Randolph. There was no escape.

They entered the church with Lady Meon beside the bride and Barnes following, blocking her retreat. They stopped for a moment while Lady Meon arranged the veil more becomingly and Arabella looked around desperately for someone, anyone who might come to her aid. There was no one up in the gallery and the church was empty save for the two gentlemen standing with the rector before the altar. She recognised Freddie Letchmore beside Teddington, as his groomsman.

'Come along.' Lady Meon gave her a little push. 'Barnes will remain by the door, to make sure we are not disturbed.'

Slowly, Arabella moved forward. The scene took on a nightmarish quality—even the vicar was smiling as she came to a halt beside Charles Teddington.

'Ah, my blushing bride.' She looked away from his smirking face as he lifted her veil. 'We do not need this, do we? I want to see my bride's beautiful smile.' He laughed at her stony countenance. 'Ah, you are too nervous, my love, is that it?'

Arabella longed to scream out that this was all a sham, but she dared not. Instead she managed the tiniest of nods, resigning herself to her fate. At some point in the future she might escape, when Teddington had lowered his guard, but that would not be for some time. Days, possibly weeks, and not until she knew Randolph's fate. Before that…she tried not to think of what would happen to her. She clung to the hope that Joseph and Ruth might yet find Ran and save him. It was too late for her.

The ceremony commenced, the words washing over Arabella in a meaningless tide as she stood beside the groom. The rector had just begun the first prayer when there was a disturbance, sounds of an altercation at the door. Teddington uttered an oath.

'What the devil—?'

A group of men bustled into the church. One she recognised as Joseph Miller; another was a police constable.

Then she saw Randolph. Gone were the dishevelled clothes, replaced by an immaculate coat of blue superfine, new buckskins and top boots that were polished to a mirror-like gloss. The only evidence of his ordeal was the bruising on his cheek and a slight stiffness in his walk. The blood had been washed away from his hair and it shone like gold in the sunlight pouring in through the windows. As he came closer, she saw his eyes blazing with blue fire.

Ran strode towards the altar, towards Bella. They had found her! He thought his legs might buckle from the sheer relief, until that was replaced with ice-cold fury for what she had suffered.

'Have we reached the point about just cause and impediment?' he drawled. 'Because I know of several.'

'Curse you, Westray!'

With a howl of rage Teddington hurled himself forward. Joseph would have stepped between them, but Ran pushed him aside. Teddington was a big man, but he was no match for his opponent. Despite his recent beating, Ran's strength was honed by years of hard physical labour. He blocked the other man's punches with ease, winded him with a blow to the stomach followed by two more to the jaw that sent his opponent crashing to the floor.

Ran stood over him, his hands clenched, but the fellow was unconscious. Only then did he allow himself to look at Arabella. She was leaning against the altar, her face as white as her veil, but she met his anxious look with a small, brave smile. She was safe.

There was noise and confusion around him. Freddie Letchmore was being dragged back from the door by two of Joseph's hirelings and Lady Meon had retreated into a box pew where a third man was blocking her escape. Miller himself, he noted, was having an altercation with the priest.

Ran took a step towards Arabella but the rector intercepted him.

'I demand an explanation, Lord Westray, if indeed you *are* the Earl!'

'By heaven if I haven't told you everything,' expostulated Joseph, coming up. He turned to Ran. 'Dashed fellow is disinclined to believe me, my lord.'

The reverend gentleman bristled with outrage and Ran put up his hand.

'Yes, I am Westray,' he said. 'As my man has explained, we came here to rescue Mrs Roffey before this fellow forced her into marriage.'

'It is true.' Arabella spoke up, her voice faint but clear enough for everyone to hear, and the priest went over to question her.

The young policeman Joseph had summoned from the street to accompany them was standing a little apart, looking bemused and faintly alarmed. Ran beckoned to him.

'Here is your man, Constable.' He pushed the unconscious form on the floor with the toe of his boot. 'Take him to the magistrate and charge him with affray, to begin with. You had better take Lady Meon and Letchmore, too. My men will help you. You will find another of their accomplices outside the door. A man called Barnes. My men apprehended him, so you had best take him with you, too.' He stepped aside as the constable helped Teddington to his feet. 'I will also be bringing charges of abduction and attempted extortion.' Teddington was standing now and Ran met his sullen glare with a contemptuous smile. 'And anything else that I can think of.'

'You can accuse me of nothing that equals your own crimes, Westray,' sneered Teddington.

'Get him out of here.' Ran waved to the constable.

He turned away, only to find the priest storming up to him, blocking his way.

'This is all most irregular!' he blustered. 'What about the wedding?'

Ran was impatient to get to Bella, who was still clinging to the altar.

'There will be no wedding,' he barked.

'Yes, yes, but there are costs to be met!'

Gently but firmly Randolph put him aside. 'My man will deal with all that, won't you, Joseph?'

'Of course, my lord.'

Having disposed of the last obstacle, Ran crossed the short distance to Arabella and took her hands. She was shaking, so he put his arm round her. To his relief, she did not resist him when he pulled her against him, and he closed his eyes as she rested her cheek against his shoulder.

'Poor Bella,' he murmured, 'I wish we could have

found you earlier, but it took a while to discover the correct church.'

'You found me in time.' She raised her head to look up at him, her eyes shining. 'That is all that matters.'

Ran could not help himself. He kissed her, hard, and she responded by throwing her arms about his neck, returning his embrace with such passion that the blood pounded through his veins. His arms tightened and he would have deepened the kiss if Arabella had not struggled against his embrace. He released her immediately and she buried her face in his coat, murmuring, 'I think we have outraged the rector, my love.'

My love!

Ran had not thought he could feel any happier, but her words caused his spirits to soar.

'Then we should remove ourselves from this place.' He put his arm around her. 'We shall leave Joseph to settle everything here and I shall take you home.'

He led her outside. Joseph and the men he had hired were shepherding Teddington and his henchmen into two of the coaches that were waiting at the roadside. Ran guided Bella towards a third carriage with the Westray crest proudly emblazoned on the door. He had taken her hand to help her into the coach when Teddington broke away from his captors and ran towards them.

'Do you think the jury will pay heed to you, Westray?' he cried.

Joseph and the constable grabbed his arms and dragged him back, but he gave a savage laugh, shouting over his shoulder as he was led away.

'You are a convicted criminal, Westray. A *murderer*!'

Ran's jaw tightened in anger. Arabella had stopped with one foot on the carriage step, looking stricken.

'I wish now Joseph had not sent your maid on to Park Street,' he muttered. 'Perhaps you would rather return alone.'

'No.' She clutched at his fingers. 'Pray do not leave me.'

'Very well.' He followed her into the carriage and sat down beside her. She was perched on the edge of the seat and looked so ill at ease that his heart twisted.

'You have no need to be anxious,' he told her. 'I will take you directly to the Roffeys. You have my word.'

Her response surprised him.

'I do not want to go,' she blurted out. 'I do not want to see them. Not yet.'

After a heartbeat's hesitation Ran nodded. 'Very well. We shall take a turn about the park.'

Arabella stared out of the window as the carriage wound its way through the traffic of Piccadilly. Ran was sitting beside her and she heard him take a deep breath.

'Bella, what Teddington said—'

'You do not need to tell me, Ran,' she interrupted him. 'You are a good man. I know that. You have proved it to me time and again.' When he would have argued she put up a hand. 'No, please. Let me speak, before I lose my courage.'

She took a deep breath. Only the truth would do now.

'I love you, Ran. I have loved you from those first days we spent together at Beaumount, only I did not know it. I had made a god out of George. He was my childhood hero, but he was never the man I had made him out to be. I realise now that I only saw one side of him, a face he kept for his infrequent visits to Revesby Hall. When we were children, he was carelessly kind to me. I think perhaps he loved me as he would a sister. He allowed me to join in his games when he was home because there was no one else. But he grew up into a wild young man with no curbs upon his appetites.

'When I went to see Dr Locke about the medicines George was taking, he was loath to talk to me, but I told him I had a right to know the truth, as George's widow. I insisted he tell me everything, however bad, however shocking. From what he told me, I realised that George attended Lady Meon's parties because he could enjoy himself without restraint. There was no one to inform his parents of what was going on and he could have his fill of gambling and drink and laudanum.' She bit her lip. 'And of women, too.'

Randolph reached out and caught her hands. 'Bella.'

She shook her head. 'I was shocked, of course, but not overset by the news. I know I have lived a sheltered life, but I am not quite so naive that I do not know of these things. What hurt me was that Sir Adam and Lady Roffey knew of it. Oh, Lady Roffey had kept George's addiction to laudanum from Sir Adam, but they both knew of his wild living and the—the consequences of it. The fact that he had contracted the pox. They ordered Dr Locke not to tell me. They wanted me kept in ignorance.'

'They were trying to protect you.'

'They wanted to protect their son's reputation,' she corrected him. 'I know they held me in affection, but they were set upon the marriage, despite knowing that the infection would pass to me. And not only me. If George had not steadfastly kept out of my bed, it would have passed to our child.' She shook her head. 'I c-cannot forgive them for that. I can never trust them again. That is why I will not return to Park Street.'

The tears spilled over and Ran pulled her into his arms while she cried.

'It was very wrong of them.' He pressed his handkerchief into her hands and tried to think of something to comfort her. 'Do not forget, if they had told you everything, you would not have taken it upon yourself to go searching for the truth and I would never have met you.'

He cursed his own inadequacy. That thought was a comfort to him, not Arabella. But she was nodding and wiping her eyes.

'There is that,' she conceded.

'They also refused to hand you over to Teddington, when he threatened to expose you. I believe they are very fond of you, Bella, in their own way.'

She sighed. 'You are right. I know it. Yet I cannot bear to live with them again.'

'But to set up your own establishment now would give rise to just the speculation we all wish to avoid.'

'Oh. Yes. Of course.'

She bowed her head. Her sorrow tore at his heart

and he said quickly, 'Oh, Bella, I would carry you away with me this minute if I could, but—'

'But you d-do not love me.'

'No!' He caught her shoulders and turned her towards him. 'I love you more than life itself, believe me!'

She shook her head. 'How can you, knowing there is so much s-scandal attached to me?'

His bitter laugh cut at her like a knife. 'If we are to talk of scandal, yours is nothing to my own. Remember, I am a killer!'

'Hush.' She reached up to cup his face. 'You paid for your crimes with six years of your life, Ran.'

'That does not make them any less serious.' When she protested, he raised his hand to silence her. 'No, you must hear me out, love. You accuse the Roffeys of not being honest with you—I would have no secrets between us.'

He settled her on the seat beside him and lapsed into silence, staring out of the window, but Arabella did not believe he was seeing anything beyond the glass.

She reached over and took his hand, saying softly, 'Tell me, then. Tell me what happened.'

They had reached the park by now, but although the sun was shining, it was not the fashionable hour and there was no traffic on the drive.

'In many ways I am no better than your late husband,' he said at last. 'I, too, was a slave to opium, when I was a young man. I used to take a great deal of it and I was encouraged to do so by a sneaking fellow who befriended me and made me a tool for his villainy. Sir Sydney Warslow. I was a mere baron then, but my family had some standing in the world and he used me to gain entrée into society, so he might pass off his counterfeit notes. I was contemptible. No more than his puppet. Even when he threatened Deborah, my sister, laudanum made me powerless to help her.' He stared down at their linked hands. 'Not only that, I almost destroyed Gilmorton. The man who saved her. The man she loved.'

Arabella held her breath. She wanted to stop him, fearful that his confession would be too much for her, that she might not be able to forgive his past deeds, once she knew exactly what they were, but there was no going back now. She remained silent and waited for him to continue.

'I owned a warehouse near London dock, the remnants of my family's shipping business. Warslow used it to hide the counterfeit notes he planned to release into the capital. I knew it was wrong and I wanted to put an end to it, but Warslow ensured my silence by keeping me drugged with laudanum. We were at the warehouse when Deborah turned up, looking for me.

'Warslow attacked her. He thought I was unconscious, too full of opium even to care what was happening, but I was not. I knew I had to protect her, or at least to try. We were on some sort of balcony, and when I rushed at him, we both fell against the rotted railing. It gave way and we went over the edge together. Warslow landed beneath me. He broke my fall, but he was killed.'

'You had not intended to kill him.'

'He was dead, nevertheless, and we were in my property, surrounded by forged notes. Gil, Viscount Gilmorton, arranged for me to be spirited away to

France.' She felt his fingers tighten on her hand. 'He was in love with Deborah, I was her brother and she loved me, little though I deserved it. Because of that he was prepared to take the blame to save me. That was when I finally came to my senses. I gave myself up. I was convicted of manslaughter for Warslow's death, but the passing of counterfeit notes was far more serious. I should have been executed, but by turning King's evidence and, I suspect, with a little help from the Viscount, my sentence was commuted to transportation.' He looked at her, his eyes dark with grief and guilt. 'I was a damned fool, Bella!'

Her heart went out to him.

'You were, but you paid the price for it.' His smile was perfunctory. She said, 'I want to marry you, Ran, if you will have me. If you think we might be happy.'

'Happy!' He looked at her, hope beginning to lighten his eyes. 'You think we might be happy, even though you know the worst of me?'

Daringly, she climbed on to his lap.

'The worst and the best, my love.' She wound her arms about his neck. 'So, will you marry me, darling Ran?'

His kiss gave her the answer and this time there was no priest to disturb them. Her lips parted beneath the onslaught of his mouth; her body trembled with the delightful sensations he roused deep inside her. When at last he raised his head she leaned against his shoulder, gazing up at him through half-closed eyes.

'Must we wait to be married?' she whispered, her voice husky with desire.

Blue fire danced in his eyes and she half-hoped he

would take her there and then, on the cramped bench seat, but instead he kissed her nose.

'I am afraid so, my love. I will not have more scandal attached to my Countess.'

She gave an exaggerated sigh. 'You had best take me back to Park Street, then.'

The thought sobered her. Ran understood and hugged her close.

'Can you bear to do so? Your stay there will not be long. You have my word.'

'Yes, I can bear it,' she told him. 'As you say, we need to avoid more gossip. And besides that, I must make my peace with the Roffeys.'

After another hug he lifted her off his lap and on to the bench seat so that he could let down the window to tell the driver to make one more circuit before leaving the park. When he resumed his seat, Arabella leaned her head against his shoulder. The horror of the past few days was fading and she was able to think of the future.

'Do you really think we can be happy, Ran, with all that has gone before?'

He put his arm around her. 'I have no doubt about it. The Roffeys will give us their blessing and my sister will love you.'

'Will she? Perhaps she wants someone better for your wife.'

'There is no one better. You are quite perfect.' He glanced down at her and his lips quirked. 'At least, you would be if you weren't dressed like a sacrificial virgin! What was Lady Meon thinking of? White robs you of all your natural colour.'

'It was not my choice!' she retorted, nettled.

'When we marry I would have you wear scarlet.' He leaned closer. 'Like the gown you were wearing the first time I saw you.'

With Randolph nibbling her ear, Arabella found it impossible to remain on her dignity, but she tried.

'Scarlet is hardly a respectable colour for a widow, my lord.'

'Lavender, then, if it means I can marry you before your year's mourning is out.'

His words pleased her, but she pretended to pout.

'I do not think the Roffeys will approve of that.'

'I shall make it a condition of leaving you in their care,' he growled. 'If they will not agree, then I shall take you away and marry you out of hand. By special licence.'

He was trailing kisses over her neck and she shivered delightfully. 'I think I would like that, very much.'

'So do I.' He pushed her down on the seat and slipped to his knees beside her as his mouth and roving hands continued to wreak havoc with her senses. 'I shall return you to the Roffeys, but only for a few days, for the sake of propriety. There is a very pretty little chapel at Westray Priors. Would you object to a quiet wedding there, my love? There is plenty of room at the house for the Roffeys to stay, as well as my sister and her husband. And anyone else you want to invite to the wedding.' He laughed suddenly. 'Deb is convinced her maid and Joseph were sweet upon one another, before we left England, so I must make sure she brings Elsie with her to the Priors. Who knows what might happen?'

'Who knows indeed?' she murmured. 'After all,

love will be in the air.' She cupped his cheek with one hand and smiled mistily up at him. 'And I do love you, very much.'

'And I you.' He kissed her again. 'I want to make you my Countess as soon as possible, and not just for a week this time. I want you with me, Bella, every day, every night, for the rest of our lives.' He raised his head to look at her. 'So, what do you say, my one and only love?'

Her body was already on fire, but the glow in his eyes sent her temperature soaring even higher.

'Oh, yes, Ran,' she said, reaching up for him. 'Yes, please!'

* * * * *

*If you enjoyed this story, why not
check out Sarah Mallory's
Saved from Disgrace miniseries*

The Ton's Most Notorious Rake
Beauty and the Brooding Lord
The Highborn Housekeeper